LET X BE THE MURDERER

LET X BE THE MURDERER

A Novel of Detection

By

CLIFFORD WITTING

GALILEO PUBLISHERS
CAMBRIDGE

Galileo Publishers
16 Woodlands Road, Great Shelford, Cambridge
CB22 5LW UK
www.galileopublishing.co.uk

Distributed in the USA by SCB Distributors
15608 S. New Century Drive Gardena,
CA 90248-2129, USA

Australia: Peribo Pty Limited
58 Beaumont Road
Mount Kuring-Gai, NSW 2080
Australia

ISBN: 9781915530004

First published 1947 by Hodder & Stoughton

Series consultant Richard Reynolds

Printed in the EU

TO

ROY AND PATRICIA

CLIFFORD WITTING

AUTHOR OF

The Inspector Charlton Stories :—

MURDER IN BLUE
MIDSUMMER MURDER
THE CASE OF THE MICHAELMAS GOOSE
CATT OUT OF THE BAG
MEASURE FOR MURDER
SUBJECT—MURDER

CONTENTS

PART I

THEOREM

CHAPTER ONE

(i)

AT two minutes past nine on a grey Monday morning in early November, the telephone-bell rang in Inspector Charlton's office in Lulverton Police Headquarters. Detective-sergeant Martin, who was alone in the room, laid aside his newspaper, took his feet off his superior's desk and leant forward to pull the instrument towards him.

"Inspector Charlton's office," he announced... "No, sir, 'e's not in at the moment. Who is that speaking, please? ... I didn't quite catch it, sir ... Oh, yes, I've got it now ... Well, I'm expecting 'im in any minute. Can I take a message?"

As the low voice at the other end answered rapidly and with a note of urgency, Martin's round, red face screwed up into an expression of comic incredulity; and, when a pause in the rush of words allowed, he said:

"Yes, sir, of course. I quite agree with you that something ought to be done ... Naturally, sir. Might lead to some unpleasantness, mightn't it? ... Yes, sir, I'll certainly pass it on to the Inspector as soon as he comes in. He should be with you within the hour. Thank you, sir. Goodbye."

He hung up the receiver, pushed the instrument away from him and took up his newspaper, muttering the word, "Barmy."

Detective-sergeant Bert Martin was second-in-command of the C.I.D. men attached to the Lulverton Division of the Downshire County Constabulary. Born and bred in Camberwell, he had been transferred, as a young constable, to Downshire, where he had lived ever since. But the years had not made him a countryman. At fifty-four, and well on the way to his pension, he was still a staunch metropolitan. For him, there was no place like London; nothing to compare with the Big Smoke: and it was his purpose, when retirement from the Police Force allowed, to abandon the beauties of the South Downs for the cherished drabness of Denmark Hill. A primrose by a river's brim was "one of them yellow flowers" to him. Of medium height, with an honest, healthily coloured face, surmounted by a thin thatch of sandy hair, he was no fool. He brought to his job a shrewd brain that combined matter-of-factness with the pungent humour of the born Cockney.

Ten minutes after the telephone call, Inspector Charlton strolled into the room. He threw his hat on top of the filing-cabinet and said, as he began to take off his overcoat:

"Morning, Martin. Anything interesting cropped up?"

The Sergeant folded the newspaper and looked across at his tall, iron-grey-haired chief. He shrugged his shoulders.

"Very little, sir. Just routine stuff. Nothing out of the ordinary." He bent his fingers to examine his nails. "Small matter of an 'omicidal ghost, amongst other things."

Charlton was hanging his coat on the stand. He paused and looked over his shoulder to ask:

"What were the other things?"

Martin threw the newspaper on the desk with a gesture of exasperation.

"If it takes me twenty years," he threatened, "one of these days I'll startle you! Too cool, calm and collected—that's what you are! 'Ere am I announcing the first case of dangerous 'auntin' in the neighbour'ood within living memory, and all you can do is take it as if . . . as if . . . "

"As if what?" Charlton murmured, a smile on his handsome face.

"Oh, as if nothing," retorted the Sergeant, shaking himself impatiently. "When I work for anybody, I like 'em to show now and again such an 'uman emotion as astonishment." Suddenly he grinned. "All right, it's one to you, you pea-green imperturbable! There wasn't no other things. Only this ghost. They've got it up at Elmsdale, Sir Victor Warringham's place. It put in a session of 'auntin' last night—'auntin' with murderous intent, from what Sir Victor says. 'E was on the blower about it, ten minutes back."

Charlton sat on the corner of the desk, opened his case, threw Martin a cigarette and helped himself to another.

"Did he give you any details?" he asked, as Martin supplied a light.

"Quite a lot, though I didn't manage to catch it all. The old gentleman was a bit worked up and talked low, as if 'e didn't want nobody that end to 'ear 'im. What it boiled down to was that about two o'clock this morning 'e woke up with a start, to find two luminous 'ands come clutchin' at 'im out of the darkness. Yes, two luminous 'ands—that was 'is own description; and they was comin' straight at 'is throat as 'e lay there in bed. Seein' these ghostly 'ands comin' at 'im and thinking they might do 'im some mortal injury, Sir Victor lands out with 'is fist, but 'its nothing. So 'e jumps out of bed, but by the time 'e'd got the light on, there was no trace of anything unusual in the room. Myself, I'd say 'e was touched in the 'ead, but 'e was very insistent that we should do something about 'avin' this spook removed from the premises without any of the customary delays." He flicked the ash from his cigarette into the waste-paper basket with studied carelessness as he added, "Another of Sir Victor's phrases."

The Inspector stretched out an arm and took "Who's Who" from the book-trough on the desk. He fingered through the pages till he found the name he sought.

"'Warringham, Sir Victor,'" he read aloud. "'Manufacturer; Chairman of Victor Motors Limited. Born 1876.' That makes him about seventy. 'Knighted 1932. Married 1904. One daughter. Publications, '*A Naturalist's Notebook, Pond Life, The*

Praying Mantis, England's Haunted Houses, etc., etc. Recreations, walking, reading and writing.'"

He closed the book. Martin chewed his lip reflectively.

"'*England's 'Aunted' Ouses,*' eh?" he said.

Charlton replaced "Who's Who," swung his long leg off the desk and walked across to the coat-stand.

"Let's go and have a look at one," he suggested.

(ii)

The ugly, busy town of Lulverton lay on the seaward side of the South Downs, three miles inland from Southmouth-by-the-Sea, with which, if building-work continued, it threatened one day to merge in a single uncomely and enormous blot on the fair countryside of Downshire. A couple of miles or so from Lulverton, on the main road to the west, was the village of Mickleham. Half a mile short of the village, on the left-hand side of the road as one came away from Lulverton, was Elmsdale, the country mansion of Sir Victor Warringham. The nearest dwelling, just outside Mickleham, was Peartree Cottage, where lived a man called Tom Blackmore.

Elmsdale stood well back from the road and at right-angles to it. The wooded estate was bounded by a high red-brick wall that Charlton, with Martin by his side, had to skirt in the car for forty yards before reaching the central gates. He turned the Vauxhall between the crumbling stone pillars flanking the entrance, then had to swing the wheel still further, for the weedy, tree-verged, gravel drive did not run straight to the house, but took them some distance back in the direction they had come before it curved again in the lower loop of an irregular and somewhat flattened "S" and, after twenty yards, led them out of the trees into the open space in front of the house.

As Charlton steered the car round the central flower-bed and came to a stop at the foot of the steps leading up to the front door, Martin said:

"I feel like Prince Charming coming to wake up the Sleeping Beauty."

"Well, you don't look like him," grunted Charlton, opening the door and putting out his leg.

There was something in Martin's remark, however. It was aptly descriptive of a first impression of Elmsdale and its grounds, which had the forsaken atmosphere of *le bois dormant*. Everything was so uncared for. Even on that winter's morning, Nature seemed to be suffocating man. The house was large, Victorian, three-storeyed and, architecturally, without a trace of elegance, but the ugly straight lines and brutal angles were masked, for the most part, by a cloak of ivy so thick and uncontrolled that a number of the windows looked more like the entrances to jungle trails than openings to admit light and air to the residents of Elmsdale.

A polite rat-tat on the heavy knocker on the paint-blistered front door had to be repeated before the door was opened a crack by a young little housemaid in a soiled, crumpled uniform. She looked worried and in need of sleep.

The Inspector said: "Sir Victor Warringham?"

"Yes, this is his house, sir," she answered round the edge of the door.

"We'd like to see him, please. He's expecting us."

"Would you be the solicitors?"

"No—the police."

Anxiety left her. The plain little face broke into a smile of relief.

"Ooo! I'm ever so glad you've come! The master was nearly murdered in' is bed last night. The place ain't safe for any of—"

She stopped in mid-sentence and bit her lip. A sharp feminine voice had called from somewhere in the house:

"Who is that, Lily?"

"It's two gentlemen, ma'am. They're asking to see the master."

They heard purposeful footsteps coming along the bare-boarded hall. Then the front door was pulled wide open and Lily thrust aside.

The woman who now confronted them was tall and thin-featured. She looked fifty, yet might have been some years older. Her long dress was of mauve silk, her greying hair was done in a bun at the back, and she wore a pair of rimless spectacles with gold side-pieces. When she opened the door, she was smiling in conventional greeting, but the smile faded at the sight of two strangers on the doorstep.

"Was Mr. Howard unable to come?" she asked.

Lily looked up at her and said timidly:

"It's not the solicitors, ma'am. It's the p'lice."

If there was a reaction to this news, the woman did not show it, but there was no friendliness in the hard pale-blue eyes behind the spectacles as she answered, with no attempt at civility:

"What do you want?"

Her haughtiness irritated Charlton. He answered sharply:

"Our business is with Sir Victor Warringham. I am Detective-inspector Charlton."

For an instant he thought she would close the door in their faces. Then she stood back and ordered, rather than invited, them to enter the house.

With Martin behind him, Charlton followed her along the hall, past the foot of the wide, heavily balustraded staircase. She led them into a small sitting-room at the rear of the house, motioned them to take seats and closed the door softly, almost stealthily, behind her.

"Now," she said, sitting primly on the edge of a chair, "what is the trouble? This is my sitting-room and we shall not be disturbed."

Her tone was slightly more conciliatory.

Charlton began: "You are Lady—"

"No," she interrupted. "Sir Victor is a widower. I am Mrs. Winters, his housekeeper."

"Then perhaps you will kindly tell Sir Victor that we are here."

She shook her head.

"He is not well enough to see anyone today. I can take a message for him, if you wish."

"I prefer to speak to him personally, please."

"That is not possible," she replied bleakly. "Sir Victor is under the doctor's orders and is not to be disturbed."

"When was he taken ill?"

"Oh, quite recently."

"Last night?"

It was a moment or two before she nodded agreement.

"Was the doctor called in?"

"Yes. . . Oh, yes, he was certainly called in. He has ordered Sir Victor complete rest. He says that the least excitement may have grave consequences. It is his heart."

"Which did not seriously affect him till last night?"

Her thin lips tightened.

"The doctor diagnosed heart trouble," she said, and rose to her feet as if the abrupt evasion had put an end to the interview.

Charlton did not stir. He asked:

"Is Sir Victor's—er—mental condition satisfactory?"

Mrs. Winters was on her way to the door. At this question she turned swiftly back.

"Good heavens, yes! A saner man than Sir Victor never walked!"

There was something about the phrase; a fleeting impression that Mrs. Winters was less the indigent lady of quality than she liked it to be thought.

She went on: "Why do you ask such a curious question? And why have you come here?"

Wondering whether she already knew the answers to both enquiries, Charlton chose to reply to the second.

"A 'phone-call was received at Police Headquarters this morning. It was a request for a police officer to call at this house without delay."

A chilly smile creased her features for an instant.

What on earth for?" she demanded. "There's obviously some mistake, Inspector. We don't need the police here. Some practical joker must have—"

"The caller was Sir Victor himself."

Mrs. Winters was manifestly taken by surprise. She sank back on to the edge of her chair, sat silently biting her lip for a time, then burst out:

"But that's ridiculous! He's not left his room since he went to bed last night. The telephone is downstairs in the hall."

"The caller gave his name as Sir Victor Warringham," Charlton persisted.

She forced another smile.

"Somebody has been playing silly tricks. Sir Victor could not possibly have telephoned you. Besides, he had no conceivable reason to—"

She broke off short. There had been a peremptory double rap on the door.

"What is it, Lily?" she called.

But it was a man's voice that answered:

"Mrs. Winters, I want you a minute."

She drew in a sharp breath—Charlton thought it was in fright—and rose swiftly to her feet with the words:

When the door had closed behind her, Martin lean forward to mutter to his chief:

"Beginning to look as if the old bulldozer's right. Someone's bin 'avin' us on. Pity, you know. A dangerous spook would 'ave made a nice change."

There was a murmur of voices outside the door. Martin, with his elbow on his knee, went on:

"Not but what Lady Macbeth don't fairly ooze guilt of one kind or another, but we've all got our 'orrible secret and, when the p'lice pop up sudden, it—"

He stopped at a silencing gesture from Charlton. Outside in the passage, the man's voice had risen enough for them to hear him say:

"In future, Mrs. Winters, you will refer all such enquiries direct to me."

The door was opened and the housekeeper came back.

"Follow me, please," she snapped. "Mr. Harler wishes to speak to you in the library."

"Who is Mr. Harler?" Charlton asked.

"Sir Victor's son-in-law," she replied, and led them from her sitting-room.

Harler must have moved quickly, for there was no sign of him in the long hall. They followed Mrs. Winters round the foot of the staircase and into the library, which was at the front of the house. A few glass-fronted bookcases gave the room its name. It was large, dark and draughty. A smoky fire in the grate did nothing to dispel the general cheerlessness.

They found Harler standing on the hearthrug. He was a slightly obese man of forty-five, of less than average height, with a small moustache and sleek black hair combed back over a bald patch. He was dressed in the conventional attire of a business man, but the jacket was bulgy, as if the pockets were overladen, and the striped trousers were creaseless and baggy at the knees. Charlton summed him up swiftly as a slovenly, bumptious little man.

He smiled at them in turn.

"Good morning, gentlemen," was his greeting.

"Please sit down." He turned to the housekeeper hovering in the doorway. "Thank you, Mrs. Winters."

At this dismissal she left them, pulling the door to, but not closing it. Harler stepped across the room and banged it shut. As he came back to the fireplace, he pulled a chromium-plated cigarette-case from his pocket.

"Smoke?"

They both took cigarettes. Harler pulled a paper spill from a vase on the white marble mantelpiece and pushed it between the bars of the grate. But the fire was unresponsive and Martin's matches had to be brought into use.

"Now," said Harler as he sat down, "let's get this little matter sorted out. My name's Harler—Clement Harler. I'm Sir Victor's son-in-law. Your name is. . . ?"

"Charlton—Inspector Charlton. This is my assistant, Sergeant Martin."

"Pleased to make your acquaintance. My wife and I live here to keep the old boy company—more or less to run the show, in fact. I'm sorry Mrs. Winters took it on herself to see you this morning. She should, of course, have told me as soon as you arrived."

He pompously cleared his throat and went on:

"During my father-in-law's—er—little attacks, I assume charge of the household. Mrs. Winters exceeded her duties. She has given me a garbled account of the reason for your visit. I gather that you were brought here by a telephone call?"

"Yes," Charlton nodded. "Sergeant Martin answered the 'phone. The caller gave his name as Sir Victor Warringham."

"What time was that?" Harler wanted to know. It was Martin who answered: "Couple of minutes after nine o'clock, sir."

Pursing his lower lip with his finger and thump, Harler considered the point. He observed after a pause.

"The old boy *could* have done it. The wife and I were dressing, and Mrs. Winters was probably overseeing the breakfast preparations in the kitchen. Yes, the old boy could have slipped downstairs, made the call and got back up to his room without anyone being the wiser. When they get that way, they're as artful as a cartload of monkeys."

"When they get which way, Mr. Harler?"

"How can I put it? Well, to use a colloquial term, when they go off the rails. I wouldn't like to say the old boy's dangerously insane. He's quite harmless, but he gets funny ideas now and again. He's never been the same since the old girl was killed—and losing his only daughter at the same time didn't make things any better."

"But didn't I understand you to say, Mr. Harler, that your wife was—"

The man's answering laugh grated on them both.

"Silly of me! I should have explained. Rosalie, Sir Victor's daughter, was my first wife. The poor kid was killed with her mother by a flying-bomb in August, 1944. They'd gone up to London for the day and the bomb caught them in the open street—and a lot of other poor devils, too. Subsequently, I married again."

He turned to Martin.

"What did the old boy tell you, Sergeant? That somebody had tried to shoot him, or just that he was being slowly poisoned?"

The Sergeant did not answer, but looked at Charlton, who said:

"He said that an attempt had been made on his life—by a ghost."

Harler threw back his sleek head and laughed again with a heartiness that made Charlton yearn to hit him with something that would hurt.

"And you believed him? You believed that? I don't like to rub it in, Inspector Clayton, but I can't help smiling at you two running up here to arrest a hobgoblin! Did you bring any handcuffs?"

He guffawed once more until Charlton's next question stopped him.

"What *did* happen here last night, Mr. Harler?"

"Happen? Oh, nothing that would interest you police fellows. The old boy gets hallucinations periodically. He had us all out of bed last night with a bad attack of them. My wife and I managed to quieten him down and eventually got him off to sleep. These little bouts are generally soon over, but last night's was more—what shall I say?—more violent. So we kept him in bed this morning, just to be on the safe side."

"What form do these hallucinations usually take?"

Harler rubbed his chin.

"Pretty much the same. Last night's episode was rather different. As a rule, he thinks he sees his wife and daughter. Sometimes he holds long conversations with them. Quiet little chats, you know, as he sits by the fire. Occasionally he works himself up into a state of excitement and shouts out, 'I'm coming to you!' or 'They can't keep me away from you!' Then, after a minute or two, he calms down and behaves quite naturally. It may be a week before he gets another spasm."

"But last night's was different, you say?"

"Yes, undoubtedly. This time these mysterious They weren't trying to keep him away from the dear departed. They had actually called for him—and the old boy was to go. What amazes me is that he rang you up this morning. In the past, he's always forgotten all about it by the next—"

"Is Sir Victor's doctor satisfied with his condition?"

"No, he doesn't take too good a view of it. The human brain is a complicated piece of machinery and once it jumps a cog. . . " He threw out his hands expressively. "We've got a specialist in mental disorders who's coming down from London the day after tomorrow to have a look at him."

Charlton asked: "How is Sir Victor's general health?"

"Never better. Eats like a horse. A.I at Lloyd's.

It's his brain, not his body. The doctor says he needs quiet and no unpleasant shocks. For instance, any bad news—"

"What did the doctor think of him last night?"

Harler looked puzzled. "Last night?"

"Mrs. Winters told us that the doctor was called in."

"I. . . " He hesitated, then raised his voice to call, "Coming, darling!" He rose to his feet. "Excuse me a moment, gentlemen. My wife wants me."

"As soon as the door had closed behind him, Martin said:

"He's gone to check up with the Winters woman."

Charlton settled himself more comfortably in his chair.

"Perhaps they'll also decide," he said, "on the exact nature of Sir Victor's malady."

"If Mr. oily 'Arler calls 'im the 'old boy' again," muttered Martin, "I'll—"

The threat remained unfinished; the door had opened again. It was not Harler who came in, but a woman. She was young—not more than twenty-five—and her flamboyant physical attractions caused Charlton to put her in the night-club-hostess category.

The two men rose to their feet.

"Oh!" she said with overplayed surprise. "I thought my husband was in here. You're the detectives, I suppose? Such a silly misunderstanding, wasn't it? As if anyone would want to murder Sir Victor! A dear, sweet old man! As Mr. Harler and I told him last night, when we had ever such a job to pacify him, he hasn't an enemy in the world—and if he thought anybody was trying to strangle him in his sleep, it must have been a bad dream." She smiled brightly at both of them and asked:

"Do you know where Mr. Harler is?"

"He went to look for you," Charlton told her.

"Then *I* must go and look for *him*, mustn't I?" she answered; and, with a roguish glance that might have beguiled a Hindu ascetic from his yoga, she left them.

They looked at each other. It was Martin who broke the silence.

"Gluttons for truth, ain't they? First it's an 'eart-attack then it's a ghost and now it's a flesh-and-blood strangler."

"We must get a word with Sir Victor," Charlton said.

Just then, Harler came briskly back into the room.

"Well, Inspector Clayton," he smiled, "I'm afraid Mrs. Winters didn't tell you the truth, the stupid woman. I've just had a word with her. She says that she told you the doctor called here last night and ordered complete rest, because she didn't want you to disturb the old boy."

Sergeant Martin clenched his fist instinctively as Harler

went merrily on:

"I think that concludes our business. I'm sorry you were brought along here on a wild-goose chase, but I think you'll admit that the old boy needs not so much the police as a brain specialist. Mrs. Winters acted foolishly yet I definitely agree with her that he shouldn't see any visitors."

"I should nevertheless like to speak to him," said Charlton steadily.

Harler shook his head with decision.

"I couldn't allow it. Not for a moment. By this time the old boy's probably entirely forgotten that he 'phoned, and if you started firing questions at him now, I wouldn't hold myself responsible for the consequences." His voice took on a dictatorial note. "Anyway, it's nothing to do with you police fellows. Quite outside your province. Maybe the old boy did 'phone you, but in his present condition, he's just as likely to call up the Ministry of Pensions or the Archbishop of Canterbury."

He walked to the door and pulled it open.

"Take my advice, Inspector Clayton, and leave Sir Victor to the medical men."

To Martin's surprise and annoyance, Charlton did not press the point. They rose to leave. Harler escorted them to the front door and walked down the steps with them. Before getting into the Vauxhall, Charlton said:

"Who is Sir Victor's doctor?"

"Dr. Stamford."

"Then I shall be glad if you will arrange immediately for him to visit Sir Victor, to decide whether it is safe for him to receive visitors. Or perhaps you would prefer me to ring Dr. Stamford myself?"

The answering smile had no humour in it.

"You can safely leave that to me."

"May I trouble you to 'phone me at Police Headquarters after Dr. Stamford has seen Sir Victor?"

"And if I don't?"

Charlton opened the door of the car.

"I think you will," he said; and slid his big body into the driving seat.

(iii)

The car had left Elmsdale and travelled fifty yards in the direction of Lulverton when the two detectives saw another car approaching. They both recognised the driver, who gave them a friendly wave as he passed.

"Mr. Howard," said Martin.

He twisted round in his seat to watch the other car, which slowed down and turned into the entrance of Elmsdale.

"Callin' at the 'ouse," he told the Inspector. "The skivvy and Mrs. Winters both let out that they was expecting solicitors. Wonder if Mr. Howard'll win through to the old—to Sir Victor?"

Charlton brought the car to a stop.

"We'll wait and see," he decided, feeling for his cigarettes.

"What do you make of it so far?" Martin wanted to know.

"Not much," Charlton had to admit. "Maybe we'll get a clearer picture when we've talked to Sir Victor. We can't be sure yet that it was he who spoke to you on the 'phone. A good deal depends on that; and even more depends on whether he's sane or not. Two facts do emerge: Mrs. Winters wants us to think he's sane; the poisonous Harler would like us to believe that he's not. But however much they contradicted each other, they're both of them most anxious to keep the police out."

"And Mrs. Harler," said Martin. "She's got a different yarn for our innocent ears."

"Yes," Charlton agreed thoughtfully, "I'd like to know what did actually happen at 2 a.m. this morning. Lily, the servant, was very relieved to see us. We must have another little chat with her."

The Sergeant nodded his head slowly up and down. Then

he observed:

"That 'Arler's a wrong 'un. Talks like the chairman of a phoney company at the annual meeting of the share—"

He stopped dead. From the direction of Elmsdale had come the sound of a shot.

CHAPTER TWO

(i)

CLEMENT HARLER answered the door himself to Sir Victor's solicitor.

"Ah Mr. Howard!" he smiled urbanely. "My father-in-law told me that you would be calling this morning, but he gave me no idea of the reason."

The solicitor did not rise to the bait.

"Did he not?" he said unhelpfully.

"Can't think what it can be. All the old boy's affairs seem in apple-pie order. Did he give you any clue?"

"He asked me to call," was all that Mr. Howard was prepared to say.

Harler shrugged his shoulders.

"Have it your own way," he grunted "But in any case, he can't see you today. You'll have to postpone it."

"Postpone it? I hope Sir Victor has not been taken ill?"

"Rather seedy. He had a bit of a turn last night and we've had to keep him in bed. It's certainly not wise to disturb him with legal business just now."

His manner became more gracious as he walked down the front steps, expecting Mr. Howard to follow.

"I'm sorry you've been brought out here unnecessarily, Mr. Howard. Better make it one day next week. I'll give you a ring when—"

He stopped and turned to find the solicitor still on the doorstep.

"Mr. Harler," said the solicitor firmly, "Sir Victor was most imperative. I must ask you to inform him of—"

The noise of the shot stopped him from going on.

(ii)

"Stay where you are," Charlton said to Martin.

He jumped out of the car and, with long, swift strides, went back along the road towards Elmsdale. He reached the entrance gates and turned into the drive. Before he had gone many yards, a second shot was fired in the shrubbery to his right. He was off the drive in an instant and thrusting his way through the bushes. As he drew near to a large chestnut tree, a voice called down from above:

"Halt! Who goes there?"

He looked up. Built in the tree was a hut. It was roughly constructed from packing-case wood, with rusty sheets of corrugated-iron for a roof. In the low doorway crouched a ten-year-old boy and in his hand, pointing straight at Charlton, was a pistol.

Charlton smiled up at him and answered, falling in with the spirit of the thing, "Friend."

"Advance, friend," commanded the boy, "and be recognised."

The detective obeyed and stepped forward to stand at the foot of the tree.

"I shouldn't point that thing at anybody, if I were you," he suggested mildly.

"Oh, that's all right," was the airy reply. "It only goes off when I want it to. It's got a triffic bang. Who are you?"

"I'm a detective-inspector; and I think you'd better come down out of that tree."

"Oh, crumbs!" ejaculated the young gentleman with some apprehension.

He threw out a rope-ladder from his eyrie and, with the pistol still in his hand, clambered down to the ground.

He was wearing a blue overcoat over his knickered grey-flannel suit. On his tousled fair head was a Paulsfield College cap, in colour a vivid pink, with the peak of it well on the way round to his right ear.

"It was only a game, sir," he explained.

Charlton held out his hand.

"Give me that, please."

Reluctantly the boy handed it over: a solid-barrelled, but otherwise realistic imitation of a revolver. After further pressing, he produced a tin of blank cartridges from his overcoat pocket.

"Where did you get this fearsome weapon?" Charlton asked.

The boy looked sulky. "Somebody lent it to me."

"Who?"

"Just somebody. Have you come about last night? I heard Sir Victor 'phoning this morning."

Creating a diversion is a favourite schoolboy manoeuvre. It seemed expedient to accept this one, so Charlton asked:

"Do you live at Elmsdale?"

"Yes, I'm John Campbell. Aunt Enid got permission for me to live here."

"Is that Mrs. Harler?"

"Help, no! I wouldn't have *her* for an aunt. I wouldn't even have her as a... as a..."

The search for a sufficiently distant relation failed.

"Then who is your aunt?"

"Mrs. Winters. She's the housekeeper."

Charlton smiled down at the boy.

"More like an aunt, eh?"

John Campbell thrust his hands deep down in his overcoat pockets and kicked a stone. On consideration, he conceded:

"She's all right."

From his voice, it was to be presumed that Mrs. Winters' only claim to agreeable aunthood was that she was an improvement on the second Mrs. Clement Harler.

"So you heard Sir Victor 'phone, did you?"

"Yes—and saw him, too. He didn't see me. I was a Secret Service Agent."

"A very curious business," Charlton said in a man-to-man tone, and went on without too much regard for accuracy, "I was just on my way to see Sir Victor about it. What's your opinion?"

John looked important.

"Very late last night"—he pulled back his coat-cuff and examined the watch on his wrist with a great display of frowning concentration—"well, I don't know exactly what time it was, but it was trifficly late—I was woken up by someone shouting and banging on a door. I stayed where I was for a little while, then, when the noise didn't stop, I got out of bed, went across to the door and poked my head out. Sir Victor's room is at the other end of the passage from mine. I sleep in the room next to Aunt Enid's. When I looked out, Aunt Enid was in the passage and Mr. Harler was just opening the door of Sir Victor's room, which Sir Victor was still thumping on like billy-oh. Then Aunt Enid turned round and saw me and told me to go back to bed. I trifficly wanted to see what was happening, but I had to do as Aunt Enid said, so I went back to bed. I heard them talking for a long time. Sir Victor sounded very angry. Then it got quieter and I fell off to sleep and don't remember anything else."

"And this morning?"

"I was playing round, waiting for breakfast, when Sir Victor came downstairs in his dressing-gown. I'd say it was about. . . "

He consulted his wristwatch again, this time with more success.

"It was just about nine o'clock."

"That's a nice watch, John," Charlton smiled.

"Yes, isn't it?" John held out his arm so that Charlton could inspect it more closely. "It's got jewels in it. Sir Victor gave it to me for my birthday last week. I was ten." Under this weight of years, he continued: "Sir Victor looked as if he didn't want anyone to see him out of his bedroom. He was behaving very fugitively. He went to the telephone in the hall and was put through to the police. All the time he was talking, he was looking over his shoulder to make sure nobody was coming. I don't think he wanted Mr. and Mrs. Harler to know he was 'phoning you."

"Can you remember what he said?"

"Well, I wasn't very close and, of course, he didn't shout. All I really heard was that ghostly hands had tried to strangle him and he wanted police protection, to see it didn't happen again. He was trifficly frightened about it—and so should I have been! But I don't think there could have been ghostly hands, do you, sir? It must have been a nightmare. I have nightmares sometimes. They always finish up with me falling off something trifficly high, but I wake up before I hit the ground. I've never seen ghostly hands, though, have you, sir?"

"No, I don't think I have... Then I suppose, Sir Victor went back upstairs again?"

"Yes—and Aunt Enid called me to breakfast just afterwards."

"Thank you, John. That's been very helpful. Not at school today?"

"No. Half-term holiday. Go back tomorrow, worse luck! Can I have my revolver, please?"

Charlton still had it in his hand. He looked at it doubtfully.

"I don't think you should. They're dangerous things, you know, even though they don't fire bullets. And they frighten nervous people when they go off. No, John, you'd better leave it with me."

"But, sir—"

"You say it was lent to you?"

"Yes, sort of."

"What do you mean—sort of?"

Young John looked extremely uncomfortable.

"Well, they... They don't *know* they lent it to me."

"In other words, you pinched it?"

"Yes, sir, but only for today. I was going to slip it back this evening."

"Does it belong to Mr. Harler?"

"Crumbs, no! I wouldn't take anything of his! Not likely!" There was more distaste than fear in his tone. "No, I got it from... from down the road." He looked up at Charlton with an appealing expression on his open young face. "It's going to be trifficly 'barrassing for me sir, if you keep it."

Charlton quite saw that; and he had been a boy himself once, though rather longer ago than he cared to think about.

"I'll tell you what we'll do," he said. "You shall have this back now, but only after you've promised me: (a) that you'll not fire it off again, and (b) that you'll return it to wherever you got it from by this afternoon, at the latest. Is that a deal?"

The boy's face lighted up.

"That's simply wizard of you, sir! I promise—on my word of honour!"

Charlton felt in his pocket for the tin of blanks.

(iii)

Meanwhile an awkward situation was developing on the front steps of Elmsdale.

The reactions of Harler and Mr. Howard to the pistol shot were not so positive as the Inspector's. Shotguns were common enough in that country district, and, after a momentary pause, Mr. Howard began his last sentence again.

"I must ask you to inform Sir Victor of my arrival."

The pompous little man began to bluster.

"Look here, Howard! I'm the best judge and I'm telling you that he can't see you today. Whatever tomfoolery he's thought up can wait."

"I gather from Mr. Blackmore—"

"Blackmore!" snorted Harler. "Your dealings are with me, not with the blasted gardener! Don't you realise that Sir Victor's not normal? He's mad, I tell you! We've got a brain specialist coming down on Wednesday. For God's sake, man, don't make things more difficult than they are already!"

Mr. Howard said slowly and with incredulity in every word: "Are you trying to tell me that Sir Victor—"

The sentence was cut short. A voice had spoken behind him. He turned round to find Mrs. Winters standing in the doorway.

"Mr. Howard," she said in a low, tense voice, "please don't go. Sir Victor is most anxious to see you."

Harler gave the solicitor no chance to reply. He shouted from the foot of the steps:

"You keep out of this, Mrs. Winters! Get back to your work!"

"I shall do nothing of the kind," she retorted calmly.

"Sir Victor wishes to speak to Mr. Howard on an urgent business matter and it is my duty to see that he does so."

"Do as I tell you!" raged Harler. "It's about time you realised that you're a paid employee."

"But not of yours, Mr. Harler. You are deliberately obstructing Mr. Howard." She turned to the solicitor. "Mr. Howard, if you will please come in and sit down for a few minutes, I will tell Sir Victor that you are here."

"He's asleep in bed, I tell you!" Harler said wildly.

The observant solicitor noticed that the man was no longer angry, but perturbed.

"He can be awakened," Mrs. Winters replied, then went on with tight lips, "provided that you and that wife of yours have not been up to some more of your devil's work."

"You damned old fool!" yelled Harler. "What are you talking about! And why are you so anxious for Howard to see the old maniac? Devil's work! I like that! If there's any devil's work in this house, you're the one who's doing it, you old harpy!"

Mr. Howard coughed.

"I'm afraid this is getting us nowhere," he said uncomfortably. "I suggest that if I call back—"

They both answered together.

"One day next week," said Harler.

"You must see him *now,*" said Mrs. Winters.

The solicitor was fingering his collar when a new voice broke into the discussion with:

"What *is* all this excitement about?"

Mrs. Harler had come up behind Mrs. Winters. She pushed past the housekeeper and stepped out to face Mr. Howard with a winning smile.

"Why, Mr. Howard! It's so nice to see you again! Are you calling on Sir Victor?"

Down on the gravel drive, Clement Harler was almost dancing with a mixture of rage and fluster.

"I've told him he can't see him!"

"Clem, darling," she reproved, "stop making an exhibition of yourself. I could hear your voice right at the back of the house. Of course Mr. Howard can't talk to Sir Victor today, but surely we can fix another appointment without having such a scene?"

She turned back to Mr. Howard and intensified the charm till the needle pointed to "Max."

"Mr. Howard, I'm so *sorry* about all this. I'm afraid we're not quite ourselves today. Sir Victor was—a little difficult last night and we're all rather worried over him. I'm sure you'll leave it to us to ring you when we think he's well enough, won't you?"

This sweet reasonableness left the solicitor with no alternative but to consent. Mrs. Winters, however, was not yet vanquished.

"I'll give you until this time tomorrow," she said. "If Mr. Howard is not allowed to see Sir Victor then—"

Mrs. Harler interrupted her with a merry peal of laughter.

"Well! That's too delicious! Since when have you been delivering ultimatums in this house, Mrs. Winters?" She went on to Mr. Howard, "The impertinence of the old family servant!"

"You cannot provoke me with your insults, Mrs. Harler," was the housekeeper's unruffled retort. "But if you don't do as I say, I shall ask that police inspector to call again—and you two won't be the only ones to get a nasty surprise."

"What a horrible threat! You mustn't take her too seriously, Mr. Howard."

Mrs. Winters tossed her head in scorn.

"Giggle all you want, my fine lady! You'll not prevent me from doing everything I can to protect an honourable, trusting old gentleman from a pair of cheap confidence tricksters!"

CHAPTER THREE

INSPECTOR CHARLTON left young John Campbell in the spinney and walked back to his car. He had not finished telling Sergeant Martin about John's dummy revolver when Mr. Howard pulled up alongside them. After they had exchanged greetings, Charlton said:

"Can you give me a few minutes, Mr. Howard, if I come back to your office now?"

"I was about to suggest the same thing. I imagine"—his tone was dry—"that your presence here is not a coincidence."

The two cars returned to Lulverton.

Mr. Howard, a portly man in the middle fifties, who combined the dignified demeanour of the town's most eminent solicitor with the hail-fellow-well-met manner of the golf club, was the senior partner of Messrs. Dickson, Parrish, Willmott & Lister, whose offices were in Bank Chambers, over the Southern Counties Bank in Lulverton High Street. He and Charlton knew each other well, both professionally and socially.

The interview began on a strictly formal level in Mr. Howard's thick-carpeted, mahogany-furnished, quietly impressive office—the sort of room in which nothing had moved quickly and no one had shouted for a hundred years; a room of intimate, murmured conferences, where the picture-hung walls heard much, but never prated.

Mr. Howard sat at his big desk, with Charlton and Martin, his bowler hat on his lap, sitting opposite.

"I trust," the solicitor opened the conversation, "that you will regard what I have to tell you as confidential and—er—*inter nos*. Sir Victor is a client—I may say an extremely valuable client—of ours. As chairman of Victor Motors Limited and its affiliated companies, Sir Victor is a gentleman of substance. Last Saturday morning—the day before yesterday—I received a letter from him. It contained a request for me to call upon him without fail—those two words were underlined—and suggested that ten o'clock this morning would be a suitable time. Sir Victor added that the matter was important and pressing."

"Did he say what it was?"

"No. Having regard for the obviously serious nature of the summons, I cancelled another appointment for ten o'clock this morning and drove out to the Warringham home. I gathered from a chance remark of one of the household that you yourself had called there a few minutes before I arrived."

"Quite so," Charlton agreed. "Please go on."

"Sir Victor—have you met him, by the way?"

"Never."

"He is not a businessman, in the accepted sense of the phrase. He is not the great magnate of popular imagination. He is more a man of the study than of the boardroom a man also, one might say, of the drawing-office, for it was he who designed the first Victor motorcar, the latest models of which still retain many of the features—unique in those days—of the original Victor. With capital put up by his life-long friend—a man called Andrew Blackmore—he started a small company and went into production. From those small beginnings has grown the immense concern that Victor Motors Limited is today. Sir Victor is a man of varied interests, sober habits and lucid mind. I have known him for twenty-five years, so can speak with some authority. I mention these points, Charlton, as a necessary introduction to what I am going to tell you now."

He leaned forward with his elbows on the red-leather arms of his chair and his hands clasped across his plump body. His face was grave.

"When I arrived at Elmsdale, I was refused admittance by Sir Victor's son-in-law, an objectionable fellow by the name of Clement Harler. The reason he gave was that Sir Victor was unwell. Had this explanation come from any other man in this neighbourhood—I might almost say in Great Britain—I should certainly have accepted it and come away without question. Once again I must ask you to look on these remarks as in confidence."

He looked rather dubiously at Martin.

"Naturally, sir," answered that offended man, and flicked a non-existent speck from the crown of his bowler before settling it with both hands more firmly on his lap.

With this assurance, the solicitor resumed:

"In my considered opinion, Harler is a thoroughly unscrupulous and completely stupid man. You may perhaps know that he was once in the employment of Victor Motors. Quite an unimportant position—something in the accounts department, if I remember rightly. How he came to meet Miss Rosalie Warringham, I cannot say, but he managed it somehow, and they were married some twelve or thirteen years ago."

"With her parents' consent?"

"Oh, yes. Sir Victor and Lady Warringham, who was then alive, favoured the match—or perhaps I should say that they did not stand out against it. Mark you, in those days Harler was not so—well, not so disreputable in appearance as he is today. He dressed smartly and, with a certain confident manner that cloaked an entire lack of real intelligence, was able, as it were, to put on an act for long enough to achieve his purpose."

He leant back in his chair.

"Harler did not last much more than a year in Victor Motors. After the marriage, Sir Victor took him out of the accounts department, or wherever it was, and put him in charge of another section. No great promotion, but a step in the right direction that would have enabled a man of any competency at all to rise, without invoking a charge of family favouritism, to a high administrative post in the company. But Harler failed. He neglected his work. He abused his position as the chairman's son-in-law. The time he took for lunch was limited only by licensed hours. The result was inevitable. He was transferred from the company's head office in Birmingham to the London branch, where, in a position of complete unimportance and lack of responsibility—I believe Sir Victor invented a sinecure especially for him—he continued for a time on a salary that was, in the circumstances, criminally generous."

The two detectives were listening closely. The quiet, precise voice went on:

"I have never been entrusted with the facts, so I cannot give you the reason, but something over ten years ago, Harler left this country. The official account put out was that he had gone as the company's representative to South America. Extremely doubtful, in my view. For some time, I heard no news of him, then a report came through that he had been killed in a train smash in Brazil—a report that I am sure the whole Warringham family greeted with sighs of relief. Rosalie had come to live with her parents at Elmsdale. She continued to do so until her tragic death. Probably you know that she and Lady Warringham were killed by a flying-bomb."

They both nodded without speaking.

"Some months after the capitulation of Japan, Harler was seen again in Lulverton. He took up residence at Elmsdale and later brought there his second wife, whom he had met and married in Brazil. If one admires that lush type of beauty, Gladys Harler has her attractions. To my mind, she is like a fine-looking apple with a big, fat maggot in the centre of it. What she was before Harler married her, I can only surmise. . . And they both came to live with grief-stricken Sir Victor."

He was silent for a time. Martin shifted uneasily on his chair. Charlton's face was stern; the story was not pretty.

"On that evidence alone," Mr. Howard began to speak again, "and with nothing save suspicions—however well-founded—as to Harler's departure abroad and sudden return after an absence of many years, there is something evil, something sinister, about the whole thing. One cannot rid one's mind of the grim picture of those two vampires—perhaps the word is too strong for Harler, but it undoubtedly describes Gladys—

battening on the old gentleman."

He thumped his fist on the desk.

"I say with complete conviction, Charlton, that Sir Victor would never willingly have permitted Harler across the threshold of Elmsdale. While his daughter lived, he might have agreed to meet her wishes, but with her in her grave and with Harler married to a wife no better than a woman of the streets—never!"

His voice became less excited as he continued.

"You will understand that it would be a breach of professional etiquette if I were to disclose to you the provisions of a client's will. But in order to impress you with the gravity of the present situation as I see it, I feel justified in telling you that, as matters now stand, Harler would profit handsomely by Sir Victor's death. . . Now let me tell you what happened an hour ago. Harler himself opened the door to me and wasted no time in trying to find out why Sir Victor had summoned me. Naturally, I should not have told him, even had I known. Having failed to pump me, Harler informed me that my appointment must be postponed until next week because Sir Victor was unwell. Frankly, I did not believe him. I insisted on being shown in to Sir Victor. Then Harler made the astounding statement—an impertinent, flagrant falsehood—that Sir Victor's malady was not physical, but mental—in short, that he was insane!"

"You don't agree?"

"A thousand times no! As I told you, I have known Sir Victor for twenty-five years. During the whole of that period, I have met him constantly; and I am prepared to go into the witness-box and swear to his sanity."

"But it would be very much to Harler's advantage if he weren't?"

"Of course it would. Granted that a man who has been certified insane can make a new will if he wishes, or cause a codicil to be added to an existing will; but the beneficiaries would have an uphill fight to have it admitted to probate in preference to the previous will. Yes, Harler would be safe if Sir Victor could be proved to be out of his mind."

"Harler told me that a brain specialist is coming down from London on Wednesday."

"He said the same to me. The man's obviously lying."

"I wouldn't be too sure about that. What did you do when he still tried to turn you away?"

"At that point there was an interruption. Mrs. Winters, the housekeeper, appeared and there was an embarrassing scene between her and Harler. She seemed as anxious that I should see Sir Victor as Harler was that I should not. Harler became extremely heated and abusive; and the sound of the altercation brought out Mrs. Harler, who tried to succeed where her husband had failed. Mrs. Winters' response was to accuse them to their faces of being a pair of confidence tricksters, and went on to threaten them that, if I was not permitted to see Sir Victor at ten o'clock tomorrow morning, she would come and see *you*."

Charlton smiled grimly, but made no comment.

"So," Mr. Howard concluded his story, "I came away—not to wait until tomorrow, but to anticipate Mrs. Winters in reporting the whole extraordinary affair to you. My own opinion is that Sir Victor is in real danger."

"Would you say that Mrs. Winters had her own reasons for wanting your interview to take place?"

The solicitor did not answer at once.

"It is clear that she shares my own views about the Harlers and that she is extremely suspicious of their motives. She has been in Sir Victor's employment for many years and it could be said that she showed no more than a natural desire to protect his interests."

"You haven't quite answered my question, Mr. Howard. You've told us that Harler has reason to be satisfied with Sir Victor's existing will. Is Mrs. Winters equally content?"

"She will receive an adequate annuity on Sir Victor's death."

Charlton looked at him steadily.

"Mr. Howard, I appreciate the need for professional reticence, but you are being evasive. If you don't want to answer my question, please say so."

The solicitor grimaced.

"Sorry. You're quite right. May I put it like this: Mrs. Winters has found cause for complaint against the terms of the existing will. It is possible that she has prevailed upon Sir Victor to alter them."

Charlton rose to his feet.

"Thank you, Mr. Howard. I'm obliged to you for passing on all this information so promptly. There's nothing much for the police to act on yet, but we'll keep our eyes open."

And, with Martin at his heels, he left Bank Chambers before Mr. Howard remembered to question him about his own visit to Elmsdale.

They got into the Vauxhall. As Martin raised himself in his seat to tuck his overcoat beneath him, he remarked:

"Bit of excitement, one way and another, outside Elmsdale this morning."

His chief grunted agreement and pressed his finger on the starter-button. As the engine came to life, Martin went on meditatively:

"Shots going off, arguments, people shouting and so forth."

The car moved off along the High Street.

Martin ruminated: "Funny it didn't rouse Sir Victor."

CHAPTER FOUR

(i)

AFTER Mrs. Winters had told the Harlers precisely what she thought of them, she turned and swept off down the hall, a mauve-gowned Alecto, leaving Mr. Howard to take his leave. Husband and wife watched the solicitor drive away, then went back indoors. As Harler closed the front door, Gladys said:

"Come upstairs."

Dutifully he followed her up the staircase to the first landing and round to the right to their sitting-room. She sank into an easy chair while he lighted the gas fire. She began to manicure her nails.

"You know something, Clem?"

He adjusted the tap to stop the gas from roaring and stood upright.

"Yes?" he replied without much animation.

"You're a fool, Clem. And do you know something else? I'm a bigger fool than you are." She carefully filed a section of nail, then examined it critically as she added: "If that's possible."

"There's no need to get rude, Glad," he grumbled.

"What did you tell the detectives this morning?"

His manner was a mixture of apology and self-vindication as he replied:

"The only thing I *could* tell 'em; that the old boy was going through one of his sessions of heeby-jeebies and that, if he saw fit to ring up the police about some homicidal hobgoblin, they shouldn't take him too seriously. I said that his was a case for the brain specialist, not the police. That got rid of them."

"Were they satisfied?"

"How should I know? I got 'em out of the house for the time being anyway. Isn't that enough till we can think of something? They caught me on the wrong foot, Glad. What did the old fool want to go and ring up for?"

"Did they say they were coming back?"

"Course they're coming back! Warringham 'phoned for the police. That started the machinery going—and you know what that means, don't you? I don't like the look of that Inspector Clayton, or whatever his blasted name is. He's too smooth, too much the—gentleman. It put the fear of God in me when the Winters woman got hold of him first. How much d'you think she knows?"

"Not nearly as much as she suspects."

"That 'confidence tricksters' crack was a kick in the teeth, Glad. The first time she's ever come out in the open. What beats me is, why did she tell Clayton that old Stamford called here last night?"

"Did she? I didn't know that. Probably the first thing that came into her head She'd tell any lie to keep Father from being disturbed."

Harler shook himself.

"I wish you wouldn't call him that," he complained uneasily. "It gives me the shudders. Too damned callous."

Gladys Harler laughed gaily and picked up her orange-stick.

"Father twice removed," she said. "Father once removed would suit us better, wouldn't it, Clem, darling?"

"Shut up!" he retorted roughly. "It's not a thing to make funny jokes about. I'm asking you, why did Winters lie about the doctor?"

"I've just told you."

"And I don't believe it. Look at it like this, Glad. Winters has got her eye on us. Right? She's been with the family long enough to know all about *me.* Right? She knows that I didn't get back under this roof without putting some sort of screw on the old boy. Right? She knows that the old boy'd give his right hand to be shot of us. Right? She knows—"

"I wish you wouldn't keep on saying 'Right'."

"She knows," pursued Harler undeterred, "that so long as the old boy doesn't tear up his will, you and I are sitting pretty—or will be when he snuffs it."

"*Does* she?"

"You bet she does! That woman'd find out anything. Now, look, Glad. It would suit her book if something unpleasant happened to you and me, wouldn't it? She'd be the boss here, like she was before we crashed in. Then why did she send the police away—or try to? I think she's got something up her sleeve, Glad."

"Purple secrets?"

"No, seriously, why did she try to send Clayton packing?"

"Clem, darling, I'm thinking. Forget Winters for a minute. I told the police this morning—you know, I think that inspector's rather nice; like a diplomat at a British Embassy somewhere, with his grey hair and sort of distinguished face. I quite fell in—"

"Stick to the point," growled her husband.

"I told him this morning that your dear father-in-law thought he was being murdered last night."

"Well, he did, didn't he?"

"Yes, I know. But thinking you're being murdered by a ghost is very different from thinking you're being murdered by a real, live person. And he *did* think he was being murdered by a real, live person. But we don't want other people to get that impression, Clem."

She stood up to face him.

"We'd better have that inspector back," she decided, Harler slid the forefinger of his hand along the side of his mouth and chewed at the nail.

"Asking for trouble, isn't it?"

"I don't fancy the police any more than you do, Clem. They always depress me so—and they ask such coarse questions. But this Clayton man is sure to come back, whatever we try to do about it. Why not take the bull by the horns? We could probably turn it to good use, Clem. Don't forget that specialist."

"But supposing Clayton believes the old boy's yarn?"

"Stamford thinks he's mad, doesn't he?"

"Yes, but—"

"Then we'll work on Stamford and turn Clayton over to him before he gets a chance to see Sir Victor first. Stamford will assure Clayton that he's got a loony to deal with—and there you are, Clem. You'd better telephone the doctor now."

"Did you put the old boy to sleep?"

"Yes, I slipped him a tablet in his breakfast coffee, just in case he got difficult when the solicitor came."

"Pity you didn't do it earlier. It would have stopped him from 'phoning. That detective fellow wants me to ring him as soon as Stamford's given the O.K."

"Then get on to Stamford quick."

Obediently Harler stepped to the door. His wife's next remark made him pause with his hand on the knob. She said:

"Blackmore was with Sir Victor for an hour on Friday evening."

Harler snorted, "I'm not frightened of Blackmore."

"You are, you know," Gladys told him, holding her hand away from her, palm-forward, to inspect her manicure.

Her husband snorted again and went downstairs to telephone Dr. Stamford. When he came back, Gladys was busy on the other hand. She looked up as he entered.

"Clem," she said, "I've been thinking about Mrs. Winters."

(ii)

Inspector Charlton did not wait for Harler to act. He drove straight from Bank Chambers to the house of Dr. Stamford and was fortunate enough to find him at home.

By a section of Lulverton's townspeople, this elderly medico was known as Old Mortality, a cynical and disrespectful description, yet, as the section was no small one, there must have been more than a grain of truth in it. It was said that he had not had a new patient for twenty-five years, and, with the steady dwindling of his once flourishing practice—a dwindling that had, in fairness, to be attributed in part to deaths from old age—now found himself with a mere handful of aged survivors. He was nearly seventy and walked with a stoop. His lower jaw, by its tendency to wobble, gave the impression that it had been filletted. And in his shuffling, fidgety fashion, he was a thoroughly stubborn old gentleman.

Charlton made himself known and introduced Sergeant Martin.

"I understand, Doctor, that Sir Victor Warringham is a patient of yours?"

"Quite so, Inspector. I have—um—attended him for many years. I have, in fact, just received an urgent—um—summons on the telephone from his son-in-law, Mr.—um—Harler. He gave me no details. I trust, Inspector, that there has not been some—um—serious accident?"

Charlton shook his head with a reassuring smile.

"As far as I know, Sir Victor has not been injured, but I've called on the same matter. This morning, Doctor, a 'phone call came through to Police Headquarters. It was from Sir Victor. He said that an attempt on his life was made in the early hours this morning."

Dr. Stamford tut-tutted and his chin quivered with distress.

"I drove out to Elmsdale immediately, Doctor. I was received, first by Mrs. Winters, the housekeeper, and then by Mr. Harler. They both considered it unwise for me to interview Sir Victor, so I came away, after receiving Mr. Harler's assurance that I should be allowed to see Sir Victor if you, as his medical adviser, were satisfied with his condition."

"You say that Sir Victor was not injured in any way?"

"I think not, though, of course, I haven't seen him. Mr. Harler suggests that there was no attack on Sir Victor—that he only imagined it. Would that be likely, Doctor?"

The old man got up from his untidy roll-top desk and walked up and down the consulting-room a couple of times before he answered:

"In—um recent months, Sir Victor has been causing me um—concern. He is no longer a young man and his heart—well, in—um—unmedical parlance, is beginning to wear out. I do not say that its condition is critical or—um—immediately dangerous, but I have advised Sir Victor to rest as much as possible and not to take exercise of—um—too strenuous a nature."

With bowed shoulders and hands clasped behind his back, he took another turn up and down the room.

"Unhappily, that is not the full extent of Sir Victor's—um—indisposition. I fear that his brain is also affected. As I have already mentioned, in recent months he has caused concern, not only to myself, but also to his—um—family. As you may be aware, in the summer of 1944 Sir Victor suffered a tragic—um—bereavement. In one—um—merciless blow, he lost his beloved wife and only daughter. Since that time, Sir Victor has been a changed man. Evidence of this is to be seen in his home, particularly in the—um—grounds, which were once his pride and—um—joy, and in which he spent many happy, industrious hours. Perhaps you have seen them recently?" He threw out his hands. "It is very—um—sad. Sir Victor has retired more and more into himself. He used to be so . . . spry is not quite the right word. Vigorous is more—um—correct; vigorous both physically and mentally. Now he is a dreamer with an inner life of his own."

He shuffled towards the fireplace and poked the coals in the grate, then turned back to the seated detectives with the poker still in his hand.

"I have been a general practitioner for well-nigh half a century, Inspector. My work has been in the—um—sphere of physic rather than psycho-pathology."

He leant the poker against the blue tiles of the grate. It slipped and fell with a clatter. With an ejaculation of annoyance, he tried to pick it up. Martin had to help him. When things had been put to rights, the old man reseated himself and passed a hand across his brow.

"What were we discussing?" he enquired.

"That you are more of a physician than a psychiatrist."

"Ah, yes! It was—um—Hamlet, I think, who said that there are more things—yes, it was Hamlet, in the play of the same name—more things in heaven and earth than are dreamed of in our philosophy. With that I am the first to—um—agree. I cannot condemn psychomancy—the cult of—um—spiritualism—out of hand, because I have not studied it sufficiently—um—deeply. I should add, nevertheless, that spiritualism would not have found so many—um—adherents had it not been for the First World War, when so many—um—unfortunate people lost their nearest and dearest and were—um—reluctant to think—"

Sergeant Martin had coughed a trifle pointedly. Dr. Stamford's mind groped its way back to the main theme.

"But that is by the way. It is a fact that after the death of his wife and daughter, Sir Victor did—um—develop strong spiritualistic—um—tendencies. He visited mediums; even, on more than one occasion, arranging for *séances* to be held at Elmsdale. That the—um—mediums were honest men and women, or that the so called *séances* were free from—um—trickery, I myself gravely doubt. Whether Sir Victor was convinced of their—um—authenticity, I do not know. I can merely—um—conjecture. Suffice it to say that he has since acted strangely. On the—um—testimony of reliable witnesses, whom I have questioned in order to arrive at some conclusion as to Sir Victor's—um—mental condition—"

"Who were these witnesses, Doctor?"

"Mr. Harler and his wife; Mrs. Winters, the housekeeper; the maidservant; a gentleman named Blackmore.

I even tactfully sounded the housekeeper's—um—nephew, who lives in the house."

"Who is Mr. Blackmore?"

"A friend of the family, who is—um—*persona grata* at Elmsdale. I know very little about him, except that he has had numerous—um—opportunities of observing Sir Victor's behaviour. All these people—um—have testified that Sir Victor is not the mentally balanced man that he was before the—um—tragedy."

"In what way was his behaviour abnormal, Doctor?"

"To take one example, I had it from little John Campbell, the—um—housekeeper's nephew, that one morning during the summer, Sir Victor took the boy on one side and asked him to procure—um—a dead frog. Yes, indeed—a dead frog."

"Perhaps Sir Victor is interested in physiology."

Martin shifted restlessly in his chair. All these physios and psychos were bothering him.

"One would hardly use a *dead* frog for such purposes," Dr. Stamford reminded the Inspector gently. "And when I tell you that, during the same morning, Sir Victor instructed the housemaid to fetch him a quart of—um—goat's milk, I think you will concede that Sir Victor could not have been engaged on—um—normal scientific research."

As one who had scored a telling point, the good doctor pulled down the dandruffy lapels of his morning coat.

"On another occasion," he continued, "Sir Victor produced a planchette. No doubt you are acquainted with the toy. I call it a toy advisedly. It is a board supported at two points by—um—small wheels and at the third by a pencil. Sir Victor—um—persuaded Mrs. Winters to join with him in resting her hands on the board, in the—um—hope that, through the medium of their fingers, the pencil would write a message from—um—the other world. Mrs. Winters has told me that she had an extremely difficult—um—time with him on that particular occasion."

"What happened?"

"Sir Victor asked the question, 'Are you both happy?' and under their fingers, the—um—planchette spelled out the answer, 'Very.' At first, according to Mrs. Winters, Sir Victor expressed great delight at this result, but—um—almost immediately he became—um—suspicious and demanded to know whether she had—um—played fair. Under his angry interrogation, the poor woman broke down and admitted that she had deliberately—um—directed the course of the pencil. Sir Victor then became so—um—unmanageable that Mrs. Winters had to cry out for—um—assistance. Fortunately, Mr. Harler and his wife were within call. Mr. Harler has informed me that he entered the room just in time to prevent the angry old gentleman from—um—belabouring the housekeeper with the planchette board. The Harlers got it away from him and ultimately—um—succeeded in pacifying him."

This attractive picture of Clement and Gladys purveying balm in Gilead did not impress Charlton. However, he let it go without comment.

"One day last week," the old doctor went on, "Mr. Harler called upon me. In the past we had had a number of serious—um—discussions on the question of Sir Victor's mental state, and we had decided that he had not reached the—um—critical juncture where eccentricity ends and—um—insanity begins. It was now Mr. Harler's conviction that that—um—juncture had been reached. Having had the same thought in my mind for some time past, I agreed with him. Naturally the unfortunate old gentleman's removal to a suitable—um—institution was not to be thought of without another—and more expert—opinion than my own. I decided, therefore, to call in a specialist in mental disorders. I expect you know the name of Sir Ninian Oxenham? I have been lucky enough to secure his services and have—um—arranged for him to visit Sir Victor at eleven o'clock in the forenoon of Wednesday next—that is to say, the—um—day after tomorrow."

"Was Sir Ninian's visit acceptable to Mr. Harler?"

"Not at first. His main objection was on the score of—um—expense. Sir Ninian's fees are not—um—negligible. But when I explained that, in any case, if a reception order were to be made by the judicial authority, the original petition by Mr. Harler would have to be accompanied by—um—a statement of particulars and two medical certificates, Mr Harler quite saw that it would be a decided—um—advantage if one of the certificates were signed by such an acknowledged—um—authority as Sir Ninian Oxenham. I must, in fairness, admit that I myself would not have considered going to—um—so high a source as Sir Ninian had Mr. Blackmore not put the—um—idea into my head."

"Was Mr. Blackmore at your conference with Mr. Harler?"

"No. In my last remarks, I have—um—telescoped two talks with Mr. Harler into one. It was not until my second talk with him that I put forward the suggestion which, since our first talk, had been made to me by Mr.—um—Blackmore."

To Charlton it seemed that there had been a good deal more conflict of human wills than Dr. Stamford wished him to imagine. He made a mental note to seek out Blackmore.

Grunting from the exertion, Dr. Stamford got himself out of his chair.

"So until Sir Ninian has made his—um—diagnosis, we can do nothing. I shall, of course, call at Elmsdale immediately after lunch, but I fear that there will be little that I can—um—do."

Charlton stood up and buttoned his overcoat.

"May I leave it to you, then, Doctor, to let me know as soon as I can see Sir Victor?"

"I can answer that question now, Inspector. I do not consider it either desirable or—um—necessary for you to see him at all."

"I don't agree with you." Charlton's voice was firm.

The old doctor's chin wobbled with displeasure.

"You have told me yourself," he sputtered angrily, "that Sir Victor was not—um—injured in any way. It should be obvious to a normal—um—intelligence that this so called attack was a figment—the merest—um—figment—of my patient's diseased mind. As his medical adviser, I cannot countenance—in no circumstances will I—um—permit him to be placed in a position that would still further endanger the—um—stability of a human brain which has already—um—um—um—deviated so far from the normal! If, in spite of my warning, you insist on disturbing Sir Victor with your—um—um—ill-timed rigmarole, I shall hold you entirely responsible for the—um—consequences. That is my last word."

Charlton said quietly: "Very well, Doctor."

Outside in the street, after the front door had been closed un-gently behind them, Martin said, not without a note of naughty elation in his voice:

"It's turning—um—colder."

CHAPTER FIVE

AT the time when Inspector Charlton was accepting his dismissal from Dr. Stamford, the conversation between Clement and Gladys Harler was coming to a stormy finish. Harler's last words were:

"Giving him the jitters is one thing, but dammit, the other would be sheer madness!"

His wife did not restrain him as he jumped to his feet and pulled open the door.

In the passage stood John Campbell.

"What are you doing hero?" Harler questioned sharply.

"Nothing much," replied the boy with studied unconcern. "Just walking along the passage."

He was wearing his overcoat and carrying his pink school cap.

Harler said: "You were standing still when I opened the door."

"Oh, I'd just stopped, Mr. Harler."

"Why?"

"There was a spider on the wall and I was looking at it. It ran away just as you came out. I think you frightened it."

"Well, you run away, too! You know you're not supposed to be in this part of the house."

"All right, Mr. Harler."

Still with assumed self-possession, John turned to walk away towards the main staircase. As he did so, something slipped from beneath his overcoat and fell with a thud on the linoleum. It was the imitation revolver. Swiftly the boy bent down and picked it up, but before he could slip it away in his pocket, Harler got hold of his arm in a grip that made him wince.

"What have you got there?"

"It's a toy pistol, sir."

"Give it to me."

He gave the boy no chance to protest, but wrenched the thing from his hand.

"*Toy* pistol!" he scoffed. "This is a dangerous weapon. Were you firing this off in the spinney this morning?"

John gulped out: "Yes, sir."

"Mad young fool! It's about time somebody took you in hand. Where did you get this thing from?"

"Somebody lent it to me."

"Well, you tell that somebody that I've confiscated it."

"But, sir!"

"Don't argue with me! Where are the caps—the shots, or whatever you call 'em?"

"I—I—There aren't any left, sir."

With unnecessary roughness, Harler shook the boy. There was a tell-tale metallic rattle. Harler dived his hand into John's overcoat pocket and pulled out the tin of blanks.

"You lying brat! If I catch you up to anything like this again, I'll thrash you within an inch of your life! I'm master of this house now. Remember that! . . . Now tell your Aunt I want to see her immediately." He pushed John away from him and went back into the sitting-room.

"Clem," his wife complained from the settee, as he slammed the door, "I wish you wouldn't be so damn violent. You remind me of Laughton on the quarterdeck of the *Bounty*. And you can kid yourself all you like, but you're *not* master of this house."

"Perhaps not, but I soon shall be."

"Changed your mind already, Clem?" his wife enquired sweetly.

Meanwhile John Campbell went off to find Mrs. Winters with murder in his young heart.

Soon after the Harlers had finished lunch, Dr. Stamford called at Elmsdale. Harler received him in the library, while the seductive Gladys went off to give instructions for Sir Victor to be got ready.

"I didn't give you any details on the 'phone, Doctor," said Harler, "because it's not the sort of thing to shout from the housetops, but we had a bad time with the poor old fellow last night. The wife and I had been sitting up late, playing crib, and we hadn't been in bed very long—round about two o'clock, I would say—when the most fearful yelling, accompanied by thumping on a door, started in the other wing. The wife said, 'That's Sir Victor!' I leapt out of bed and rushed along to his room. When I went in, he was standing there in his nightshirt, looking like death. I asked him what the devil was the matter and managed to get out of him some yarn about spooky hands trying to strangle him. I tried to tell him that it was all imagination, but I couldn't do anything with him, he was so worked up. He even tried to bring *me* into it."

He smote his chest dramatically.

"Me, of all people! Said I'd like to see him dead, or some such nonsense."

"Very worrying," Dr. Stamford sympathised. "Such cases—um—not infrequently develop into persecution mania."

Harler shrugged his shoulders philosophically.

"All in the day's work, I suppose, though I'm beginning to be sorry I accepted his invitation for the wife and me to come and live here. Anyway, while I was endeavouring to cope with him, the wife and Mrs. Winters appeared. Between the three of us, we persuaded him—or so we thought at the time—that he must have been dreaming; and he got back into bed. I can't explain the happy knack some women have, but the wife seems to have a way with her on these occasions. Sir Victor has a childish trust in her. Pathetic, really."

"Did you give Sir Victor one of the tablets I supplied?"

"Oh, yes, of course. That reminds me, Doctor, I carelessly dropped the box in the fireplace and wasn't able to salvage more than two or three tablets."

"I will let you have some more, Mr. Harler, but please do not administer them more often than is absolutely necessary."

"The father-in-law will see to that, Doctor! We have to use a lot of trickery to administer the tablets at all. I think the old boy's got the impression that we're slowly poisoning him!"

"Most distressing for you. Now if I may, Mr. Harler, I will go up to Sir Victor—not, I am afraid, that I shall be—um—able to do much for him. I earnestly hope that an authoritative—um—decision on the part of Sir Ninian Oxenham will relieve you of your present heavy—um—responsibilities."

"So do I, Doctor—very fervently," the worried little man agreed from the bottom of his heart. "Let's go up, shall we?"

"By all means—but wait. There is one other thing. This morning I received a visit from the—um—police."

Harler's hands clenched convulsively.

"You did, did you?"

"A visit that—um—ended on an unpleasant note. A certain Detective-inspector Charlton—a very persistent and overbearing—um type of man—insisted on interviewing Sir Victor. I, of course, flatly refused to allow it. We cannot—um—"

"But Dr. Stamford!" Harler gave a helpless gesture.

"The Inspector left here this morning on the understanding that, as soon as you had agreed—"

"And I do *not* agree, Mr. Harler! Sir Victor is my patient, my—um—responsibility. I left the Inspector in no doubt on that score—no doubt whatever. You can rest assured that he will not—um—trouble you again."

"But supposing something happened to Sir Victor? Suppose he died? Just suppose he was murdered tonight? I should be in a spot, shouldn't I?"

The old doctor tapped him on the shoulder encouragingly.

"Calm yourself, my boy! This miserable business is affecting your nerves. Keep cool. Why should any—um—evil befall Sir Victor?"

"But after last night—"

"Nonsense! As I told that—um—offensive detective, no normal person would attach—um—credence to a poor old gentleman's wild—um—imaginings. No, I think you will hear nothing further from the police. Which will be a very good thing, if you ask my—um—opinion. I do not like the look of

Inspector Charlton."

Harler walked across and opened the door.

"Neither do I," he muttered.

CHAPTER SIX

(i)

TOM BLACKMORE stuck his garden-fork in the ground, pulled a box of matches from the pocket of his well-worn sports coat and relighted his big briar pipe.

November is an uninteresting month for the gardener, yet a month when there is much solid work to do. Digging and clearing, for the most part. Dead stalks to be cut away and burnt, leaves and rubbish to be collected for the compost heap, roses to be transplanted, phloxes to be divided and moved, gooseberry and currant bushes to be pruned—and so with the pear tree on the wall of the cottage. Yes, there was a lot to be done, yet Tom Blackmore loved it all. Orators may be made, but gardeners, like poets, are born that way. This fair-haired giant of forty-five had the green thumb, a gift that was manifested—perhaps not in November, but certainly in the more fruitful months—by the small, beautiful garden of Peartree Cottage.

The cottage itself, which was just outside Mickleham village, was no architect's dream. Give a child a pencil and instructions to draw a house, and the finished sketch will be, in general design, a facsimile of Peartree Cottage: box-shaped, two-storeyed, with a central front door, a window on each side of it and two windows above; and a couple of single-potted chimney stacks, one to the right, the other to the left, of the common-gable roof. Having got so far with the elevation, the normal child will draw a front fence with a gate in the middle of it, a straight garden path so entirely out of perspective that the house seems to stand on top of it, like a dove-cote on a pole; and will add a homely touch to the two-dimensional residence by great clouds of ponderable, 'press-hard', black smoke from the chimneys, and a dog whose size is governed only by the extent of the front garden. In these last two respects, Peartree Cottage differed slightly; only one chimney was smoking, very modestly, and the dog was not a spindle-legged monster in the front garden, but a normal-sized cocker spaniel, answering to the name of Bugle, in the back garden with his master.

With his pipe going again, Tom Blackmore put another fork-load on the bonfire, then went back to his digging, while Bugle interested himself strenuously in a series of exciting delusions, as only the young can do. After another half an hour under the heavy grey sky of the winter's afternoon—it was growing colder and there was frost about—they went indoors for tea.

The interior of Peartree Cottage was as simple in pattern as the outside. As one entered through the front door, one was faced by the stairs. To one's left was the door leading into the kitchen, to one's right, the door of the sitting-room which Tom Blackmore called his den. Similar doors at the head of the staircase gave access to the two bedrooms. From the kitchen a door opened on to the back garden. In modern amenities, the cottage was entirely lacking; no gas, electricity, water supply or main drainage. For cooking and lighting, Tom Blackmore had paraffin stoves and lamps; for water he was dependent on a well outside the back door; for bathing he had a galvanised tub, filled with great labour from a copper in the outhouse; and the other important domestic need was met by a *cabinet d'aisance*—to use the graceful French phrase—at the bottom of the garden.

But with this unpromising material, Tom Blackmore had worked wonders. When he had taken over the cottage some years before, he had stripped off the abominable floral wallpapers, that had extended from wainscot to ceiling; had fitted picture-rails, then whitewashed above and distempered below; had banished the copper to the outhouse; had adjusted the windows so that they opened—an innovation not envisaged by previous tenants: and had broken the flat façades at front and back by building porches for the doors. The furniture was old and solid, his few pictures good. The den was well stocked with books on a wide range of subjects. Under one window was a flat-topped desk, under the other, a couch. In a corner was a cabinet-gramophone and on a table by the fireplace was a battery-radio within arm's reach of Tom Blackmore's easy chair. The fireplace had once been of Victorian design, with a black-leaded, barred grate, violent blue tiles and a painted cast-iron mantel. Tom Blackmore had prised the grate from its moorings, fitted a barless grate in its place, removed the mantel and tiles and built a surround of red bricks.

With Bugle fussing around him, Tom Blackmore removed his mud-caked shoes in the back porch and entered the kitchen in his socks. Bugle was not so meticulous; he enthusiastically lolloped and slid on the linoleum that Mrs. Tucker, from the village, had so painstakingly polished only that morning. Tom found his slippers, then lighted the oil-stove. While the kettle came to the boil, he went into the den, put a fresh log on the fire and dropped into his easy chair with a thankful sigh.

"Hard work digging, Bugle, my boy," he said to the spaniel, who had stretched himself out on the hearth-rug with as deep a breath as his master's.

Bugle raised his head. "Nothing to what I've been up to," his eyes might have said.

They were good friends, these two. A man who lives alone has need of a dog, if only to lend a sympathetic ear. One feels so foolish, talking to oneself. It was a dull life—or would have been if Tom Blackmore had let it. He had to make his own amusements these days—gardening, reading, the gramophone, the radio. There was much to be forgotten—and still more to be remembered. Those years of marriage, they were to be forgotten. Sometimes he wondered if his wife was still alive. Then he would shrug his shoulders; she wasn't the sort of woman to die easily. At other times he would speculate idly whether she was still living with that Valentine fellow. Probably not. She would have run through years ago whatever money he had had. Yes, all that was to be forgotten. Memory should be for those pleasanter things.

But that afternoon Tom Blackmore was neither remembering, nor trying to forget. His mind was serenely concerned with the pleasures of the moment. A day's work in the garden, to be followed by an evening with pipe and radio. He sighed again, this time with quiet satisfaction, and levered himself out of his chair as the kettle-lid began to rattle in the other room.

While he was transferring a spoonful of tea from the caddy to the pot, the latch of the front gate clicked. He went to the window and looked out into the gathering dusk. Young John Campbell was walking up the path.

(ii)

Blackmore put down the tea-pot and went to open the door to his visitor.

"Hullo, John!" he welcomed him with a broad smile. "I didn't expect to see you along today. Got yourself expelled or something?"

The boy's answering smile was not so effortless.

"Hullo, Uncle Tom. No, it's half-term. I forgot to tell you. Are you trifficly busy?"

"Yes, busy making a cup of tea. You're just in time. Come in and get your coat off, while I finish the mystic rites."

John went into the den, with Bugle dancing round him, his ears flopping in an ecstasy of friendliness. When Blackmore came in, a few minutes later, with the teatray and a plate of Mrs. Tucker's cakes, the boy had his overcoat off and was sitting by the fire.

"Well, John, what have you been doing with yourself today?"

He put the tray on the desk and began to sort out the china.

"Oh, just stooging around, Uncle Tom."

The avuncular title was honorary. It had been adopted some years before as a less formal mode of address than "Mr. Blackmore."

"A very refreshing way of passing the day, I always think. It invigorates the brain." He held out the plate. "Cake?"

John shook his head.

"No, thank you. Just a cup of tea, please. I'm not trifficly hungry."

"Rubbish! There's no such thing as a ten-year-old boy who's not hungry. Come on—they're some of Mrs. Tucker's specials."

Under this pressure, John took a cake from the proffered plate and bit off a piece the size of a pea. Blackmore busied himself with the teapot. He turned his head with the pot poised over a cup when John said in a stained voice:

"Uncle, I've got something to tell you. Something rotten."

With his attention distracted, Blackmore let the spout stray. The pot tilted and some tea ran on to the tray-cloth. He put the pot down and turned to John.

"Let's hear what it is," he suggested quietly.

The reply took him completely by surprise

"You know that dummy revolver of yours? The one in your desk-drawer with the little tin of blanks?"

"Yes."

"Well, it isn't there any more, Uncle Tom. I—I stole it when you weren't here yesterday."

The big man stood looking down at the worried boy.

"That wasn't a very nice thing to do, John."

"I know it wasn't but I—I wanted to hear what sort of a bang it made, and I knew you wouldn't lend it to me, so I borrowed it I swear on my word of honour that I was going to bring it back and. . . "

Blackmore finished the sentence for him.

"Slip it away in the drawer when I wasn't looking. Is that it, John?"

"Yes," the boy admitted with a gulp. His lip was quivering and he was very near to tears.

"I needn't tell you what I think about behaviour like that," said Blackmore with a severity hard to maintain.

"And why didn't you do it while I was in the other room, making the tea?"

"Because I haven't got it," John answered desperately. "Mr. Harler caught me with it and confiscated it."

"So now what are you going to do?"

"I don't know. He'll never give it back to me . . . I suppose you wouldn't like to . . . I mean, would you trifficly mind. . . "

His voice trailed off.

"You want me to go and tell him you stole it from me and please would he let me have it back?"

"No, not exactly. But if you could. . . Well, if you could say you'd sort of—*lent* it to me . . . "

He stole a swift glance at Blackmore, then went on quickly:

"You see, Uncle Tom, I'm in a triffic jam, because I promised on my word of honour that I'd put it back today in the place I'd got it from—and now I can't do it."

"Who did you give this promise to?"

"A detective. But he was trifficly decent and said if I—"

"Where did this happen?"

"At Elmsdale, in the spinney."

"The spinney? What was the detective doing there?"

"He was on his way to see Sir Victor."

Blackmore turned back to the tray and poured out two cups of tea. It was not until he had handed one to John and sat down with the other that he asked:

"Do you know why this detective was going to see Sir Victor?"

A tiny ray of hope pierced the gloom of young John's cloud of black despair. Here, for the second time that day, was a heaven-sent diversion. Eagerly he told Tom Blackmore all he knew about the previous night's happening and Sir Victor Warringham's telephone-call to the police that morning. Blackmore listened in silence and, when the tale was finished, lay stretched back in his chair with his hands in the pockets of his gardening flannels, thoughtfully puffing at his big briar. John waited for him to speak, then asked with boyish diffidence:

"You don't like Mr. Harler, do you, Uncle Tom?"

The big man answered with half his mind:

"What? Oh, Harler. No, I don't much care for him."

"Do you think he and Mrs. . . Uncle Tom, giving anyone the jitters means frightening them, doesn't it?"

The question was answered by a nod.

"And can anyone be frightened to death?"

Blackmore sat up and took the pipe from his mouth.

"Why do you ask that, John?"

"Well, this morning I heard Mr. and Mrs. Harler talking. They didn't know I heard because I pretended it was a spider I'd stopped to look at outside their sitting-room. I heard Mr. Harler say it was one thing to give *him* the jitters, but that the other thing was sheer madness. He didn't say Sir Victor—just *him*, but that's who he must have meant, mustn't he? I don't know what the thing that was sheer madness was. It was probably something Mrs. Harler'd suggested. I'm not frightened of Mr. Harler. I don't like him, that's all, just as I don't like the squiggly things under stones in the garden. But I *am* frightened of Mrs. Harler . . . Uncle Tom, do you think Sir Victor's *safe* at Elmsdale?"

The answer was an attempt at reassurance.

"Yes, I should think so. You've probably got the wrong end of the stick, John. That's the worst of over hearing scraps of conversation. Mr. Harler was probably probably talking about something quite different."

"Aunt Enid is trifficly suspicious of them, Uncle Tom. I heard Lily saying to Mrs. Gulliver this morning that Aunt Enid told Mr. Howard, the solicitor, that Mr. and Mrs Harler were a pair of confidence tricksters. Lily heard her say it, right in front of Mr. and Mrs. Harler."

"Mr. Howard was at Elmsdale?"

"Yes, he came to see Sir Victor, who'd written to ask him to call. Mr. Harler answered the door to Mr. Howard and wouldn't let him in. He said Sir Victor wasn't well enough. Then Aunt Enid butted in. You know what she's like, don't you? She told them Mr. Howard had got to see Sir Victor and that, if he didn't, Aunt Enid would go to the p'lice."

Blackmore finished refilling his pipe, took a spill and bent forward to light it from the fire. When the pipe was going, he asked:

"Did Mr. Howard eventually see Sir Victor?"

"No. Aunt Enid was trifficly ratty, Lily said, but Mrs. Harler joined in and talked Mr. Howard into going away. He's coming back at ten o'clock tomorrow morning, or else Aunt Enid is going to the police. I think she would, too, Uncle Tom. And she said that if she did go to the police, Mr. and Mrs. Harler wouldn't be the only ones to get a nasty surprise."

Tom Blackmore thought this over. When he spoke again, it was about the dummy revolver.

"When did Mr. Harler take it away from you, John?"

John looked crestfallen. He had been beginning to hope that it had been forgotten.

"This morning, a little while before lunch."

"What's the detective's name?"

"Aunt Enid said it was Inspector Charlton. He's a trifficly tall man though not so tall and big as you, Uncle Tom, and he's got grey hair and a kind face, and he didn't talk to me as if I was a kid. I like him trifficly."

"You're very fond of that word, John!"

"Trifficly? It's a very useful word, Uncle Tom. You can use it for almost anything."

Blackmore smiled and got out of his chair

"You'd better leave this business to me, John," he said.

What had he promised himself? An evening with pipe and radio. a pity; he would have enjoyed that. But now there were other things to do. Tom blackmore had made his decision.

CHAPTER SEVEN

(i)

AT six o'clock that evening, Charlton and Martin were in their room in Lulverton Police Headquarters. They had been talking for some time about the Elmsdale affair and had arrived at one conclusion: that, although the Harlers were undoubtedly playing some deep game, Sir Victor Warringham was not in any immediate danger of his life.

"Put it this way," Martin was saying. "Something out of the ordinary took place there last night. Old Warringham gets on the blower and gives us the story. We make for Elmsdale 'ot-foot—and the 'Arlers is took by surprise. What more likely than that pair of 'ighly dubious characters, 'avin' in mind that old Warry was, as you might say, well on the way to the funny-'ouse, didn't stage a bit of Grong Gignol last night, to 'urry 'im up a piece?"

"Agreed," nodded Charlton.

"Well, then. By some curious twist of Fate—"

"Martin, *please*!"

"I say again, by some curious twist of Fate—with a capital eff—two members of the C.I.D., in the well-set-up persons of you and especially me, get to 'ear about this Grong Gignol performance and come to certain definite conclusions, about which C. Harler and wife can't rest in no doubt. With that knowledge in their black 'earts, are they going to do old Warry in, the following night? Not on your life!"

"I hope you're right, Martin. I think you are. Apart from that, there's one thing puzzling me. Why didn't Harler ring for Dr. Stamford last night—or even first thing this morning? That ancient G.P. is definitely pro-Harler. He's also convinced in his own mind that Warringham is certifiable. Wouldn't it have strengthened Harler's case with Sir Ninian Oxenham—and there's no doubt he's worried about Wednesday's visit—

wouldn't it have strengthened his case if Dr. Stamford could testify—"

He broke off to answer the telephone.

"Inspector Charlton speaking. . . Yes, Mr. Harler. . . Right, I'll be there … Goodbye."

He hung up the receiver.

"He says Stamford has seen Warringham and considers he needs perfect quiet. Harler's taken it on himself to go against the doctor, and suggests I call at nine-thirty tomorrow."

The Sergeant opened his mouth to reply, but the telephone-bell rang again. This time it was the duty sergeant on the desk downstairs. A gentleman, he said, had called to see the Inspector.

Charlton asked: "What's his name?. . . Send him up."

(ii)

Tom Blackmore had changed out of his gardening clothes into well-cut Harris tweeds, over which he wore a thickly lined, belted, extensively storm-flapped trench-coat. Round his neck was a woollen muffler in the blue and orange colours of his old school; and on his feet were heavy brown shoes. Altogether, he was too inconveniently massive for Charlton's small room.

"Inspector Charlton?" he asked, identifying him from John's description.

"Yes. You're Mr. Blackmore, I believe? Sit down, won't you. This is my chief assistant, Sergeant Martin."

Blackmore exchanged nods with the Sergeant and took the chair that Charlton had indicated. He slipped his green pork-pie hat under the chair, unbelted and unbuttoned his rain-coat, removed the muffler from round his neck and laid it on his knee.

"Means to make a session of it," Martin thought ruefully, with his mind on his tea.

"There's colder weather on the way, I think," said Blackmore.

Charlton agreed and asked to know the reason for the call.

"I've come on a rather curious errand, Inspector. A young friend of mine—his name is John Campbell—met you this morning."

"Quite right."

"You caught him in possession of a stage revolver, which is far too dangerous a toy for a ten-year-old."

"He promised to return it."

"That's what I've come to see you about. The thing belongs to me. The little monkey pinched it when my back was turned yesterday. I'd have done the same at his age! I blame myself for leaving it about. A relic of my old amateur dramatic day. John came to to me in great distress this afternoon and confessed his crime like a man. The difficulty was that he couldn't keep his word to you, because the gun had been taken away from him. Confiscated is the schoolmaster's word for it. So promised young John that I'd come along and explain matters to you."

"Those dummy weapons are not very dangerous in themselves, Mr. Blackmore, but the solid barrels can be drilled without much trouble. Do you know who has it now?"

"I'm sorry to bother you with all these trivialities. Inspector, but there are certain difficulties. The pistol was taken away from John by Mr. Harler. I expect you know the set-up at Elmsdale?"

"Yes. Please go on."

"Mr. Harler was perfectly justified in confiscating the pistol. In his position, I should have done the same. But I can't go to him and ask for it back. If I tell him that John was playing with it with my permission, he'd have cause for complaint against me, which I want to avoid. Alternatively, if I tell him the truth—that John pinched it—the poor little devil would be in much hotter water than I'd care to see him in. So it amounts to this: do you mind if things are left as they are?"

"I suppose the pistol's as safe in Mr. Harler's keeping as it is in yours," Charlton answered, ending on a note that was cunningly half-questioning.

From the promptitude with which the point was taken up, he surmised that John Campbell's little peccadillo was not the only reason for Blackmore's visit.

"Quite frankly, Inspector, I wouldn't trust Harler any further than I could see him. I'm not suggesting he'd drill that barrel and shoot someone through the ear with a rusty nail! That's too fantastic. But I don't like the present situation at Elmsdale. When John told me a few things this afternoon, I was horrified. D'you mind if I smoke?"

"Not a bit."

The two detectives waited while he carefully filled and lighted his pipe. Martin, anxious to be off home, whistled faintly and untunefully between his teeth. Charlton was weighing his visitor up. He assessed him as not easily hurried; a reflective man, not given to hasty judgments, and of great dependability.

The spent match went into the ashtray on the desk.

"I've known Sir Victor Warringham," Blackmore resumed, "for a good many years and I can claim to be his friend. To me he has been more than a friend. My married life was a miserable failure. My wife ran up debts that brought me on the verge of bankruptcy, then left me for another man. During that anxious period of my life—and since—Sir Victor has been my friend and benefactor. To give you one example, the cottage where I live—a bachelor with no legal standing as such, worse luck!—is the property of Sir Victor. The rent I pay is ridiculously low. In return, I do my best to keep the grounds of Elmsdale in some sort of order." He shrugged his broad shoulders. "A labour of Hercules for one man. There was a time when Sir Victor himself was a keen gardener, but. . . You know of his great personal tragedy, I suppose?"

Charlton nodded and Martin grunted sympathetically.

"You'll gather from what I've told you, Inspector, that I owe Sir Victor a debt of gratitude—a debt that I'll never be able to repay in full. But I *can* pay small instalments now and again—and that's my real reason for crashing in on you now."

He pressed down the tobacco in his pipe.

"There's some sort of funny business going on at Elmsdale and the Harler people are undoubtedly behind it. I'm sufficiently in Sir Victor's confidence to have certain information. Perhaps I'm breaking faith by passing it on to you, but I'm convinced the occasion demands it. A will made by Sir Victor many years back bequeathed the bulk of his personal fortune—which is considerable—to his wife and daughter in equal shares. On her marriage to Harler, Rosalie arranged with her father—more than probably at the suggestion of Harler himself—that he should add a codicil to the will to the effect that, if Rosalie died before her father, her share should go to Harler. Rosalie died in 1944. The will and codicil have never since been revoked.

"The marriage was as big a failure as my own. Harler's a rotten type. He sponged on Sir Victor without shame; he was persistently unfaithful to his wife; and finally got himself so hopelessly involved with wine, women and dud cheques that he had to get out of the country. Rosalie, poor girl, was mighty glad to see the back of the fellow. But it left her in an awkward position. A scandal in a family so much in the public eye as the Warringhams was to be avoided at almost any cost. So she had to remain a grass widow. The story was circulated that Harler had gone to Brazil on the Victor Motor Company's business; and so the matter rested until news came of Harler's death in a train smash. A Brazilian paper printed a list of casualties. Among the killed figured the name of Clement Harler. The London papers reprinted the report. The family caused enquiries to be made on the spot and it was established to the satisfaction—and relief—of everyone concerned that it was one and the same Clement Harler—and Rosalie assumed her formal widowhood."

Another match was used on the big briar.

"You can imagine Sir Victor's feelings when Harler reappeared at Elmsdale. His story was that he'd actually been in the train smash, but had lost his memory and wandered away from the wreck into the tropical forests of Matto Grosso—or some such tarradiddle—and lived in a state of blissful amnesia that did not end, by one of those curious coincidences, until the appearance in a local paper of a news paragraph concerning the death of his wife.

"So, like the proverbial bad penny, he turned up again. I have never been able to discover the method by which he prevailed on his father-in-law to let him live at Elmsdale. A still greater mystery was Sir Victor's acceptance of that flashy piece of merchandise, the second Mrs. Harler. Rumour has it that Harler picked her up in Santos, while she was on tour with a theatrical company. That's as it may be . . . A possible reason for Sir Victor's hospitable gesture—I say, am I detaining you with all this chatter?"

"Far from it."

"A possible reason—only my theory, mark you—was this: Assume that Sir Victor had, figuratively speaking, kicked the resurrected Harler down the steps of Elmsdale and told him not to show his face in Lulverton again. And assume that Harler could have substantiated, if necessary, his amnesia yarn. It would have been a toothsome titbit for the gutter-press, wouldn't it? You see, officially, Harler took with him to South America the good wishes of the Warringham family. What harsh, unreasonable, un-Christian treatment, then, of the mentally restored, greatly bereaved husband, refused sanctuary by an inhuman father-in-law!"

He waved his pipe in semi-dismissal of the idea.

"Even that doesn't justify glorious Gladys. Now, that brings me at last to my main theme. I've explained how Harler will come into a large fortune on the death of Sir Victor, provided the old gentleman does not do what he should have done years since—tear up his will and make a new one. Two things would prevent Sir Victor from doing this. The first, naturally, would be his death. The second would be—how shall I describe it?—legal powerlessness. If Sir Victor were to be certified insane, he wouldn't have much chance of making a new will, and Harler would be safe. That opens up certain sinister possibilities, Inspector."

A pause gave Charlton the opportunity to speak. He merely grunted non-committally. Blackmore waited a moment before he spoke again.

"I don't want to see my benefactor in a mental home. If he were a dangerous lunatic, that would be different. If I thought that a period in an institution run on enlightened lines was necessary, I should be the first to agree. But in my view, Sir Victor is not insane—*yet*."

This time Charlton took advantage of the break.

"I was talking this morning to Dr. Stamford. He mentioned you, Mr. Blackmore, as one of the people who can testify that Sir Victor is not so well-balanced mentally as he was before the loss of his wife and daughter."

"Stamford is a foolish old man—a public danger. He ought to have retired years ago. He's got the idea into his head—and I know who put it there—that Sir Victor is not responsible for his actions; and he's twisted my actual words round so that they mean what he wants them to mean. What I said was that Sir Victor's mental powers had deteriorated. And they have. He's getting an old man. You can't expect him to have the same keen brain as he had when he first put the Victor car on the road. The loss of his wife and daughter took something away from him, but it wasn't his sanity."

He refolded his muffler and put it back on his knee.

"So there you have it, Inspector. If Harler and his wife succeed in getting him put away in a home for the remainder of his life, those two vultures will live in comfort for the rest of their days. I've tried to put a spoke in their wheel by forcing old Stamford to call in one of our greatest brain specialists, Sir Ninian Oxenham. It may succeed. On the other hand, it may put Sir Victor in greater danger than he is already. What the devil really happened last night? John had got hold of some story about ghostly hands trying to strangle Sir Victor in the dark. If that wasn't the Harlers up to their tricks, I'm a Dutchman! Can't you do something about it, Inspector?"

"Just before you arrived, Mr. Blackmore, I arranged on the telephone with Mr. Harler to call and see Sir Victor at nine-thirty tomorrow morning. I'll try then to get the whole thing sorted out." He smiled in a friendly fashion. "I don't think you need disturb yourself too much over Sir Victor."

There was something in his tone that inspired confidence. With apologies for having kept them, Blackmore felt under the chair for his hat. Charlton asked:

"Are you a relation of Mr. Andrew Blackmore?"

The big man nodded. "He was my father. He's dead now. He and Sir Victor were great friends years ago."

When their visitor had left, Charlton sat in deep thought for some time before he said with a tired sigh:

"You know, Martin, this business irritates me. There's nothing I can get my teeth into."

"You've all my sympathy," grunted the Sergeant. "I feel the same about my tea."

(iii)

Martin had his tea. Afterwards he took his wife to the cinema. At eleven o'clock they retired to bed. At a quarter-past seven the following morning he was called from the bathroom to the telephone, which he answered with the lather still on one side of his face.

It was Charlton who rang him, and his voice had lost its usual deep, unhurried note.

CHAPTER EIGHT

(i)

LILY HIGGINS, the little housemaid, was always first astir at Elmsdale. At the best of times, it was hard enough to get up at six o'clock, but when the alarm-clock aroused her on that Tuesday morning, Lily found it even more difficult, for the recent muggy weather had changed overnight to almost Arctic conditions. When, after five delightful minutes of stolen bliss, she crawled shivering from between the sheets, the window panes of her little room on the top floor were opalescent with frost. She switched on the light, performed her sketchy toilet, finished dressing and went downstairs into the kitchen.

There were two things to be done first; setting the fires, and taking a cup of tea up to Mrs. Gulliver, the cook, who slept in a room adjoining her own. Lily filled the kettle, lighted the gas-cooker, raked out and refuelled the domestic-boiler, then went off to clear the grates in the other rooms. By the time she came back to the kitchen with her pail of cinders, the kettle was boiling. She took down the teapot from the dresser, made the tea and left it on the table to draw while she disposed of the cinders.

Outside it was dark and bitingly cold. The handle of the pail numbed Lily's fingers, as she opened the back door and hurried along to the dustbins, keeping close to the wall of the house. On her way back with the empty pail, her eyes were becoming accustomed to the darkness, and she pulled up suddenly with a frightened, "Oo-er!" and made a careful detour before scurrying back into the warm kitchen.

The tea was ready to pour out. Lily went to the dresser for cups and saucers for Mrs. Gulliver and herself. The first cup that she took off its hook slipped from her cold-stiffened fingers and smashed into many pieces on the tiled floor.

"Oh, lor," lamented Lily. "That's the *first* thing."

(ii)

Mrs. Gulliver was awakened by Lily's tap on her bedroom door. She called out, and the little housemaid came in with the tea, much of which had slopped into the saucer on the long climb up from the kitchen.

"That's a good girl, Lily," said Mrs. Gulliver. "I will say you've bin better at getting up since Mrs. W. gave you that talking to."

She was a large, homely woman, was Ada Gulliver. In the service of the Warringham family since girlhood, she was now in the late fifties; an excellent cook, an irrepressible windbag, adoring slave of Sir Victor and bosom enemy of Mrs. Winters.

Lily stood timidly by as Mrs. Gulliver, after a second's doubt as to which was more expedient, transferred more tea to the saucer and sipped it with noisy enjoyment.

The girl said at last: "Mrs. Gulliver."

"Yes, love?"

"I've broken a cup."

"Then all I c'n say is, you're a careless girl, that's what you are, Lily. Which service?"

"Only one of the white kitchen ones, Mrs. Gulliver."

"Oh, well, that's not so bad. 'Ave you cleared up the bits?"

"Yes, Mrs. Gulliver. I put 'em in the dustbin."

"Make sure you cover 'em up with cinders, love. You know what *She* is fer nosin' round."

"I did that, Mrs. Gulliver. . . Course I mighter known somethink like that was goin' to 'appen. They say it always does when you walk under one."

"Walk under what, ducky?" She handed back the empty cup and saucer to Lily. "A ladder?"

Lily nodded vigorously.

"And when've you bin walkin' under ladders?" Mrs. Gulliver wanted to know as she threw back the bedclothes. "Lummy, it's cold!"

"Just now, Mrs. Gulliver. It was leaning upper gainst the wall'n I walked right under it, I did, going out wither cinders. I didn't know it was there till I come back."

In her flannel nightdress and hair-curlers, Mrs. Gulliver sat on the edge of the bed and looked at Lily in a way that made the girl uneasy.

"There wasn't no ladder there last night, Lily. 'Ere! Gimme me dressing-gown from be'ind the door!"

They went down together into the kitchen. Mrs. Gulliver took a flashlamp from the dresser-drawer and, leaving Lily shivering with cold and apprehension in the open doorway, flapped out into the cement-surfaced yard in her carpet-slippers.

The beam from the flashlamp found the ladder and travelled upwards, to play on a first-floor window. The lower sash had been pushed up as far as it would go. Mrs. Gulliver hissed a low summons to Lily, who reluctantly came out and stood by her side.

"You know 'oose window that is, don't you?"

"Yes, Mrs. Gulliver," Lily answered through chattering teeth. "What're we goin' ter do?"

"Why, go up, er course!" Mrs. Gulliver spoke with a confidence she was far from feeling.

With the girl now a prudent pace behind, she retraced her steps through the kitchen, along the hall and up the stairs. Outside a door on the first floor, she stopped and knocked. In her other hand was the flashlamp. There was no reply. She knocked again, louder this time, but there was still no answer from the room.

Mustering all her courage, Mrs. Gulliver turned the knob and cautiously pushed open the door. An icy draught swept across from the window. The room was in darkness. With a trembling hand, Mrs. Gulliver felt round the corner for the light-switch. It was already pressed down.

Then she remembered the flashlamp.

When the wavering beam reached the bed, Mrs. Gulliver screamed, and Lily, peering round her at the dreadful sight, screamed in a higher key.

(iii)

"Martin," said Charlton's voice urgently from the other end of the line, "can you be ready for me to pick you up in fifteen minutes?"

"Yes, sir," Martin answered briskly. "Something serious?"

"There's been some trouble at Elmsdale."

"What sort of trouble?"

"Murder, by the sound of it."

"Good God! So they got the poor old beggar after all!"

"No, not Sir Victor," Charlton told him. "It's Mrs. Winters."

PART II

HYPOTHESIS

CHAPTER NINE

(i)

A CONSTABLE was posted at the gates of Elmsdale, another stood guard at the front door and a third was stationed at the back of the house. In Mrs. Winters' bedroom, the police surgeon had confirmed that life was extinct, and the photographer had then busied himself with his camera and flashlights. Now, with Charlton and Martin standing by, the surgeon was carrying out a more detailed examination of the dead woman.

Dr. Lorimer, the police surgeon for the Lulverton Division, was a tall, alert, horn-rimmed-spectacled young man—a very different type from doddering old Dr. Stamford. He and Charlton had worked together on a number of previous cases and knew each other's ways.

Lorimer straightened his back and examined the thermometer in his hand.

"Eighty-nine," he read. "The window was wide open at the bottom, but she was fairly well covered over by the bedclothes. Difficult to be definite. I'd say she died of strangulation somewhere between midnight and two o'clock this morning."

Charlton grunted and went roving off round the room. His usual composure had been rudely shaken by the tragedy. He felt that he could have prevented it; that he should have sensed, from the previous day's events, that murder was in the air, and ought to have taken proper precautions. He had confessed as much to Martin on the way out from Lulverton, but the Sergeant had poo-pooed the idea with:

"'Ow the 'ell was you to 'ave guessed, unless"—with a shrewd, sidelong glance at his chief—"you'd 'ave forecast it before'and with the 'elp of a dead frog and a quart of goat's milk?"

Mrs. Winters' bedroom was of fair size. The door and window were opposite to each other, and were centrally placed in the longer sides of the room. Between them, with its head to the third wall, was the oak bedstead. Against the fourth wall, alongside the fireplace, was a chest-of-drawers, also of oak. To the left of the window, across the corner of the room, was the housekeeper's dressing-table. In the other corner, near the head of the bed, was a small escritoire. Between the escritoire and the bed was a small table with a single drawer in it.

From the ceiling, a yard or so from the window, hung a light pendant. A two-way adaptor in the socket at the end of it had enabled Mrs. Winters to have one light, with its own switch, over the dressing-table, and another—a parchment-shaded table-lamp—for use either on the escritoire or on the bedside table.

On that Tuesday morning, however, the lamp was on neither desk nor table; it was lying on the floor by the side of the bed. Nor was the plug still in the two-way ceiling adaptor, for the flex was around Mrs. Winters' throat. It had been made to bite into the flesh by means of a garotte slipped through the knot in the flex. The garotte was a paper-knife of some green plastic material. At one end of it was a circular brass seal with the initial "W" engraved on it. The strangled woman's jaw had prevented it from unwinding.

Mrs. Winters wore a crocheted hair-net of brown silk and a white cambric nightdress. Just below the left shoulder of the nightdress, they found a small brown stain.

The bedclothes were disordered, partially covering the body, which was lying on its right side diagonally across the bed, the feet nearest the door and the head just off the pillow and facing the window. The loose end of the flex, with the plug still attached to it, hung over the side of the bed. On the table were a silver pocket-watch and a china beaker bearing traces of having contained a beverage of the colour of beef-extract.

The front writing-flap of the escritoire was open. The letters and other papers in the pigeon-holes were not as tidy as Charlton would have expected of Mrs. Winters. Below the flap were two drawers. Both were half open. The upper one contained various papers. Charlton went carefully through them. Apart from old theatre programmes, Christmas cards and the like, there were Mrs. Winters' marriage certificate, a Southern Counties Bank chequebook, some Admiralty documents relating to her husband's death on active service during the First World War, and a small packet of letters written by him before and after their marriage. The lower drawer was empty, but the lock of it had been forced.

None of the other drawers in the room was locked, and there were no signs that drawers or contents had been tampered with.

The lower sash of the window had been pushed up as far as it would go. The top sash was open a few inches. The window was heavily framed outside with ivy. A leafy tendril ran along the window-ledge. Two feet below the ledge was the top of the ladder. Ledge, ivy and ladder were all thickly coated with frost.

"Martin," instructed Charlton from the window, "make a note that the frost is levelly coated and unmarked—and that the ivy is not crushed or damaged. We'll have to find out what time the frost started to come down."

As the Sergeant wrote as directed in his notebook, Charlton threw back his head to examine the underside of the lower sash.

"No marks on lower sash to suggest window levered open from outside," he dictated. "Some form of leverage necessary to do this when window closed. No sashlifters on inside. Query, did deceased normally sleep with lower sash raised?

Upper sash found opened three inches at top."

He turned back into the room.

"You 'phoned for Peters?"

"Be 'ere any minute, sir," the Sergeant replied.

Sergeant Peters was the fingerprint expert attached to the Downshire County Constabulary. He was stationed at the county town of Whitchester, which was away to the north-west, on the landward side of the South Downs.

"Right, Martin. I'm going down into the garden to have a look round. If Peters comes before I'm back, tell him I want him to get working *pronto* on—you'd better write them down." Martin poised his pencil. "Drawers and handles of the bureau, the bedside table, the chest-of-drawers and the dressing-table. The lower sash of the window, with particular attention to the upper rail—just where anybody would get hold of it to open the sash from the inside. Interior window sill and—"

"Turn it up!" protested Martin. "I'm a human being, not a perishing dictaphone!"

"Better learn shorthand."

"What, at my age?"

He was given time to catch up, before Charlton went on, more slowly:

"Interior window sill and frame for prints of person pulling himself up from top of ladder outside. China beaker on bedside table. Letter-opener. Electric table-lamp, plug at other end of wire and two-way adaptor in ceiling-pendant. That should be the lot—oh, and the light-switch inside the door."

With Martin still busily scribbling, Charlton turned to Dr. Lorimer.

"Have you finished here, Lorimer?" The police surgeon nodded. "When we've got the flex off, I'd like you to have a closer look at that neck. I want to make sure that the strangling was done with the flex and not with something else."

"Certainly. I'll go with the body to the mortuary."

"Martin, please ring the mortuary for the ambulance. Also notify the coroner. I shall want the public analyst to tell us what was in the beaker and whether the same stuff—it looks like beef-extract—caused the stain on the nightdress. When Peters comes, get him to take the fingerprints of all the members of the household. And give me a cigarette."

The Sergeant pulled out a packet of Player's. Charlton took two and, with a nod to Dr. Lorimer, strode out of the room

Martin jerked up his head in a what-a-life movement.

"All for six-ten a week," he said.

Dr. Lorimer grinned: "He's a bit touchy this morning."

The Sergeant shook his head sadly.

"It's smoking before breakfast. I've told 'im about it."

(ii)

Half an hour later, with his examination of the yard and ladder completed, Inspector Charlton began his interrogation of Elmsdale's residents. He interviewed them one by one in Mrs. Winters' sitting-room, which was at the end of the hall and adjoining the kitchen.

Mrs. Ada Gulliver, the cook, was the first to be called. She gave her account of the discovery of the body. Charlton then asked:

"You say that, when you went into the room, the lights didn't work. Was the switch at the door on or off?"

"It was on, sir. So I used the torch which I'd—"

"Yes, Mrs. Gulliver." It was not the first time he had had to curb her tendency to go over the same ground again and again. "Now—"

"It's always kep in the same drawer of the dresser," Mrs. Gulliver assured him affably.

"Now, tell me—"

"You never know when you might need it, do you?"

"Quite. Now, did Mrs. Winters have a hot drink every night?"

"As regular as the clock. Always beef-extract. Not what you might call everybody's night-cap, but there's no accountin' for tastes. Every man to 'is own poison, as the saying goes. I could never take it meself, last thing at night, but Mrs. W., she may 'ave bin made different. We can't be all alike, as I was only tellin'—"

"Did Mrs. Winters prepare the beef-extract herself?"

"Oh, dear, no! What, Mrs. W.? The very idea! It was, 'Ada, this' and 'Ada, that,' from mornin' to last thing at night. No, I 'ad to take it up to 'er. She 'ad notions about 'erself, 'ad Mrs. W."

"So when you took it up, that was the last time you saw her alive?"

"Yes, I—just a minute, though. What am I saying? Now you come to put the question, sir, the last time I saw 'er was a long while before I mixed the beef-extract for 'er. Soon after dinner, it was, when she came into my kitchen to tell me the sweet 'adn't bin to Sir Victor's liking. Not to 'is liking! Why, the dear old gentleman never knows what 'e's eating. More's the pity, after the trouble I go to. No, according to Lily, 'oo was doing the waiting at table, there was a bit of a tiff between Mrs. W. and the Aitches. Lily says they got the best of it, and wanting to take it out of somebody, Mrs. W. comes into my kitchen and tries to take it out of me. 'Mrs. Winters,' I says to 'er—"

"Didn't you take the beef-extract up tor Mrs. Winters?"

"Only part of the way. Mrs. W.'s drink is the last thing I do at night and I take it in to 'er on me way up to bed, to save me legs. Last night, I got as far as the first-floor landing, when along comes Mrs. Aitch. 'Ah, Mrs. Gulliver,' she says, all airs and graces and la-di-blinking-da."

"What time was this?"

"Ten-thirty. 'Ah, Mrs. Gulliver,' says Mrs. Aitch. 'I was just going along to 'ave a word with Mrs. Winters. I'll take that if you like.' 'Ta,' I says to 'er, thinking it wasn't like 'er, and I gave 'er old of the saucer and went upstairs to bed."

"The beaker was in a saucer, was it?"

"Oh, yes, they're a set. Mrs. W. bought it specially for the purpose."

"Were you and Mrs. Winters on friendly terms, Mrs. Gulliver?"

"No, she wasn't the sort to encourage that kind of thing. Kep' 'erself very much to 'erself, she did. She and I never did 'it it off. Not that we didn't try to be pleasant with each other. Armed neutrality, as they say in the papers."

"Do you know if she had any relatives?"

"Yes, there's a sister. That's the only one she's ever mentioned in my 'earing, probably because this sister's done well for 'erself, and Mrs. W. wanted me to know it. Shocking snob she was."

"Did she tell you the sister's name?"

"Yes, it was. . . Now, what was it?. . . Freshwater. Yes, that was it—Freshwater."

"Can you give me her address?"

"Only that she lives in Croydon. The 'usband was an Air Raid Warden, as far as I remember."

He made a note of it. His next question was on a different theme.

"Did Mrs. Winters keep any valuables in her bedroom?"

"I don't doubt but what she did. Must 'ave somethink put away. Never spent a penny if she could avoid it. Was there anything took?"

"Did she always keep the lower drawer of her bureau locked?"

"Not never 'aving tried to open it," replied Mrs. Gulliver virtuously, "I reely couldn't say. I do know that she got in a state some months back, when she thought she'd lost the key of it. Fair crazy she was, till she found it."

"In Mrs. Winters' room this morning, we found a bedside lamp, Mrs. Gulliver. It had a polished oak base and a buff-coloured parchment shade. Is that part of the room's usual furniture?"

"Yes, sir. Mrs. W. usually kep' it on the little table by the side of the bed. When she wanted to write, she stood it on top of the desk."

"And the lead was taken from the ceiling-pendant?"

Mrs. Gulliver agreed, then, feeling there might be still room for doubt, agreed again. Charlton thanked her for the information she had given him, and asked for the housemaid to be sent in.

Lily Higgins was, by nature, as timid as a mouse, but Charlton, quiet-spoken and reassuring, gave her courage. As she told Mrs. Gulliver afterwards in the kitchen:

"Just like a big, kind doctor, didn't you think, Mrs. Gulliver? One of them doctors as make you feel better as soon as they come in the bedroom." A dreamy expression came over her plain little face. "I thought 'e was ever so nice, didn't you, Mrs. Gulliver?"

The cook was peeling a potato at the time.

"Quite the gentleman," she agreed, ruthlessly gouging out an eye.

Lily told Charlton her story. When she came to the finding of the body, she said:

"Troubles always come in threes, 'aven't you noticed, sir? First I broke a cup, then we found Mrs. Winters murdered. I wonder what the third'll be. I do 'ope it's nothink serious, like one of the best tea-service."

"I think you waited at dinner last night, Lily?"

"Yes, sir."

"Who was at the table?"

"Sir Victor, Mrs. Winters, Mistrermissizarler and Master John."

"There was an argument, wasn't there?"

"Yes, sir, between Mrs. Winters and Mistrermissizarler. I was in and out of the room, so I didn't catch much of it, but what I did 'ear was Missizarler say, 'One of these days you'll get what's comin' to you, you snake in the grass!'"

"That was to Mrs. Winters?" Lily nodded. "Did you get any idea what the conversation was about?"

"No, sir. Probably about yesterday morning's dust-up. They didn't talk when I was in the room. I only caught that bit when I came in quiet."

"Do you look after Mrs. Winters' room, Lily?"

"Yes, sir. I go over it with the vacuum every morning."

"Then you can tell me something else. Did Mrs. Winters sleep with her window open?"

"Oh, always, sir. Not open much, you know. Just an inch or two at the top."

"She never slept with it open at the bottom?"

"Not in the winter-time, sir."

"Thank you, Lily. Now, there's another thing. Did Mrs. Winters ever use a letter-opener?"

"You mean the one what the wire was twisted round 'er neck with? That green thing with a 'W' at the end of it? Yes, that was 'ers. She kep' it in the writing-desk."

"You're sure it's the same one, Lily?"

"Oo, yes, sir. I crep' in an' took a peep this morning before Sir Victor locked up the room. Didn't she look awful, sir?"

"You should have stayed out," he told her. "Did you find an odd saucer lying round anywhere this morning?" Lily gaped at him as if he had supernatural powers.

"What a funny thing you should say that, 'cause I did. It was on the table in Mistrermissizarler's sitting-room."

"Was it any particular saucer?"

"Yes, it was the one Mrs. Winters uses. It goes with the mug. You can tell it by the rings on it, which are the same pattern as on the mug. I took it back to the kitchen." She looked at him in sudden fright. "That wasn't wrong of me, was it, sir?"

"No, Lily," he smiled, "of course not. Now, you'd better run along and do some more clearing up." He wagged a warning finger at her. "But keep away from Mrs. Winters' room."

"I 'ad to slip in an' look at 'er," Lily explained solemnly. "It's somethink to write to me Mum and Dad about."

(iii)

Young John Campbell was next. Because of the serious state of affairs at Elmsdale, he had been kept away from school. He told Charlton how he had gone to bed at half-past eight and had slept soundly until aroused by the disturbance that had followed the discovery of the body.

"When I came out of my room—it's next to Aunt Enid's, you know—Mrs. Gulliver and Lily were standing just inside Aunt Enid's room, screaming like anything. Sir Victor's room is along on the other side of the passage, near the stairs. He came out in his dressing-gown and wanted to know what all the noise was about. He was trifficly ratty. Mrs. Gulliver couldn't speak, but she pointed in at Aunt Enid lying on the bed. Sir Victor went in and looked at Aunt Enid. He didn't say anything, but got Aunt Enid's hand-mirror from her dressing-table and held it in front of her mouth. I s'pose it was to see if she was still breathing. Just then, Mr. and Mrs. Harler came pelting along from their own bedroom. They pushed past us into the room and both of them got trifficly excited. Sir Victor told them not to be so silly, 'specially Mr. Harler, who kept on shouting, 'Some swine shall pay dearly for this!' But he's always like that. Then he noticed the open window and swore that somebody must have broken into the house. He was working out what he called a theory, when Sir Victor shoved us all from the room, then took the key from inside the door and locked it from the outside."

"Did your aunt sleep with her door locked, John?"

"No, never, sir. Sir Victor told me to run and fetch an envelope and some sealing-wax. When I brought them back, he put the doorkey in the envelope and stuck it down. Then he went along to his bedroom and sealed the envelope with the ring off his finger. When all that was done, he told Mr. Harler to go and ring for the police."

This simple tale interested Charlton immensely. Sir Victor Warringham, who, if certain persons were to be believed, was hovering on the brink of mental collapse, had seemingly been the only adult in the house to deal with such a critical matter in a sane and common-sense fashion. It had been Sir Victor who had received them at the front door on their arrival that morning and had handed over the sealed envelope; and Charlton had been struck then by the old gentleman's restrained and unaffected manner.

His next question to John was:

"Have you seen the ladder leaning up against the back of the house?"

"Yes, sir, Mr. Harler said the murderer must have used it to get in."

"Does it belong here?"

"Yes, it's usually kept on the wall of the wash-house. The roof sticks out to keep the rain off it, and it hangs on two pieces of wood fixed into the wall."

This confirmed the conclusions Charlton had drawn when he had gone out to look round. There was a cemented yard at the rear of the house. At one end of it, ten feet or so from the kitchen door, was the brick-built washhouse that John had mentioned. The ladder-hooks were on the far side of the building, but the cementing extended beyond it and be had found no recent footprints, either on the frost-covered yard, or in the garden paths and beds beyond.

He pondered over his next question. He would have liked to ask John for his version of the quarrel at the dinner table between the Harlers and Mrs. Winters. He decided against it, however, and asked instead:

"Have you any other relations, John?"

"I don't quite know, sir. I suppose I must have, though I've never really thought about it. I've lived with Aunt Enid since

I was trifficly young. I asked her once whether I ever had a mother and father. She said, yes, of course I had, but she hadn't heard from them for a long, long time and they must be dead. There was another aunt that Aunt Enid took me to tea with ages ago. I think she was Aunt Connie, but I didn't like her very much because she wouldn't leave me alone. Trifficly 'barrassing."

"We must try to find her, John."

He got up and put his hand on the boy's shoulder.

"I'm sorry about all this," he said quietly.

"It *is* rather rotten, sir," John answered, and fled from the room with his bottom lip between his teeth.

CHAPTER TEN

(i)

UNLIKE the carefree amateur sleuth, who can arrive at his objective *via* any expeditious short cut that may present itself, the professional investigator is forced to go the long way round. There are solid reasons for this. When the amateur has unmasked his villain to the wonderment of his friends and the mortification of the blockheaded police, his job is over; but it is only at that point that Scotland Yard's real work begins. It is one thing to know who did the crime at the Old Mill; it is quite another thing to prove it at the Old Bailey.

To ensure that the policeman plods steadily along the winding highway of cold fact, and does not scamper madly across the green meadows of intuition, certain precautionary measures have been taken. Among these are Judges' Rules. Statements by witnesses are not admissible in evidence unless they have been made voluntarily. It is laid down, therefore, in Judges' Rules that, should the police have decided to charge a person with a crime, they are strictly forbidden to question him without first telling him that he need not reply. This timely reminder is of great advantage to the criminal, for it is a warning that he is under suspicion. It can also be a tremendous handicap to the detective collecting evidence. The alternative, it must not be forgotten, is the Third Degree—or worse.

With these considerations in mind, Inspecter Charlton deferred his interrogation of the Harlers until such time as the reports from the fingerprint expert and the public analyst were in his hands. Meanwhile he interviewed Sir Victor Warringham.

(ii)

The conversation took place in the library. With Sergeant Martin discreetly in the background, with notebook and pencil at the alert, the Inspector and Sir Victor sat in easy chairs on each side of the fireplace, in which there was no cheerier a blaze than on the previous day. Martin, withdrawing as far as possible into his overcoat, considered that the frigidity of the room demanded an urgent call for the sweep and a severe rebuke for the coal-merchant.

The chairman of Victor Motors Ltd., author of *The Praying Mantis* and *England's Haunted Houses,* was a man on the verge of three score years and ten. Tall and thin, clean-shaven, with a splendid mane of pure white hair, and of benevolent countenance, his appearance was more that of a high ecclesiastic than of a manufacturer of Cars For the Million. He would have made, thought Charlton on first sight of him, an admirable archdeacon of today or an impressive Prime Minister of the day before yesterday. His voice had a resonance that gave his most casual utterance the rich impressiveness of the best rhetoric.

Charlton was about to put his first question when Sir Victor said:

"I want to give you all the assistance within my power, Inspector, and I think I can best achieve that end by giving you some account of the events leading up to this lamentable climax. Then, if you have afterwards any questions, I will answer them to the best of my ability. Is that agreeable to you?"

Assent came readily. "Get 'em to talk," had always been Charlton's motto.

"Then let me begin. Please smoke if you wish . . . The police are not concerned with opinions, but with facts. Yet, in spite of that, I should like to say now that I am convinced that this terrible tragedy is linked with my own harrowing experience on Sunday night, to which I will return later. I am a sensitive man, Inspector, quickly responsive to impressions. For some time past, I have sensed the existence of a heavy shadow hanging over Elmsdale. Evil has been in the air, if I may so put it. I hasten to add that I imply nothing transphysical."

"Getting on to that stuff again," thought Martin dourly and defensively turned up the collar of his overcoat.

"No, Inspector, the evil was of this world. It was in human minds. I have felt that those black thoughts would be translated into black deeds. My fears have been terribly justified by events. Last night, for the first time in my long life, I had my bedroom window fastened and the door locked. My son-in-law—it angers me to be forced to admit the relationship—my son-in-law and his wife, who has the poisonous beauty of the meadow saffron, would doubtless have you believe that those precautions were to keep out demons and other supernatural folk."

His lips twisted in a humourless smile.

"My intention was far more matter-of-fact. It was to prevent Mr. and Mrs. Clement Harler from getting up to more of their devilish work. It is a great grief to me that I only partially succeeded."

Martin's head jerked out of his collar. This was a direct indictment.

"May I take it, sir," Charlton asked, "that you are accusing Mr. and Mrs. Harler of murdering Mrs. Winters?"

Sir Victor inclined his head in a nod of grave agreement.

"It is a dreadful charge to make, Inspector, yet I am forced to make it.

"Have you any evidence to support it, sir?"

"I have no direct evidence, in so far as I was not present when the crime was committed. I believe I am correct in saying, however, that most murderers are convicted on circumstantial evidence alone?"

"In a number of cases, yes," Charlton conceded.

"Then let me give you such circumstantial evidence as I can put forward. Mrs. Winters has stated on more than one occasion in my presence that she is, or was, a very light sleeper, awakened at the slightest sound. In spite of that, she was murdered without a chance to cry out. Her nephew, little John Campbell, sleeps in an adjoining room; my own room is not far distant. Neither of us heard a sound. Surely, Inspector, any intruder in her bedroom would have aroused the unfortunate woman in time to give the alarm before her voice was stilled for ever?"

Evidently he did not expect a reply, for he went straight on:

"A few minutes after half-past ten last night, I was in my bedroom, preparing to retire. I overheard a short conversation between Mrs. Harler and my cook, which took place on the landing adjacent to my bedroom. Mrs. Gulliver, the cook, was on her way with Mrs. Winters' customary cup of beef-tea. Mrs. Harler intercepted her and suggested that she should take it along instead. In the first place, I cannot think, with my knowledge of the young woman, that Mrs. Harler would go out of her way to perform small acts of kindness without some ulterior motive. In the second place—and this is something more definite than personal prejudice—she did not go at once to Mrs. Winters' room. It was some minutes before I heard her footsteps passing my door. What's more likely than that, before proceeding to Mrs. Winters' room, she took the beverage along to her own apartments on the other side of the landing, in order to dose it with some soporific compound, as a preliminary to the foul deed which was to follow?"

Again the question was rhetorical. Sir Victor switched suddenly to another matter.

"The ladder. Was there ever a more palpable red herring? Would any intending murderer wishing to enter the house place a ladder against the wall, enter the room through the victim's window, then quit the scene of his crime without closing the window and removing the ladder?"

"His intention might not have been murder," Charlton reminded him.

"You mean he came to rob? Really, Inspector, that won't do! A thief with any intelligence at all does not break into bedrooms at night. He might do so when the family are at dinner, but surely at night he confines himself to the downstairs rooms. Why erect ladders, with the danger of waking the whole household, when the pantry window is open—I speak hypothetically—and there is silver on the sideboard? No, Inspector, I submit that the ladder was placed there by the Harlers with the sole intention of creating the impression that Mrs. Winters was killed by some person not resident in the house. Do you find it too cold in here?"

"Not at all, sir," Charlton lied manfully.

"We come, then, to opportunity. Who had more opportunity than the Harlers? *There* was this poor woman in a drugged sleep in a room on the other side of the landing. *There* was the electric light wire ready to hand.

There was the letter-opener in or on her bureau—"

"It *was* her letter-opener?"

"Certainly it was. I gave it to her myself as a Christmas present, a year or two ago."

"Where did you buy it, sir?"

"If I remember rightly, at Messrs. Horwill, Adams & Company. They are very dependable stationers. So you see, the opportunity was there, the materials for the commission of the crime were there and, furthermore, the *motive* was there."

The old gentleman sat back in his chair and looked at the two detectives in turn, as if to relish their reactions to a startling announcement. Their lack of response must have disappointed him, for he said somewhat lamely:

"I see I have not surprised you."

Charlton replied: "We shall be glad to hear about it."

"I will tell you, then. Under my will as it is worded at the moment, my son-in-law will inherit a considerable sum of money on my death. I have decided that I have no wish that this should happen. A few days ago, I informed Mrs. Winters that it was my intention that my son-in-law's interest should be transferred to her."

"Did Mr. Harler know this, Sir Victor?"

"I did not tell him myself. I strongly suspect that Mrs.

Winters was imprudent enough to inform him. There was a distressing battle of words at the dinner table last night. Though the will was not mentioned and though no one not conversant with the facts would have understood their remarks, there is no doubt in my mind that my decision to see my solicitor on the matter of a new will was the real cause of the dissension."

"Did Mrs. Harler call Mrs. Winters a snake in the grass?"

The old gentleman raised his eyebrows in astonishment. "Indeed she did! Could it have been, Inspector, that you were concealed behind the curtains?"

Charlton smiled in reply, but did not explain.

"Yes," said Sir Victor, "she undoubtedly described her as a snake in the grass. She also said—an extremely sinister remark in the light of subsequent events—that one of these days Mrs. Winters would get what was coming to her. Please do not attribute that deplorable phrase to me. I merely quote the words of Mrs. Harler . . . That, then, was the situation. By a piece of shameful trickery, my son-in-law prevented me from seeing my solicitor yesterday morning. As he could not postpone the meeting indefinitely, he ended last night all chance of Mrs. Winters becoming a beneficiary by taking her life. You may ask, why did he select Mrs. Winters as his victim instead of myself? My answer is that he has other plans for me."

His thin sensitive fingers gripped on the arms of his chair.

"I intend, Inspector, that those plans shall come to nothing—nothing but the undoing of himself and that depraved and vicious woman, his so-called wife!"

"Aren't they married?"

"I should imagine not. I have never seen a marriage certificate. Perhaps it is an improper thing to say, but the sanctity or legality of their association is a matter of the utmost indifference to me."

The Inspector asked bluntly: "Why have you allowed them to live here, Sir Victor?"

The fine old face took on a troubled expression.

"It is not easy to explain . . . It is mixed up with other things . . . Personal, intimate things. They concern my daughter. You may know that she—died. I would rather not discuss it. The subject is very painful to me."

"As you wish, sir. Has Mrs. Winters been in your employment long?"

"It must be twenty years. Until my dear wife's death, Mrs. Winters was her paid companion. Since then she has acted as chatelaine. It would have been my wife's wish that Mrs. Winters should be left amply provided for on my own decease."

"Are you communicating with her relatives, sir?"

"Unfortunately, I have no precise information about them. Mrs. Winters was never very informative on that subject. Her husband, I know, was in the Royal Navy and was killed in the Great War. I believe she was deeply attached to him."

"Mrs. Gulliver, your cook, informs me that there is a sister living in Croydon—a Mrs. Freshwater."

Sir Victor looked surprised.

"Is there indeed? Does Mrs. Gulliver know her address?" Charlton shook his head. "I must try to find it out. This Mrs. Freshwater should be written to without delay."

"The young nephew, sir? How does he come in?"

"Little John Campbell? A very bright and promising boy. He came to live in this house when he was quite a little toddler. I was not entrusted with all the facts. I recall that Mrs. Winters came to my wife in great distress about eight years ago and told her the sad tale of this small child with no one to care for it. Probably Mrs. Winters told my wife the whole story. If she did, my wife respected her confidence. I was not curious. It was sufficient for me that there was a child in the house. I have always been passionately fond of children."

"Do you know whether there was an actual relationship between Mrs. Winters and John?"

"On that point, I cannot be sure. He came into our home as her nephew and I, for one, never thought to question it."

"Very likely Mrs. Freshwater can tell us."

"Mrs. Freshwater? Oh, yes, the sister. Yes, that is quite possible. Not that there need be apprehension about the boy's future. I shall attend to that." Sir Victor looked grim as he added: "And my first care will be to get him out of the clutches of those two monsters!"

CHAPTER ELEVEN

CHARLTON turned the conversation to the subject of the ghostly hands. Sir Victor Warringham responded with the animation of a man for ever ready to leap into the saddle of his hobby-horse. With his elbows on the arms of his easy chair, he locked his fingers together. Charlton and Martin philosophically prepared themselves for a discourse.

"Perhaps," Sir Victor began, "you have read my book, *England's Haunted Houses?* . . . No? Neither, I imagine, has my son-in-law. It might have been to his advantage if he had—though not, possibly, to mine! *England's Haunted Houses*, gentlemen, is the product of years of patient psychical research. It is an attempt—I can claim it as a successful attempt—to disprove the existence of"—he gesticulated with his hands as he quoted sonorously—"the 'evil thing that walks by night in fog or fire, by lake or moorish fen.' How does it go on? Something about witches, if I remember aright . . . Oh, yes: 'Blue meagre hag, or stubborn unlaid ghost that breaks his magic chains at curfew time.'"

He turned in his chair to say to Martin:

"Milton, I believe."

"I wouldn't put it past him, sir," replied the shivering unregenerate, more concerned, as he told his chief afterwards, with his stubborn thirst at opening time.

Sir Victor reclasped his hands.

"I have read extensively on the subject—Podmore, Myers, Swedenborg, Sir William Crookes, Schwenkfelt and a score of others. I visited alleged haunted houses. I questioned hundreds of old country folk about ghoulies and ghosties and mysterious poltergeists that not only went bump in the night, but also broke crockery and threw furniture about. I ultimately reached the conclusion, gentlemen, that the poltergeists were mischievous persons, probably small boys, and that the ghoulies and ghosties were produced either by trickery or hysteria."

Charlton and Martin exchanged furtive glances. Martin examined his wristwatch with elaborate attention. Sir Victor, however, had got well into his stride.

"I have had expounded to me an interesting theory to explain ghosts. It is based on the workings of the human eye. When we say we *see,* we mean that there has been formed on the retina of the eye an image which has been transferred to the brain through the optic nerve. If the optic nerve is functioning as it should—that is, in one direction only—all is well. But let us assume that the optic nerve suddenly begins to work in the opposite direction. There appears to be no chemical reason why it should not. What happens then?"

"I wouldn't know," Martin muttered under his breath.

"We all of us have a 'mind's eye.' We see pictures, faces, things we have seen, things we have only imagined. If I tell you now to imagine a ghost—a white phantom, let us say, with flapping arms and long fingernails—you will undoubtedly see it in your mind's eye. Now, we will take it that, with this imaginary picture in your mind, your optic nerve goes into reverse, to use a motoring term. Your mind picture is immediately registered on the retina of the eye—and back it comes to the brain, not as a mind picture, but as something your eye has actually seen. Do you understand what I mean?"

"Most ingenious," Charlton agreed. "And do you think this is what happened in your case, the night before last?"

"Definitely not!" Sir Victor retorted. "I mentioned some minutes ago that my son-in-law has certain plans which I play no small part. I am, in fact, cast for the role of victim. He is endeavouring to consolidate his position—it might even be his intention to gain control of my financial affairs—on the grounds that I am not in *compos mentis.* I need hardly tell you, Inspector—you can judge for yourself—that I am perfectly sane and in my right mind. But by cleverly playing on the credulity of various other persons, including the family doctor, he is well on the way to getting me certified insane. In order to hasten my—er—mental disintegration, he enacted a small performance for my benefit during the small hours of yesterday."

"Have you proof of this, Sir Victor?"

"The rascal was too smart for that. I ought to have said that his wife was too smart. She is the brains of the infernal partnership. She plays, if I may so put it, Lady Macbeth to his doltish and unwilling thane . . . I do not know what awakened me, but I opened my eyes to see two glowing, clutching hands approaching me from out of the darkness. I was—"

"These hands, sir. From which direction did they come?"

"I was lying on my right side—that is to say, facing the door. I would say they were the hands of a person standing by the side of the bed and leaning slightly over me."

"You say they were glowing?"

"Yes. My opinion is that Harler was wearing a pair of gloves to which he had applied luminous paint. There was a rough, sketchy quality about the outline of the fingers and palms which suggested that the paint had not been applied with any great care—a fact stamping it as the work of my son-in-law, who is a slovenly, messy, unconscientious fellow . . . For a fraction of time, I was alarmed—very naturally, in the circumstances. Then the silly man gave an insane cackle of laughter. It should have frozen my blood, but it had just the opposite effect. I reached out for the bedside light, but my groping hand found nothing save a bare table. Before commencing his ghostly antics, our very practical spectre had removed the fitting from the table to the floor—as I was soon to discover to my cost! Failing to find the light, I lunged out with my fist towards where I imagined the intruder to be. He anticipated me. The luminous hands were snatched back—and disappeared, leaving the room in complete darkness. I threw aside the bedclothes and jumped out of bed. As I did so, my leg became involved with the flex of the light-fitting. By the time I had sorted it out—you will understand that the incident had disturbed my normal composure—I had damaged the bulb. It did not respond to the switch. With arms outstretched, I felt my way to the door, by the side of which is the switch for the main ceiling light. When I pressed it down, the light went on—and I found myself alone in the room. The door was closed. The rascal had slipped out while I was grappling with the bedside lamp. The passage must have been in darkness, because I did not see him leave the room."

"What did you do then, Sir Victor?"

"My purpose was to apprehend the fellow. You must understand that, at this juncture, I did not suspect him to be my son-in-law. That unpalatable fact was not borne in upon me until I had time for speculation. So, with a view to following him, I made to open the door. It was locked—another example of my ghost's matter-of-fact turn of mind! I then considered it advisable to raise the alarm. I shouted for assistance and thumped the panels of the door with my fists. In a very short space of time, the key was turned in the lock, the door was opened and my son-in-law looked into the room. I will give him credit for playing his part with an ability one would not have expected from such a dullard. With well-feigned anxiety, he asked to know the cause of the trouble. In a few words, I explained to him what had happened, and insisted on a thorough search of the house being made for the miscreant. He tried to calm me with smooth words of comfort and endeavoured to get me back into bed. I protested forcibly. The arrival of Mrs. Winters and Mrs. Harler did nothing to restore my tranquillity, particularly as, barefooted and in my nightshirt, I was in no good plight to receive ladies!"

The old gentleman smiled ruefully.

"Can you recall the conversation, sir?"

"On broad lines, yes. My own remarks were to the effect that an attempt had been made on my life. I put it as strongly as that, though I have since revised my judgement. I do not now consider that the Harlers intended more than to frighten me—to make me say afterwards, to those who would draw certain conclusions, that I had been visited by a homicidal phantom."

Charlton nodded, yet did not fully share Sir Victor's opinion. There seemed an ominous relationship between the two bedside lamps. Sir Victor's might have been moved from the table to prevent his identifying the owner of the luminous hands; and again, it might not. Conversely, why the luminous hands? Intending murderers do not ordinarily advertise their presence in that fashion.

"I told them," Sir Victor went on, "that someone had tried to strangle me."

"You didn't suggest anything supernatural?"

"To the contrary. The Harlers did their best to get me to make such an assertion. It was, in fact, their curious insistence on the point that first aroused my suspicions."

"And Mrs. Winters? What had she to say?"

"Very little, if I remember. Her main concern was to get me back to bed. The poor, devoted woman always treated me like a child. I eventually consented, realizing that, by that time, any uninvited visitor would have slipped out of the house. We all retired to our rooms and, for the rest of the night, I was free from unpleasant interruptions."

While jotting down the salient points of Sir Victor's narrative, Martin still had time for independent reflection. He remembered his chief's puzzlement over Harler's reason for not ringing Dr. Stamford on the Sunday night, or early on Monday morning. Here, it seemed to Martin, was the answer. Sir Victor had refused to accept the ghost theory. Dr. Stamford, convinced though he was of Sir Victor's abnormality, might have insisted on calling in the police.

"But I was not free," Sir Victor was continuing, "from unpleasant thoughts. I do not like Clement Harler. I like his wife even less. Notwithstanding that, I had no real cause for complaint about their manner towards me, until the incident in the small hours of yesterday. I cannot say that I welcomed their presence in this house. That would be utterly untrue. Yet I am the first to concede—or would have been before Sunday night—that they behaved themselves in a reasonable fashion. On the face of it, their first thought was for my comfort. I was not blind enough to fail to detect a substantial degree of 'cupboard love' in this consideration for my well-being, but that was not unnatural. There are many people in this country today who are tenderly caring for rich relatives in the fervent hope that they will not be long a-dying! Yes, I found the Harlers' behaviour unexceptionable."

"Did Mrs. Winters share your view?"

"Far from it. She was unceasing in her condemnation. I might almost describe it as never-ending tittle-tattle. She was for ever tale-bearing. Human nature being the inconsistent thing it is, this had the effect of influencing me in the Harlers' favour. I could not imagine there could exist two such wretches as Mrs. Winters made them out to be."

He gave a helpless gesture with his heavily veined hands.

"I find, now that it is too late, how very right she was . . . That, then, was the situation before Sunday night. But when I was back in bed again after—"

"Excuse me a moment, Sir Victor. You've told us that Mrs. Winters' charges against the Harlers carried little weight with you. If that was so, why did you decide to change your will?"

The question was not to the old man's taste. His ecclesiastical features creased themselves in a frown of secular annoyance.

"It is a testator's unalienable right," he almost snapped, "to bequeath his fortune to whomever he thinks fit. Although I was not disposed to pay too much attention to Mrs. Winters' accusations against the Harlers, I considered some amendment of the clauses of the will to be desirable. Now, to return. After they had left me on Sunday night, I fell to thinking. First I recalled how anxious the Harlers had been that I should adopt the ghost theory. From that, my mind travelled back from one trivial incident to another. They all pointed to one thing: that my son-in-law and his second wife were slowly, but very surely, making the world believe that I was mad."

"Did Mrs. Winters ever mention that aspect, sir?"

"No. I do not believe she ever realised it. Their methods were devilishly cunning. Lying in bed, I reached the conclusion that I must take some step to—er—prevent my early transfer to a mental institution. I decided, therefore, to communicate with the police at the earliest opportunity. Accordingly, yesterday morning I chose a time when the rest of the household are normally engaged elsewhere, and slipped down to use the telephone in the hall. The call was made, but my plan was frustrated by the Harlers. Mrs. Winters told me later in the day that you called in response to my summons, but that my son-in-law and his wife had persuaded you to go away. Mrs. Winters also informed me that they had done the same with my solicitor, Mr. Howard, in spite of his vigorous protests. I myself was not in a position to circumvent the Harlers, as I was sound asleep. My lack of rest during the night must have been the cause. After taking a light breakfast in bed, I fell into a deep sleep, from which I did not waken until lunch-time."

"What did you have for breakfast, sir?"

"Surely a superfluous question!" Then comprehension came. "I see what you mean . . . It would explain a great deal. I had some toast and marmalade and a cup of coffee. . . . Yes, a cup of coffee. I noticed at the time that it seemed to dry on the palate, but attached no significance to it." He shook himself angrily as he added, "Serpents!"

"Has Dr. Stamford prescribed any sort of sedative?"

"No. I should not consent to take it, even if he did. I do not agree with such artificial aids, except in cases of extreme necessity. Yes, the Harlers undoubtedly drugged my coffee."

Charlton decided that nothing more was to be gained by further questioning of Sir Victor. He put an end to the interview by rising to his feet with the remark:

"I don't think I need trouble you any more for the time being. Sir Victor. I'm afraid I must ask you to put up with the police in the house until our inquiries are completed. You won't forget about Mrs. Winters' sister, will you, sir? I'm anxious to have her address."

"By all means. A Mrs. Newport, was it not?"

"Freshwater, sir."

"Of course! How foolish of me! I knew it was connected in some way with the Isle of Wight. By a coincidence, I am at present in correspondence with a gentleman living in Shanklin. It is on the subject of werewolves. Really most interesting."

He got his hands on the arms of the chair and raised himself to a standing position. His eyes were gleaming.

"There is still far too much nonsense being talked about werewolves, gentlemen, even by those who should know better. Cannibals practise anthropophagy. Whether this be done as a ritual or to satisfy a craving for human flesh does not affect my argument that a cannibal does not change into a wolf merely on account of his diet."

"Of course not, sir. Now, if—"

"I have studied the folklore of many races. I have visited zoological gardens in all parts of this country and watched the wolves for hours at a time. I maintain that werewolves are an old wives' tale. My Shanklin correspondent claims acquaintance with an avowed lycanthrope. In support of this, he says that this man howls at night—an altogether too specious argument, as you will agree!"

He beamed at each of them in turn with the geniality of one who has made a telling point at the diocesan conference.

CHAPTER TWELVE

(i)

TEN minutes later, just as Sergeant Martin was saying to his chief that it was a nice enough little murder case, but there were far too many long words in it, a constable announced the arrival of three visitors to Elmsdale: Dr. Stamford, Mr. Howard and Mr. Tom Blackmore.

Charlton interviewed them individually in the late housekeeper's sitting-room. Dr. Stamford was the first to be called in. His manner was agitated and his chin quivered like a blancmange in a restaurant-car.

"I have been brought here," he teetered, "by a startling—um—rumour that is spreading like—um—wildfire throughout Lulverton. The presence of the police here in such—um—numbers confirms it. Tell me, Inspector, how did Sir Victor meet his death?"

"He didn't," was the curt answer. "It was Mrs. Winters who was killed."

It was difficult for him to keep patience with the old doctor. The remark about 'ill-timed rigmarole' still rankled. So he went on without giving the other time to speak:

"Dr. Stamford, have you at any time prescribed a drug for Sir Victor?"

"Yes. Just a sedative, you understand. I considered that a tablet or two, on occasions when the patient was exceptionally excited, would—"

"What was this sedative?"

"Phenobarbitone."

"Who had charge of the tablets?"

"Er—Mr. Harler, I fancy. . . Yes, I recall his mentioning yesterday that he had rendered a quantity of the tablets unfit for use, by spilling them in the—um—fireplace."

"What happened to them?"

"I take it that Mr. Harler threw them away. I am at a loss to understand, Inspector——"

"When were they supplied?"

"My records will show the exact date. I would say it was about—um—a fortnight ago."

"Did you dispense the tablets yourself?"

"No, phenobarbitone tablets are supplied by a chemist on a doctor's prescription."

"How many tablets were prescribed?"

"To the best of my recollection, twenty-five."

"What is the normal dose?"

"From a half to one grain, taken at night before retiring."

"How many grains are there in a tablet?"

"I prescribed one-grain tablets. I—um—enjoined on Mr. Harler the need for—um—restraint in the use of the tablets. Great care must always be exercised with phenobarbitone, as too much recourse to the drug is liable to establish what is medically known as—um—tolerance. A constitution that has grown too—um—accustomed to—"

"What is a dangerous dose?"

"Um—I would say anything over two grains—that is, in this case, two tablets. There is a very small margin between the maximum therapeutic dose and a lethal dose."

"Did the Harlers know all this?"

"Undoubtedly. I took pains to—um—explain it to both of them . . . Your questions are—um—frightening me, Inspector. Was Mrs.—um—Winters—"

"Has phenobarbitone a noticeable taste?"

"It is bitter and tends to—um—dry on the palate. In small quantities, it might pass undetected."

"In beef-extract?"

"For a covertly administered dose, beef-extract would be an excellent—um—medium. I beg you, Inspector, to set my mind at rest. Has Mrs. Winters been—um—poisoned?"

"We don't know yet. Thank you, Dr. Stamford. I need keep you no longer."

"Would it be—um—advisable for me to see Sir Victor?"

"I leave that to you."

The old man got up and shuffled to the door, his permanently bowed shoulders accentuating his abashment. He turned back to Charlton before he left the room.

"Sir Ninian Oxenham is due to come from London tomorrow. Do you think I should—um—cancel the appointment?"

Charlton looked up from the notes he was making.

"Again I must leave it to you, Dr. Stamford," he said blandly. "You'll remember reminding me yesterday that he's *your* patient."

(ii)

Mr. Howard, of Messrs. Dickson, Parrish, Willmott & Lister, was also most distressed, though better informed than Dr. Stamford.

"This is a disaster, Charlton! I little thought, when I warned you yesterday of Sir Victor's perilous position, that the blow would fall in another quarter."

"Does it surprise you?"

"I admit that I was startled when Martin told me just now, but after the first shock, I won't say that I'm surprised. I gave you yesterday my considered opinion about two members of this household. It seems to me that their purpose is served as much by the death of Mrs. Winters as it would have been by the death of Sir Victor.

In making that assertion, I assume that Sir Victor proposed to alter the terms of his will."

"Do you think the Harlers knew his plans?"

"I would say they knew nothing definite. Wouldn't Mrs. Winters' actions yesterday morning have given them a clue?"

"Very likely . . . D'you know a Mrs. Freshwater?"

At this sudden question, Mr. Howard shot him a quick glance.

"I've heard of her. Mrs. Winters' sister, isn't she? Married to a stockbroker, I remember somebody once telling me."

"Have you got her address?"

"No . . . No, I haven't . . . Look, Charlton; I've come this morning as arranged with the Harlers yesterday. The situation's changed since, but I'd better have a word with Sir Victor. Any objection?"

"None at all—but don't go yet."

He rose from his seat at the table and paced the small room for a minute or two before he turned back to the seated, and evidently worried, solicitor.

"Howard," he said abruptly, "I didn't press it yesterday, because things weren't so serious then. Your story—and it's the same story as certain other people want me to swallow—is the nice, neat little yarn that Sir Victor's money was to be diverted from Clement Harler to Enid Winters. There was more to it than that, wasn't there? . . . Wasn't there, Howard?"

The solicitor stood up, a small portly figure by comparison with the tall, well-knit frame of the detective.

"Your question is unwelcome, Charlton. Unwelcome because I am not in a position to give you any answer. That should come from Sir Victor. You know me well enough to be satisfied that I'm not being deliberately obstructive. Be a good fellow and don't press me. Ask Sir Victor."

"Or Mrs. Freshwater?"

"Or Mrs. Freshwater."

"Or the Harlers?"

"Or the Harlers—if they know. Ask anybody you like, old man, but don't ask me. You'll find out sooner or later."

From his superior height, Charlton looked down at him. Like rival advocates, they were friends behind the scenes, and there was no animosity in Charlton's tone as he replied:

"I'm sure I shall."

(iii)

With Mr. Howard on his way to find Sir Victor, Charlton had Tom Blackmore in. The big man was dressed as he had been on his visit to Police Headquarters the previous evening. He now had Bugle with him, on a lead.

"A bad business, Inspector. I heard about it from the hired help and came straight along, to see if I could lend a hand."

"Thanks, Mr. Blackmore. Things are a bit upset here at the moment, but we're getting them sorted out slowly."

"What exactly happened? Mrs. Tucker—my char—was vague about the details."

"Mrs. Winters was found dead in bed this morning. She'd been strangled with a length of light-flex. The window was open and there was a ladder against the wall."

"Suggests an outside job, doesn't it? . . . Or does it suggest it rather too blatantly?"

"It's hard to tell at this stage. Do you know whether they keep a ladder on the premises?"

"Yes, there is one—an extending affair. I've used it myself for pruning the fruit trees. It usually hangs on a couple of pegs on the side of the wash-house. Painted green, if I remember rightly."

"That sounds like it. I'll get you to have a look at it later on. Meanwhile, there are one or two other points on which you may be able to advise me, Mr. Blackmore. Yesterday evening you gave me some valuable information. It was evident that you'd a considerable knowledge of the Warringham family's history. Mrs. Winters was with them for twenty years, so you probably know something about her, too. Can you give me any facts?"

Blackmore rubbed his chin and considered the question.

"She was a bit of a mystery. Women of that kind usually are. Decayed gentility. Forced by a change in the family fortunes to work for a living. Some of them open tea-shops; Enid Winters became a housekeeper. She was married, at one time, to a Navy man—an officer, I believe. He went down with his ship at Jutland and left her with no alternative but to find a job. I don't know what she did for the first few years, but it was about 1926 that she took up employment with the Warringhams. She and Lady Warringham—or plain Mrs. Warringham, as she was then—grew very fond of each other. When Lady Warringham died, Enid Winters carried on here as Sir Victor's housekeeper. Does that tell you what you want to know?"

"Had Mrs. Winters a sister—a Mrs. Freshwater?"

"Yes, Constance Freshwater, a younger sister. I've heard her name mentioned once or twice. Seem to remember meeting her years ago, though exactly when and where . . ." He shrugged his broad shoulders expressively. "She married a man with money, I believe."

"Where can I get in touch with her?"

"There you have me. Can't someone here tell you? Have you asked Sir Victor?"

"He says he doesn't know . . . Mr. Blackmore, your intimacy with affairs in the house may enable you to answer this: Why was Mrs. Winters murdered?"

"A question very much to the point!" He lighted a cigarette. "You're discounting the ladder, are you, and assuming that the murder was *en famille,* as it were?"

"For the moment, yes."

"Then my answer's not at all helpful. I can't even guess at a reason. If Sir Victor had been the victim, I should have been ready enough with my answer! I told you of my fears last evening. When Mrs. Tucker told me this morning that a murder had been committed at Elmsdale, my first thought was that the Har—perhaps it's better not to mention names—my first thought was that certain persons had—er—consolidated their position. Then, when Mrs. Tucker mentioned Mrs.

Winters as the victim, I was—well, thunderstruck is not too strong a word."

"Last Friday, Sir Victor sent a letter to his solicitors, asking for Mr. Howard, the senior partner, to call on him yesterday morning. Do you know why?"

The big man slowly shook his head.

"'Fraid not. It does give rise to some speculation, doesn't it, though? Maybe Sir Victor was going to alter his will. Have you asked him?"

"Yes."

"And what did he say—or shouldn't I ask?"

"He told me he intended to disinherit Clement Harler and leave the money to Mrs. Winters."

Blackmore was patting the spaniel. He looked up with an expression of amazement mingled with disbelief on his face.

"He didn't, did he? Enid Winters is admittedly an old family retainer, but there's a pound or two involved, you know. Sir Victor's no pauper. I can't see him leaving all that pile of spondulics to a housekeeper, however matey she was with his wife."

He smoked his cigarette thoughtfully for a while.

"But it does link up, doesn't it?" he eventually conceded. "Now I come to think of it, I got some sort of sidelight on it from young John yesterday. He said that Howard had actually called, but that the Harlers had sent him packing. Mrs. Winters was extremely cross about it, according to John. That does certainly suggest—but it's no business of mine to formulate theories. I'm here to answer questions. Any more for me?"

"No, that's an end of my catechism, Mr. Blackmore."

"Then maybe I can ask you one. It's not so much a question as a request. The atmosphere in this house is not healthy at the moment for a ten-year-old. Any objection to young John coming to stay with me for a day or two? It's only just down the road—Peartree Cottage."

"An excellent idea," Charlton smiled.

He had, in fact, been worried over the boy's continued presence at Elmsdale.

"Then if you'll have him fetched, we'll suggest it to him."

Charlton nodded and went to the door to send off a constable in search of John. While they waited, Charlton said:

"You understand that I can give you only police sanction. I think you should also consult Sir Victor."

"Yes, of course."

In a few minutes, the constable returned. John was nowhere to be found in the house.

Charlton got up.

"Then I can guess where he is."

(iv)

Up in their sitting-room, where they had been politely told to stop, sat Clement Harler and his wife, Gladys. They were both busy with their nails. She was manicuring hers; he was biting his.

"Why doesn't that detective fellow take our statements?" demanded Harler for the eleventh time that morning.

"Because he's still doing the others. Clem, darling, stop biting your nails. It's a shocking habit to get into."

"You'd bite your nails if you were in my shoes!"

"But I am. We're both in your shoes together!"

At her trilling laugh, he turned on her viciously.

"You sniggering, damfool bitch! Can't you see the spot I'm in? They came round and took our fingerprints. What d'you think they want those for—to start a collection? That Carlton or Clayton—or whatever his blasted name is—will be after me like a terrier after a rat."

"Darling, what an appropriate simile!"

"What chance have I got? We didn't cover our tracks, I tell you!"

"There's the ladder, isn't there? And who thought of that?

Your little wifey. I don't know where you'd be without me, my sweet!"

"Well, I certainly shouldn't be in this mess, for a start." He laughed sardonically. "Ladder, my foot! D'you think Clayton's going to fall for that?"

"Charlton, darling."

"D'you think he's going to be taken in by a ladder? Would anybody outside this dump who wanted to murder Winters have used a ladder—and left it there?"

"You should have mentioned it at the time," said Gladys serenely.

"Don't shout, Clem. They've probably got the whole placed wired with dictaphones by now."

Harler obediently dropped his voice as he asked:

"Have you got your story right? Don't forget he'll question us separately."

"My story'll be all right. It's yours I'm worried about. You know, you're such a fool, my angel child."

"Me a fool? I like that, coming from you, Glad! It's your fault we're in this jam! It was your idea, wasn't it?"

"Don't we gain by Winters' death?"

"And what good'll that do us if we both hang for it?"

"Only you'd hang, Clem. I'd get off on the plea that you coerced me."

"I believe you would, too! You'd double-cross your own mother."

Gladys's face lighted up in a smile of happy reminiscence.

"I did once," she said. "But Clem, let's be serious for a moment."

"*Serious?* What the hell d'you think I'm being—funny-ha-ha?"

"All you've got to do, Clem, is to deny everything. Tell 'em you didn't do it—and keep on telling 'em. It'll be up to Charlton to prove otherwise. Just say you didn't do it."

"And if I didn't," was her husband's very reasonable enquiry, "who did?"

(v)

Elsewhere in Elmsdale, another serious conversation was in progress. It was between Mr. Howard and Sir Victor Warringham. The solicitor was saying:

"It is difficult to imagine a more unpleasant and embarrassing situation, Sir Victor."

"You are right, Mr. Howard—you are indeed right. Do I understand that Inspector Charlton has questioned you this morning?"

"Yes, that is so."

"Did he question you—ah—closely?"

"I think you should know, Sir Victor, that he is growing suspicious about—a certain matter."

"I trust you told him nothing, Mr. Howard?"

"Your confidence was respected in every way, Sir Victor, but I am placed in an extremely awkward position. My action was tantamount to impeding the processes of the law. The Inspector has a right to know. Murder is a crime of the most serious nature."

"We will stand out against him. Only in exceptional circumstances will I agree to enlighten him on that subject."

"He was enquiring this morning as to the present whereabouts of Mrs. Constance Freshwater."

"It is regrettable that he has got hold of Mrs. Freshwater's name. He gleaned it from that garrulous woman, my cook. But without Mrs. Freshwater's address, the Inspector can do little."

Mr. Howard shook his head in sad denial.

"Believe me when I tell you, Sir Victor—if the police want Mrs. Freshwater, they will find her."

"Then let them do so, Mr. Howard!" The magnificent voice gave splendour to the phrase. "I doubt if she could tell them much."

"She could direct them to Mr. George Campbell, Sir Victor."

"Perchance she could, Mr. Howard—perchance she could."

He raised his thin shoulders in a shrug. "I am adopting a fatalistic attitude. If they find out, then they find out. But I owe it to the memory of those who have gone not to participate in the divulgation of that unhappy secret. Would you say, Mr. Howard, that, were you or I to tell Inspector Charlton all we know, he would be even nearer than he is now to laying hands on the murderer—or should I say the murderers?—of the luckless Mrs. Winters? Did they not do away with her to prevent my modest fortune from slipping from their grasp into hers?"

"Is that your considered view, sir?"

"Could an intelligent investigator put any other construction upon it?"

"But do you yourself think that, Sir Victor?"

The old gentleman shook himself with impatience. "I can conceive of no other reason. I have suggested as much to the detectives. I have informed the Inspector that my reason for asking you to come here yesterday was to discuss a new will in favour of Mrs. Winters. I was at pains to explain to him that she was a valued servant and devoted companion to my beloved wife, thereby being more deserving of my—ah—bounty than my scapegrace son-in-law, Clement Harler."

"I take it, Sir Victor, that that was, in fact, your purpose in sending for me?"

Sir Victor bestowed on his solicitor a gaze of extreme benignity.

"Good heavens no," he said.

(vi)

With Tom Blackmore and Bugle at his heels, Charlton left Elmsdale by the front door. As they started off round the central flower-bed, still thickly blanketed with frost, Blackmore bent down to unclip Bugle's lead and, with wildly flapping ears, the young spaniel scampered off ahead of them.

"Young John's a great joy to me," confided Blackmore, as he strode along beside Charlton. "Always been fond of children, especially boys. They show more intelligent interest than girls in really serious things like clockwork trains! Great disappointment to me that I've never had a noisy handful of kids round me. Still, there it is."

Charlton agreed and they chatted about children until Bugle's barks of delight signalled the finding of their quarry. John Campbell was standing at the foot of his eyrie in the chestnut when they came upon him. Bugle was dancing madly round him, demanding attention.

Clutched in John's hand was a pair of rubber gloves.

CHAPTER THIRTEEN

(i)

INSPECTOR CHARLTON was too keenly interested to waste time on preliminaries.

"Where did you get those, John?"

The boy showed no trace of confusion.

"I was just coming to see you about them, sir. I found them in Falcon's Nest."

"Where's that?"

"My tree-house, sir. I christened it Falcon's Nest because that's what the Swiss Family Robinson called theirs."

"When did you find them?"

"Only a few minutes ago. I came out here to play. They weren't there yesterday."

"Do you leave that rope-ladder hanging down?"

"Oh, yes, sir. Otherwise I wouldn't be able to get up there, unless I climbed the tree, which is trifficly difficult, isn't it, Uncle Tom?"

Blackmore smiled and turned to the Inspector.

"I helped him build the thing."

Charlton asked John: "Have you ever seen the gloves before?"

The boy creased his brows. "I *think* I have, sir, though I can't be certain. Aunt Enid had a pair very much like them. She used them to keep her hands nice when she was doing mucky jobs."

"Do you know where she usually kept them, John?"

"Yes, sir—in the drawer of the table in her sitting-room. I've seen her put them away there lots of times.

"Right." He held out his hand. "You'd better let me have them."

John handed them over with evident relief. Charlton said as he took them:

"Mr. Blackmore wants to ask you something."

"Yes, John. How would you like to come and stay at the cottage for a day or two?"

"Oo, yes! Will I sleep in the second-best bedroom?"

"No," answered Tom Blackmore with a solemn shake of his head, "the Duchess of Dantzig is in that one. You'll have to be satisfied with the blue room in the east wing. We must ask Sir Victor whether you can come."

"You leave him to me," asserted John.

(ii)

The three of them walked back to the house together. Charlton parted with the others in the hall and went off in search of Sergeant Martin, whom he found having a quiet cup of tea and a chat with Mrs. Gulliver in the kitchen. The Sergeant was soon able to prove, however, that he had not spent all his time treading the primrose path of dalliance. He reported that all the Inspector's instructions had been attended to. Sergeant Peters had done his fingerprint photography, had taken prints of all the members of the household and carried them off to Whitchester for examination and comparison. The china beaker had been sent, after photographing, to the public analyst, together with the dead woman's nightdress. Martin had also been in touch with the meteorological office and had been informed that the white frost had descended on the Lulverton district at, or about, one o'clock that morning.

"Nice work, Martin," approved Charlton. "Now, where can I find a dark corner?"

Mrs. Gulliver was consulted. She directed him to a cupboard under the stairs. Charlton retired into it and closed the door. In the darkness, the rubber gloves were still faintly phosphorescent.

He emerged from the cupboard (to the alarm of Lily Higgins, who was passing at that moment) and went back into the kitchen. He handed over the gloves to Martin with instructions for them to be sent at once to Sergeant Peters, so that the inner surfaces could be examined for fingerprints.

"And one more thing, Martin," he added.

He drew the Sergeant into the hall, out of the hearing of Mrs. Gulliver, to that lady's great annoyance.

"Send a man back to Police H.Q. with a message for them to get in touch with the police at Croydon, Surrey. I want Croydon to trace a Mrs. Constance Freshwater. All I know about her is that her husband's a stockbroker and used to be an Air Raid Warden. When they find her, she's to be told that her sister, Mrs. Enid Winters, has died and will she come down to Lulverton p.d.q."

Martin nodded. His chief went into Mrs. Winters' sitting-room. There were no rubber gloves in the table drawer. But in the fireplace—and he reproached himself for not having noticed it before—was the ragged butt of a small cigar.

(iii)

With his few necessities in an attaché-case and his pink school cap askew on his boyishly untidy head, John Campbell marched along beside Tom Blackmore on their way to Peartree Cottage, while Bugle scouted ahead. The dark shadow of Mrs. Winters' death was already lifting from the boy's mind and he chatted happily as they went down the drive of Elmsdale and turned into the main road. But they had not gone far before he was struck by a weighty thought.

"Uncle Tom, what's going to happen to me, now that I can't live with Aunt Enid any more?"

"Oh, we'll fix up something for you."

Blackmore's voice was comforting, yet he, too, was perplexed by the same problem.

"Aunt Enid told me once that I came to live with her when I was trifficly young and said that my father and mother must be dead. Now Aunt Enid's dead, so I'm like a boy in a story I read that hadn't any relations at all and was Alone in the World."

The capital letters emphasised by his tone made Blackmore smile.

"It won't be as bad as that, John. You're not alone in the world by a long way. Perhaps we shall find another relation of your mother and father for you to go and live with. They may have boys of their own, which should make life not quite so lonely for you."

"I don't think I'd like that, Uncle Tom. They might not want me and I'm sure I'd hate them trifficly, 'specially Aunt Connie."

"We all have to get used to new surroundings from time to time. Life is full of change, John. It's always strange at first, but it wears off after a week or two."

"But a week or two's simply *ages.*"

"A day or two, then. Perhaps—and it's a big perhaps, don't forget—Sir Victor will want you to stay on at Elmsdale. Then you'll be able to carry on at Paulsfield College." John stopped in mid-stride.

"No! I won't! Whatever anyone says, I won't! Not with Mr. and Mrs. Harler there! Nobody can make me stop! I'll run away and never be seen again!"

Blackmore put his hand on the boy's shoulder.

"All right, John. Don't get worked up. Sorry I suggested it."

Somewhat mollified, John resumed walking.

"I would," he threatened darkly.

They went on a few yards in silence, then John ventured, with a sideways, upward glance at his tall companion:

"Uncle Tom, d'you think I could come and live with you? I'd—try not to be a triffic nuisance. D'you think I could?"

Tom Blackmore hesitated. He was fond of John, but the boy would be a heavy responsibility. An easy-going bachelor life, eating when one felt hungry, sleeping at irregular hours, was not the existence for a growing boy to share. Besides, there were other things—terrifying things like bed-sheets being aired and chicken-pox. John's suggestion needed some thought.

John asked again: "D'you think I could, Uncle Tom?"

Blackmore temporised. "Let's not decide just yet. You're coming for a few days, anyway. Shall we see how we get on together before we decide on a long-term partnership? Can you grill bacon?"

This crafty question sent John off on a long, enthusiastic and not very truthful account of his domestic accomplishments that lasted until they drew near to Peartree Cottage.

As the thickset hedge that flanked the road gave place to the white fence of the front garden, they saw a man standing in the porch. He turned towards them, so that they saw his face. To John he was a stranger.

Tom Blackmore opened the garden gate and walked slowly up the path.

(iv)

There are men whose pathological thirsts give them pouches under eyes as full of a lively intelligence as those of a dead cod, a blotchy skin and a reticulation of blood-vessels in the flesh covering the cheekbones. Such were the signs on the face of the man standing in the porch of Peartree Cottage.

He was on the eve of forty. His figure was slim and of over medium height. The most impressive thing about him was his moustache—one of those spectacular growths curling up from the lip that have come to be associated with the Royal Air Force. In his dress, he was dandified. He wore a grey suit, a double-breasted overcoat of the same colour and cut snugly to his slender lines, patent leather shoes and, at a raffish angle, a black felt hat with an ultra-curly brim. On the doorstep by his side was a large leather suitcase pasted over with labels, the number and variety of which suggested that its owner was either much travelled or wished to create that impression.

He smiled blandly as Blackmore approached him. Since opening time, he had had several double Scotches in Lulverton and another couple in the Mickleham Arms after descending from the bus.

"How are you, Tom, old sportsman?"

Blackmore did not return the smile.

"What do you want, Valentine?"

"Just happened to be in these parts, old chappie, so I thought I'd look you up."

"Very thoughtful of you."

"Not at all. Matter of fact, I've a message for you—from Clare."

"So my wife is still living with you, is she?"

"No need to put it quite so bluntly, old darling. Not in front of our young friend, at any rate."

Blackmore had forgotten John, who had diffidently followed him up the garden path and now stood behind him, pretending an interest in Bugle.

"John, would you like to take Bugle for a game in the back garden?"

Readily the boy agreed. He did not like the look of Mr. Valentine. With Bugle at his heels, he disappeared round the side of the cottage.

"Now, what's this message?" Blackmore demanded. "The last one I received from my wife came through the King's Proctor. Now she sends you, of all people."

"Not much use bearing malice, old dear. Won't get us anywhere. 'Let the dead past'—and all that. Are you going to keep me shivering on the jolly old doorstep?"

He flinched as Blackmore took a sudden pace forward, but the big man's intention was to unlock the front door.

Suitcase in hand, Valentine followed him into the den. Without waiting for an invitation, he took off his overcoat, threw it over the back of a chair and sat down by the fire, which was beginning to burn low. Then he looked round the room.

"Comfy little place you've got here, Tom. Some of the old furniture, I see. Reminds me of days gone by."

His voice was of the hoarse variety known as gin-and-fog.

Blackmore preferred to remain standing. With his hands thrust down into the pockets of his trench-coat, he said:

"I admire your gall, Valentine. It's the only thing about you that I respect."

"Getting a tiny bit offensive, old darling. Doesn't pay in the long run, you know. We're none of us ripping old plaster saints, as you'll be the first to admit."

"Any more of that, Valentine, and I'll throw you out into the road."

Valentine pulled a packet from his pocket, extracted the last remaining "Manikin" and threw the empty packet in the fire.

"No doubt you could, too," he nodded, feeling for his lighter. "Always were a muscular brute."

He flicked a flame, but paused before lighting his cigar to say:

"But you know the story of Goliath, old prune. How does it run? . . . 'And David put his hand in his bag, and took thence a stone, and slang it.' Learnt that at Sunday school. Funny the things you can remember, isn't it?"

With carefully assumed nonchalance, he applied the flame to his cigar and blew out a cloud of smoke before going on to his silent host:

"A wee scrap too old and tottery for the David part myself. There are one or two points of similarity, though. For instance, I also have a bag."

His cigar between his fingers, he waved airily towards the suitcase.

Tom Blackmore took his hands out of his pockets and folded his arms across his broad chest.

"What are you getting at, Valentine? If I know you, it's

nothing pleasant."

"Cast your mind back to—well, it's a good many years now. I'm speaking of the time when Clare, recognizing the jolly old sterling worth when she saw it, left you for me. We understand each other on the point, old campaigner, so you won't be put out when I say that you were deuced glad when she went. Never could get on together, you two. Curious, you know, because she's a sweet kid."

If he intended to stir Blackmore to retort, he failed. "I still say, old dear, that you took it badly. Not the pukka sahib at all. Fellow doesn't divorce his wife; he let's her divorce him. The old hotel-bill stuff. More sporting. Be that as it may, we won't go any further into the ethics of the thing. Let's say you got a decree nisi against dear old Clare. Very cut up, she was, poor old darling. Publicity and all that."

This stung Blackmore into snapping back:

"Don't talk such damned nonsense, Valentine! That woman gloats over publicity. And she wanted a divorce. Why did she get the decree absolute squashed?"

"It wasn't Clare. It was the King's Proctor."

"And who put the King's Proctor up to it? Why did she do it?"

There was a leer in Valentine's voice as he answered: "You should know."

"The reason she gave, yes; but why did she do it? It wasn't vindictiveness. She'd always put her own comfort before any petty retaliation. She wanted to marry you because she thought you'd got money. So why did she smash up any chance of divorce?"

"Moral obligation, old chappie. Well-developed sense of duty. Felt she couldn't have that sort of thing going on."

"Don't be a fool, Valentine. What did she gain, except a cheap revenge? What did either of you gain?"

"Satisfaction of knowing we'd done the right thing."

"Didn't you want to marry Clare?"

"All one to me, dear boy. I didn't argue about the terms."

Blackmore got furious at that.

"You rat!" he shouted. "You drunken, verminous, dirty, slinking little blackguard! Knew you'd done the right thing! You never did the right thing in your life, Raymond Valentine! Did you do the right thing with Clare? Did you do the right thing with me? Did you do the right thing with—Rosalie Warringham?"

"Leave her out of it. Unhappy memories and all—"

"Unhappy memories, pah! You left her, Valentine—left her flat when she most needed you. And you ran off with my wife! You do the right thing Why, you alcoholic, oversexed reptile—"

Suddenly Valentine savagely crushed his half-smoked "Manikin" in the ashtray by his side. His fish-eyes had narrowed with anger.

"I've had enough of your bloody rudeness, Blackmore!" he said viciously. "It's time I put you where I want you!"

CHAPTER FOURTEEN

(i)

LATER that same Tuesday afternoon, Inspector Charlton and Sergeant Bert Martin were in conference with the Police Superintendent in charge of the Lulverton Division.

"Carthorse" Kingsley, as he was called by the lawbreakers, "Tiny", as he was called by his friends, was in civilian clothes that afternoon. He was a big Downshireman in the early fifties, in appearance more like a farmer than a policeman, in manner downright, in method without artifice. Though nominally in control of the C.I.D. men attached to his division, he usually gave Charlton a free hand to act as he saw fit, but he liked to know what was going on. His motto was "Facts—nothing but facts."

Charlton was giving him a summary of events in the Winters murder. They sat in the Super's office.

"Yesterday morning at nine o'clock, Martin took a 'phone call from Sir Victor Warringham. Sir Victor reported that, during Sunday night—two a.m., to be precise—an attack was made on him, as he lay in bed, by two clutching phosphorescent hands. He asked for police investigation into the affair. As soon as Martin told me about it, we drove out to Elmsdale, the Warringham home. The door was opened by a frightened young servant named Lily Higgins, who mistook us for solicitors."

"Some people go too far," murmured the Super with a perfectly straight face.

"I explained who we were and Lily was very glad to hear it. While she was telling us that 'the master was nearly murdered in 'is bed last night,' Mrs. Winters, the housekeeper, appeared."

"What was she like?"

"Tall, angular, fiftyish, school-marmish. Rimless spectacles. Severe hairstyle. Long mauve dress. Black shoes. General first impression, woman of good family compelled to work for a living. Second impression, not quite such good family. She, also, took us for solicitors before I'd a chance to explain."

The Super tut-tutted sympathetically.

"When I told her we were the police and had called to see Sir Victor, she very nearly slammed the door in our faces. But she thought better of it and invited us in. She took us along to her sitting-room on the ground floor. I told her that we'd called in response to a 'phone call from Sir Victor. She said it must have been some practical joker, because there was no conceivable reason why Sir Victor should need the police. I said that, for all that, I'd like to speak to him. She replied that it wasn't possible. He'd been taken ill on Sunday night and his doctor had given orders for him not to be disturbed. I asked her whether his trouble was physical or mental. She said he suffered from his heart. There wasn't any doubt from her manner that, if we saw the old gentleman at all, it would be over her dead body."

"Which is just what happened, I suppose?"

"Precisely, I failed to make contact with Sir Victor yesterday, though Martin and I had a long chat with him this morning. But I'll come to that. While we were talking to Mrs. Winters, we were interrupted by a man called Clement Harler, who is Sir Victor's son-in-law. He married Rosalie, the Warringham daughter, something like twelve years ago. She was killed by a flying-bomb. Harler married again and is now living at Elmsdale with his second wife, Gladys."

"Damned unnatural set-up," was the Super's dry comment. "Description?"

"Gladys? Twenty-five or six. Luscious Lovely. Front row of the chorus, West End. Tired businessman's refuge. Hardworking gold-digger, I'd say."

"And Harler?"

"Seedy middle forties. Fleshy. Small moustache. Thinning hair brilliantined back over a bald patch. Manner a combination of furtiveness and bluster. Very much under the red-nailed thumb of Gladys, I should imagine. Charley Howard described Harler as 'thoroughly unscrupulous and completely stupid.' To get back to the story, Harler called Mrs. Winters out of the room and gave her a curtain-lecture for not referring us direct to him when we'd arrived. She came back into the room, looking extremely put out, and took us along to the library, where the Harler man was waiting for us. His purpose was identical with Mrs. Winters'—to keep us away from Warringham. His yarn was different, however. *He* wanted us to think that Sir Victor was as fit as a fiddle, but as mad as a hatter; that the luminous hands were a product of the old gentleman's diseased mind. I mentioned the doctor. Harler said that no doctor had been called in on Sunday night. I told him that didn't agree with Mrs. Winters' statement. With a flimsy excuse, he hurried out of the room to compare stories with the housekeeper.

"While he was away his wife came in, apparently in search of him. She was archly surprised to find us there and managed, during her few minutes in the room, to contradict both her husband and Mrs. Winters. Mrs. Winters would have liked us to believe that Sir Victor had had one of his heart attacks. Harler's explanation was that Sir Victor had complained about a murderous phantom. But Gladys's version was that the old gentleman had asserted that he had been attacked by a human being.

"In a few minutes, Harler returned. He'd seen Mrs. Winters and she'd admitted that she'd lied about the doctor calling. She said she had done it to protect Sir Victor from being disturbed by the uncouth constabulary."

He paused to light a cigarette.

"After that, Tiny, there didn't seem much we could do, so we came away—but not before I'd got Harler's assurance that I should see Sir Victor as soon as he'd been passed as fit to receive visitors by Dr. Stamford."

"Old Mortality," grunted the Super. "Dithering lump of uselessness. I'd rather call in the devil himself."

"We'd only just left Elmsdale when Charley Howard called there. I got his story afterwards. He had much the same reception as we did. Harler told him to come back tomorrow."

"Why had Howard called?"

"Sir Victor wanted to make a new will."

"Who would have benefited?"

"Winters would have gained; Harler would have lost. This is supported by their actions when Howard called. Harler tried to get rid of him; Winters wanted him to stop."

"And Harler won."

"Yes. There was quite a scene on the doorstep, according to Howard. Gladys joined in and it was really she who persuaded Howard to put off his interview until this morning."

"By which time Winters was dead and Harler's legacy was safe."

"Safe from Mrs. Winters, at any rate."

"But a cast-iron motive for the murder."

"Let's say a reasonable motive. And there's more to it . . . To what extent Dr. Stamford has been worked on by the Harlers is difficult to estimate, but the old idiot is prepared to give his certificate that Sir Victor is insane. He'd made arrangements for Sir Ninian Oxenham, the London brain specialist, to come down tomorrow and give a separate opinion. If Oxenham agrees with Stamford, Harler will have a strong case to lay before the magistrate, or whoever is called on to make the reception order. Then, with Sir Victor comfortably tucked away in a mental home, Harler's legacy under the will should be pretty safe. Charley Howard says that anyone who's been certified as insane *can* make another will, but the beneficiaries wouldn't find it too easy to get it admitted to probate."

Superintendent Kingsley nodded his head slowly up and down.

"So we get this situation," he reasoned. "The Harlers were fighting against time. Warringham had to be certified, with no time wasted, to stop him from altering his will. The brain specialist was to come tomorrow, but Howard was to come today. So their hand was forced. Winters had to be stopped from inheriting. Either Winters or Warringham had to be put out of the way—and quickly. Killing Warringham would have been too obvious, so they chose Winters. There's your motive, Harry. Now, what about evidence?"

"Here's what I've pieced together so far. The household comprises Sir Victor Warringham, Clement Harler, Gladys Harler, Enid Winters, Mrs. Gulliver, who is the cook, Lily Higgins, the housemaid, and a boy of ten called John Campbell, who is a nephew of Mrs. Winters. When I say he's a nephew, that's what he's living there as. Whether it's a real relationship, I've yet to find out.

"The first to get up this morning was Lily Higgins. While taking some ashes out to the dustbin, she noticed a ladder standing against the back wall of the house. She went up to tell the cook, whose suspicions were immediately aroused. She went down with Lily, saw that the ladder was under Winters' window and that the window was open. She came back indoors, went up to Winters' room and discovered her lying in bed with all the symptoms of having been strangled. I'd say myself that she had. When I saw her, her face was mottled and congested and the colour of a nearly ripe mulberry. You remember the Cadogan woman, Tiny? . . . Well, somewhat worse than that. Strangulation was certainly indicated, though there's a faint possibility that she was poisoned first. We'll come to that later. Round Winters' neck had been twisted the flex of her bedside lamp. A plastic paper-knife had been used as a garotte. The flex, when I came to examine it, was half buried in a dull red weal that ran in a narrow, slightly raised ring around the woman's neck. Lorimer's working on it now and I'm hoping he'll have something interesting to tell us."

He stubbed out his cigarette-end and lighted another. "The screams of the cook and housemaid brought the rest of the household out of their rooms. I gather from young John Campbell that both Harler and his wife overacted their dismay. Harler kept shouting, 'Some swine shall pay for this,' and was at particular pains to draw attention to the ladder and the open window. Sir Victor, on the other hand, remained calm. He first made sure that the woman was dead, then locked up the room and put the key in a sealed envelope, which he handed to me on my arrival."

"Doesn't sound like a man on the waiting-list for an asylum. What's your view of him, Harry?"

Charlton stroked his chin.

"It's difficult to say with certainty. Some of these mental cases are very odd. I read some time ago of an old gentleman who appeared at breakfast stark naked and shouted, to the consternation of his family, 'I'm Adam. Where's Eve?' He'd gone through seventy years of life without doing anything so blatantly unconventional, but enquiries revealed that, for forty of those seventy years, he'd been suffering from delusions. As a result of this Garden of Eden performance, he was certified, yet, if it hadn't been for that, he would probably never have been found out. It may be the same with Sir Victor."

Sergeant Martin stirred in his chair.

"Them werewolves."

"Yes," Charlton agreed, and turned to explain to the Super: "After a perfectly reasonable conversation with Martin and me this morning, Sir Victor mentioned quite casually that he was looking into the question of werewolves. He argues that they're just an old wives' tale."

"So do I," said the Super, "but I'm not crazy."

"Sir Victor is endeavouring to prove," said Charlton patiently, "that human beings cannot be turned into wolves.

Would any perfectly sane person consider such investigation necessary? Would it be rational, do you think, Tiny, for a man to grow scarlet runners with a view to refuting the story of Jack and the Beanstalk?"

The Super nodded. "I see what you mean."

"I think myself that Sir Victor is normal for ninety-nine percent of the time and abnormal for the other one percent. It looks as if the Harlers have been trying to adjust the ratio. I've no proof yet, but everything seems to point to Harler—or his wife—having been Sir Victor's luminous visitor on Sunday night. Evidence so far is a pair of rubber gloves brushed with luminous paint."

"Did you catch the Harlers with 'em?"

"No . . . But even if the gloves don't directly incriminate the Harlers, their very existence suggests that somebody did have fun and games with Warringham on Sunday night. The Harlers want the credulous world to think that the old gentleman was just seeing things."

"Where did you find the gloves?"

"They were in the possession of the boy, John Campbell. I found him with them this morning in the Elmsdale grounds."

"What was his story?"

"He has a structure that he calls Falcon's Nest in one of the chestnut trees. It's reached by a rope-ladder. He told me that he'd just discovered the gloves in Falcon's Nest and was on his way to me with them when I met him."

"Any reason to disbelieve him?"

"He seems a very honest, straightforward kid."

"A typical boyish prank, you know," warned the Super, "frightening the lives out of people. Could the kid have got into Warringham's room on Sunday night?"

"He could have done; his room's only just along the corridor. But somehow I can't see him doing it. He'd have been more likely to try putting the breeze up the Harlers. Even then, it wouldn't have been very probable.

He's too scared of them to play tricks. No, Tiny, I'm inclined to rule John out. The Harlers are my bet and I'm ready to lay long odds. Peters has the gloves now. I'm hoping he'll find some useful fingerprints inside them.

. . . We've drifted away from the main story."

"You'd got to the point where Warringham handed you the key of the room in a sealed envelope."

"Oh, yes . . . When Martin and I went into the room, this is what we found. Martin, will you read your notes?"

"'Bedroom of deceased on first floor back, facing west. Boy's room adjoining. No communicating door.' I've got a plan 'ere, sir. The room's twenty-two foot by fifteen, with the window in the centre of one long wall and the door in the centre of the other. That's west and east respectively, sir." The Super nodded and Martin resumed reading. "'Fireplace in centre of south wall. Single bed against centre of north wall. Small table on window side of bed. Other furniture, dressing-table, chest-of-drawers and small writing desk with flap. When examined, state of room as follows: Lower sash of window pushed up to fullest extent. Top sash open three inches. Ivy on outside window-ledge. Frost on ledge and ivy levelly coated and unmarked. Ivy not crushed or damaged.'"

Charlton threw in here:

"The meteorological office say the frost came down at one o'clock in the morning. The ladder, up against the wall below the window, was also coated with frost when I examined it. If it was used at all, Tiny, it certainly wasn't used after the frost descended. From the condition of the ladder, the window-sill and the ivy, I'll stake my oath nobody scaled the ladder and got in through the window after one o'clock this morning; and I'm willing to make a sporting bet, on the evidence of the undamaged ivy alone, that nobody climbed through the window at all."

"A blind, eh?" grunted the Super. "Carry on, Martin."

"'Witness Lily Higgins testifies deceased had habit of

sleeping with lower sash closed and upper sash open a few inches. When examined, no marks found on lower sash to suggest levered open from outside. Some form of leverage necessary when window closed. No sash-lifters on inside of frame. Sergeant Peters found fingerprints on upper rail of lower sash."

"Whose were they?" the Super wanted to know.

"I haven't had Peters' report yet, Tiny," Charlton told him. "It should be in soon."

At a sign from the Superintendent, Martin read on:

"'Deceased found lying on right side, partly under disordered bedclothes. Position diagonal across bed, with head just off pillow on window side of bed. White cambric nightdress. Small brown stain on left shoulder of it.'"

The Super interrupted to ask the nature of the stain. "I imagine it was beef-extract," Charlton replied. "It's being analysed. Martin."

"'Medical evidence, died of strangulation between midnight and two a.m. Light-flex twisted round neck of deceased by means of letter-opener of green plastic. Witness Lily Higgins confirmed letter-opener was property of deceased and usually kept in bedroom writing-desk. Witness Sir V. Warringham identifies it as Christmas present from him to deceased. Light-flex attached at one end to table-lamp. Polished oak base and standard. Buff-coloured parchment shade. Flex coloured gold. Other end of flex fitted with bayonet plug. Found unattached. Witness Ada Gulliver confirms lamp usually on bedside table, with plug fitted into ceiling pendant. Lamp found lying on floor alongside bed.'"

"Some interesting points arise there, Tiny," Charlton commented. "A murder is either premeditated or done on the spur of the moment."

"I'll make a careful note of that," responded the Super gratefully. "It'll help me in my work."

The interruption was disregarded.

"Had Mrs. Winters been murdered on the spur of the moment—say by some sneak-thief who'd broken into the house and had to quieten her tongue to avoid being caught—the use of the light-flex and letter-opener would have been quite natural. I can think of easier ways of subduing Winters, but, if the intruder preferred garotting, there were the materials all to hand. That applies not only to a housebreaker—and such gentry don't resort to violence if they can possibly help it—but also to any other person suddenly deciding to liquidate Winters . . . Now assume that the crime was premeditated. My assertion is that the intending murderer would have come supplied with his own homicidal equipment, unless he knew with certainty that he would find it on the spot. Therefore I say that the murder was done by someone acquainted with two facts: one, that Winters had a bedside lamp with enough flex for the purpose; and two, that the letter-opener was kept in, or on, the bureau."

"Agreed," said the Super. "And who's more likely to know both those things than one of the household? That's in keeping with the ladder-and-window evidence. If it wasn't an outside job, it must have been done from the inside."

"Your deductions are breathtaking," murmured Charlton, getting his revenge.

"And who had more reasons for doing it than the Harlers? All we've to do now is to pin it on to them . . .

But how?"

"A lot depends on Peters . . . Getting back to our theme, there were one or two other things worth noting in the room. The flap of the desk was found open. Nothing unusual in that, of course, but the papers in the pigeonholes weren't as neatly arranged as I should have expected. Winters seems to have been a pernickety sort of person. I ran through the papers. Nothing of interest in them. There were two drawers in the lower half of the desk. The upper one was unlocked. It had some papers in it:

Christmas cards, theatre programmes, a cheque-book—"

"Any interesting counterfoils?"

"No . . . A packet of letters from her late husband, some documents concerning his death in the Great War, and Mrs. Winters' marriage certificate. The lower drawer was completely empty, but the lock of it had been forced. It's worth noting that it was the only drawer in the room that Winters had kept locked. I'll forestall any brilliant inferences, Tiny, by suggesting that the contents were removed when the drawer was forced."

"If I have any more of that," growled the Super, "I'll get you back on the beat. And you can take that idiotic grin off your face, Bert Martin! The discipline in this damn division is going right to pieces. Things have got to be tightened up."

Whereupon the despot began a new reign of tyranny by handing round his cigarettes with an iron hand and 'phoning downstairs for three cups of tea in the voice of one not lightly to be disobeyed. Then he said to Charlton:

"Proceed."

"The rim of the drawer and the rail above it had been levered apart until the bolt was clear of the hole in the rail. By the marks on the wood, I'd say an ordinary screwdriver was used. The fellow took it away with him. There was nothing else in the room that would have suited the purpose . . . There's no doubt that Winters kept something of value in that drawer—money or jewels or important papers. Mrs. Gulliver, the cook, told me how, on one occasion, Winters mislaid the key and 'fair crazy she was till she found it.' What the drawer contained, I've not been able to discover yet, but it was clearly of some consequence to Winters—and, presumably, to someone else."

"Not necessarily," Superintendent Kingsley disagreed. "The drawer may have been rifled to give the impression that the house had been broken into by some casual crook; that the real motive was theft and the murder only incidental."

"In my experience," Charlton replied, "when people try that game, they invariably overdo it. They leave the room looking as if a typhoon had hit it. I'd say this was a case of genuine robbery—not just a normal robbery for financial gain, because there was a silver watch of some value on the bedside table that any thief would have slipped in his pocket before he left, but the purloining of a definite thing—or things."

"Then it comes to this, Harry. We have (*a*) a murder and (*b*) a robbery. The two incidents must be connected with each other; they can't be isolated acts. Whoever did the murder, did the robbery as well. We're agreed that the Harlers had a strong motive for killing Winters. Now, what was their motive for robbery? You don't think it was for pounds, shillings and pence?"

"I doubt it. Much more likely to be important documents—incriminating letters and so forth . . . Which brings us to something else."

He was about to go on when a uniformed constable came in with three cups of tea on a tray. As he passed them round, he said to Charlton:

"Message for you from Sergeant Peters, sir. 'E's on 'is way over with the stuff. Be 'ere in fifteen minutes."

Charlton thanked him and, when he had left the room, went on to Superintendent Kingsley:

"We were talking about the papers that might have been in the bureau drawer. What I'm going to say is wildly suppositional. It springs from a chat I had this morning with Charley Howard. He told me yesterday, after some prompting on my part, that Winters was not satisfied with the terms of Warringham's existing will and that it was possible that Warringham had summoned him in order to draft a new will more to her liking. This was confirmed this morning by Warringham himself, who told me that he had decided to cut out Clement Harler and leave the money to Winters."

The Super was going to speak, but Charlton held up his hand.

"Wait a minute, Tiny. This morning I had a second talk with

Howard. I put it to him bluntly that there was more to it than that. He admitted as much, but flatly refused to give me the details. He said I'd find out sooner or later, but that he wasn't going to be the one to tell me."

He sipped his tea.

"I was just wondering whether there were papers in the bureau drawer that might have thrown some light on that little mystery."

The Superintendent shook himself impatiently.

"Don't let's get involved in speculation. Let's stick to the facts. Let's get the Harlers tied up so they can't wriggle free. What else have you got against them?"

Charlton sat for a while in thought before he answered: "Mrs. Winters was a light sleeper. It's reasonable to suppose that, in the normal way, she would have been awakened by an intruder in good time to avoid being strangled. Dr. Stamford prescribed phenobarbitone for Sir Victor. The supply of tablets was kept by the Harlers. Stamford told me so himself... It was Mrs. Winter' custom to have some beef-extract in bed before she went to sleep. Not everyone's choice of night-cap, but that was Mrs. Winters' custom. She drank the beef-extract from a special china mug with its own saucer. The drink was always prepared by the cook and taken up by her to Winters' room. Last night the cook was intercepted on the landing by Gladys Harler, who took the mug from her and said she would see that Winters got it . . . Sir Victor, whose room adjoins the landing, overheard the conversation. He told me that such considerate behaviour was not in keeping with Gladys's character; and he also told me that there was a considerable pause between the end of her chat with the cook and the sound of her footsteps passing his room on their way along to Mrs. Winters' room . . . When the cook handed Gladys the drink, the mug was standing in the saucer. We found the empty mug on Winters' bedside table this morning, but no saucer. Lily Higgins says she discovered the saucer in the Harlers' sitting-room while she was tidying up this morning. I'm having the residue of beef-extract analysed.

If it contains any phenobarbitone, counsel for the defence won't find it easy to brush aside that little piece of circumstantial evidence!"

"No report yet from the analysts?"

For answer, Charlton reached for the 'phone and asked for a number. He made his enquiry, held on for a time, then, with a word of thanks, replaced the receiver.

"They'll ring us back in half an hour."

They returned to their discussion, which went on until the arrival of Sergeant Peters with the results of his fingerprint tests. He had written them on a sheet of paper, which he passed over to Charlton, who studied them so long in silence that Sergeant Martin almost exploded with exasperation. At last Charlton said:

"Extremely interesting. The main points are that Gladys Harler's prints were on the tumbler and Harler's prints were on the bureau drawer and the top rail of the window-sash. Harler's prints were also found inside the rubber gloves and on—"

"The paper-knife?"

"Yes."

(ii)

Prompt to the minute came the analysts' report. They were not ready yet with a decision about the stain on the nightdress, but they were able to confirm that the residue of beef-extract in the mug contained phenobarbitone.

"What strength?" Charlton asked.

"Up to the maximum pharmaceutical dose," was the answer, "but not strong enough to be lethal."

Superintendent Kingsley rubbed his hands together in glee when Charlton passed on this information, then leapt to his feet like an eager schoolboy.

"It's sewn up!" he exulted. We'll run out to Elmsdale, hear what lies these Harler people have to tell us, then arrest 'em on suspicion." He looked at his watch. "We'll have to look sharp about it, though. I'm taking the missis to the first house at the pictures."

CHAPTER FIFTEEN

(i)

THEY interviewed Gladys Harler first. The scene, once again, was the late housekeeper's sitting-room. Gladys set out to be charming. How could any man, even a policeman, stand out against her? Was she, whose life's work was twisting men round her little finger, to be dismayed by a trio of flatties? Even when Charlton gave her the warning required by Judges' Rules, she giggled prettily:

"Inspector! What a terrifying man you can be! Is he always like this, Superintendent? You don't have to threaten poor little me! Of course I'll tell you all I can. What's question number one? Just like the radio quizzes, isn't it?"

"You are Gladys Harler, wife of Clement Harler?"

"Yes. Don't look so stern, Inspector! I really am married to him."

"Where were you married?"

"In the English church in Rio de Janeiro. I have the certificate upstairs, if you'd like to see it."

"What were you before your marriage?"

She answered with a pert toss or her blonde head:

"A spinster."

"Were you in employment?"

"Yes. I gave up a very promising stage career to marry Mr. Harler. It's marvellous what love can do, isn't it?"

"And on your return from South America, you and your husband came to live in this house?"

"Yes. Sir Victor—he's my husband's father-in-law, you know. I've never been quite sure whether he's *my* father-in-law as well. I'd like him to be. Such a dear, gentle old man. He wanted company in this big house, so Clem—that's my husband—and I agreed to come and live here with him. A big wrench, stuck in this one-eyed place after gay Rio. Have you ever been to Brazil?"

"Please tell me what happened yesterday evening, Mrs. Harler."

"You mean—last night?"

"No, yesterday evening."

"Well, we had dinner at seven o'clock."

"Do you and your husband dine by yourselves?"

"No, it's the one meal of the day that we all have together. Sir Victor likes it that way. There was"—she enumerated with her fingers—"Sir Victor, my husband and I, Mrs. Winters and her nephew, little John Campbell. Five of us altogether. My husband and I found it embarrassing eating with servants when we first came here, but Mrs. Winters was a very old employee of the family and expected little privileges like that."

Each of the three men restrained an unchivalrous impulse. Martin got as far as raising his hand, but diverted it to smoothing down his sandy poll.

"Did the meal proceed on the usual lines?"

"Oh, yes. Just like every other day. Frightfully dull."

"Was Mrs. Winters her normal self?"

"She seemed to be. Of course you never know with women like that."

"Did you and your husband have a difference of opinion with her at the table, Mrs. Harler?"

"Oh, good heavens, no! Whatever put *that* idea in your head?"

"I've been given to understand that you did."

"Who by? The servant, I suppose? I do think you police ought to stop snooping round questioning servants! They always dramatise everything so. My husband and I certainly had an argument with Winters, but it was quite a friendly one on a purely personal subject that wouldn't interest you people."

"Did you say to Mrs. Winters, 'One of these days you'll get what's coming to you, you snake in the grass'?"

"Of course I didn't! . . . Well, I may have said it, but I only meant it quite jokingly."

By this time, she was not looking so carefree as when the

interrogation, had started. This twisting-round-the-little-finger business was not proving so easy.

"What gave rise to the remark, Mrs. Harler?"

"Oh, something she'd said. I forget exactly what."

"Was it anything to do with the visit of Mr. Howard, Sir Victor's solicitor?"

"No . . . Yes, now you mention it, it was."

She leant forward in her chair and, with her big languorous eyes, welcomed them into the small and honoured circle of her dearest friends.

"I see I must take you into my confidence," she purred. "It is not a thing we like to talk about, but Sir Victor is not—well, he's not quite normal. A dreadful thing to have to say, but I'm afraid it's only too true. My husband and I have been very concerned about him. His medical adviser, Dr. Stamford, is so? worried over his condition that he is getting a brain specialist down from London—the famous Sir Ninian Oxenham. Poor Sir Victor has been acting very strangely. In the last few weeks, his manner towards Clem and myself has changed very noticeably. Sometimes he has been quite rude to us, for no reason at all. My husband and I have put this down to two things. The first is that the poor old man is suffering from what I believe is called persecution mania. The second is—I don't like having to say it, but I must—that Mrs. Winters has been poisoning his mind against us."

Whatever else was lies, thought Charlton, this, at least, was true. He had Sir Victor's word for it.

"We none of us like to sing our own praises," Gladys Harler went prattling on, getting more sure of herself as she proceeded, "but my husband and I do claim that we have been good angels to Sir Victor. We shouldn't be human, should we, not to expect some sort of return? We've been ready to wait for our little reward. Neither of us ask for a penny now, but we do say—and I'm sure you'll agree—we do say that we should have our fair share of Sir Victor's money when he dies, which I hope won't be for a long time yet. Don't you think it's reasonable?"

Her eyes made another sweep, but failed to claim a victim.

"Nobody could think otherwise . . . Now, under Sir Victor's will, my husband will inherit quite a large fortune. I oughtn't to speak ill of the dead, but Winters didn't like this arrangement. She thought she should have the money herself. For the *life* of me, I can't see why. She was only a servant, not a close relation like Mr. Harler is. I know she'd been with the family for a long time and deserved some sort of recognition. In fact, my husband had decided to give her a small annuity when he inherited. But to expect the whole lot! It was really *too* impertinent!"

She laughed like a lady.

"Winters caused us a lot of trouble. By tittle-tattling to Sir Victor, she turned him against us to such a tremendous extent that he agreed to disinherit his own son-in-law!"

"Have you any proof of this, madam?" demanded the Super.

"She told me so herself, yesterday morning—soon after these two gentlemen called. And she was proud of it! Proud of having talked a poor, insane old man into cutting his own family off with a shilling! Can you wonder that I called her a snake in the grass? She's dead now, so I really shouldn't say it, but she was a scheming old woman! A treacherous, ungrateful—"

"What did you do after dinner?" Charlton interrupted briskly.

"Oh, the usual deadly, dreary things. Mr. Harler and I went up to our sitting-room—we have our own suite on the first floor—and listened to the radio. We switched it off after the news-summary at nine o'clock and played crib till about half-past ten, when we went to bed. Not devastatingly exciting! Then, at soon after six o'clock this morning, I was suddenly awakened out of a beautiful—"

"Mrs. Harler," Charlton pulled her up again, "I understand

that, before you went to bed last night, you took Mrs. Winters along a cup of beef-extract. Was that so?"

Gladys was visibly shaken. The question took her completely by surprise. She stammered a denial, then thought better of it.

"As a matter of fact, I did. You're making me confused with all these sharp questions. I want to help you all I can, but it's difficult to remember every little detail. Yes, I met Mrs. Gulliver on the landing. I was going along to Mrs. Winters' room, so I offered—"

"You were on your way to see Mrs. Winters?"

"Yes, I was. She—I—I—that is, I wanted to apologise for the snake-in-the-grass remark at dinner. Sometimes it's best to swallow your pride, isn't it?"

"Was Mrs. Winters in bed?"

"Yes."

"Did she drink the beef-extract while you were in the room?"

"No . . . I was only there a minute or two. She was so insulting that I came away."

"Mrs. Gulliver has told me that the beaker was in a saucer when she handed it to you. Was that the case?"

"Yes, I believe there was a saucer."

"We found no saucer in Mrs. Winters' room this morning."

"Then there couldn't have been one, could there?"

"Did you bring it away with you from Mrs. Winters' room?"

"Why ever should I do that? Mrs. Winters hadn't finished with it."

"The housemaid confirms that she found the saucer in your sitting-room"—Gladys caught her breath—"early this morning, Mrs. Harler. Can you explain how it got there?"

"What a ridiculous question! No, of course I can't."

"When Mrs. Gulliver handed you the beaker, did you take it straight along to Mrs. Winters' room?"

"Yes."

"You didn't take it first to your own room?"

"No . . . I mean yes. Are all these entirely pointless enquiries really necessary?"

"Why did you take the beaker to your room?"

"Why on earth shouldn't I?" She was becoming desperate. "Have I got to give a reason for everything?"

"You don't have to answer my questions if you don't wish to, Mrs. Harler. Why did you take the beaker to your room?"

"I—I—I suddenly remembered something I wanted to ask my husband before I saw Mrs. Winters. So I took the beaker with me. I couldn't very well leave it on the floor, could I?"

"Dr. Stamford has told me that he prescribed a drug called phenobarbitone for Sir Victor and that the supply of tablets was held by you and your husband. Traces of a strong dose of phenobarbitone were found in the beaker this morning, Mrs. Harler. Did you put it there? I remind you once again that you need not answer."

"I don't mind answering, if it really pleases you, Inspector. No, I did *not* dope Winters' drink. And you'll never prove that I did, Mister Clever! Anyone could have done it. She might even have done it herself to cure insomnia. Or it might have already been in the beef-extract when Mrs. Gulliver passed it over to me. And if it *was* doped as you say it was, it must have had a very funny effect on Winters, because, when I went back to her room about half an hour later, the beaker was empty, so she must have drunk the stuff—and it had acted on her in such a curious fashion that—"

"Why did you go back, Mrs. Harler?"

"Why, why, why! Will there be no end to your stupid questions? I went back to tell her that my husband and I had decided that, if Sir Victor altered the will in her favour, we'd take the matter to court."

"What was her reply?"

"That's what I was coming to, when you interrupted so rudely. When I went back to her room, she wasn't there!"

(ii)

Further questioning on the point elicited nothing. Gladys Harler's story was that, on finding Mrs. Winters' bedroom unoccupied, she had gone back to her own room and retired for the night. Whether Mrs. Winters had dressed herself before leaving the room, Gladys expressed herself unable to say.

Clement Harler would doubtless have liked to compare notes with his wife after her interrogation and before his own. He was, however, given no opportunity. When Charlton put an end to the interview with Gladys, Harler was brought straight in, without a chance to speak to her.

"Mr. Harler," Charlton began, "I'm going to start by telling you that you're not obliged to say anything at all, but if you wish to reply to my questions, your answers will be written down and may be used later in evidence."

After a good many hours of nail-chewing suspense, waiting for the ordeal, Harler was in a terrible state of nerves. All his bluster had deserted him and his manner was conciliatory, almost cringing.

"Naturally I will do my utmost to answer your questions, Inspector Clayton," he said with a wan smile. "I'm only too anxious to help you all I can to lay hands on the ruffian who murdered the poor, helpless woman. Ask me anything you like."

"Thank you, Mr. Harler." Charlton's manner had all the paw-patting friendliness of a cat for a mouse during the secondary stage of their encounter. The victim had been caught; it was not yet time to administer the *coup de grâce.* "First of all, let us go back to yesterday morning. We—"

"I must apologise for my behaviour on that occasion," the little man hastened to assure him. "Perhaps you will let me tell you the circumstances leading up to that unfortunate scene. It may help to show you"—he gave another thin smile—"that I'm not quite such a scoundrel as I'm afraid you imagine!"

"Carry on, Mr. Harler. Take your time. Tell us everything

you think has some bearing on this matter. We want to give you every chance."

"To clear myself, I suppose? Yes, I am well aware that I am in a not too favourable position over this terrible murder. I can only tell you, quite simply, that I didn't do it. I ask you, do I look the sort of fellow to murder an elderly woman in cold blood?"

"We won't go into that, Mr. Harler. Let us have your story, please."

"The whole thing hinges, gentlemen, on my father-in-law's will. By that I am not suggesting that the will was the cause of the murder, because I know nothing about that. I can guess neither the murderer, nor the motive. What I mean is that the will was the bone of contention between Mrs. Winters and myself, and the cause of the unpleasantness yesterday morning. Now, you already know my position under the will. In case you do not, I will try to clarify it for you. I married Rosalie Warringham, Sir Victor's only child, at the end of 1933. At that time, I was in the employment of Victor Motors Limited, the company of which Sir Victor was—and still is—chairman. You will appreciate that he is a very rich man. By the will as it stood before my marriage, his fortune was to be divided, on his death, equally between his wife and daughter. When I married Rosalie, Sir Victor added a codicil to the will. It provided that if my wife died before her father, I was to have a life interest in her share of the estate. There was also a proviso that, if there were any children by our marriage, the money should go to them and not to me, but that I should act as sole trustee until the children—or child, as the case might have been—came of age. This was a very understandable proviso, because, naturally, Sir Victor wanted his fortune to be enjoyed by his descendants. As things turned out, the proviso wasn't necessary, as my wife and I never had any children. If we had, things might have turned out differently. Our marriage was not a happy one. There were faults on both sides. I was unlucky with Victor Motors. Couldn't do a thing right. Of course, the cards were stacked against me. When a junior clerk—which was all I was—marries into the firm, every other employee is only too anxious to stab him in the back. My colleagues were very successful at this type of manœuvre and eventually I was forced to get out. Leaving my wife behind, I went to South America, to try and make good there, so that, in due course, she could join me."

This was not quite the story Charlton had heard, but he did not interrupt.

"No sooner was I out of the country—and I hate to have to repeat this—than my wife began an affair with another man."

"Can you tell me his name, Mr. Harler?"

"Fellow called Valentine. Raymond Valentine. I never met him. When news of it came to me, I was deeply shaken. Victor Motors had finished with me. Now my wife had thrown me overboard. What had I to come back to? By that time, I was doing fairly well in Brazil—in the coffee trade. I decided to stop there . . . And then there happened one of those strange things for which there is no accounting. I got involved in a train smash. I came through with nothing more than a few scratches, but the local newspapers got my name confused with that of another unfortunate fellow who was actually killed in the accident. So my name appeared in the newspapers as one of the victims. My first impulse, of course, was to get the report contradicted. Then I had some second thoughts. Wasn't this my opportunity to start a new life? My wife would be only too pleased to be rid of me. The Old Country held out no promise. So I cut adrift—I imagined for ever."

The detectives were listening intently. This sounded like the truth. Harler was not an accomplished liar.

"Years passed. The old life became just a dream. Then I met a girl in Santos. She was with an English travelling theatrical company. You have met her, too. She became my second wife—but not until after the death of my first wife. I am no bigamist, gentlemen! I must admit frankly that we lived together for some time. What was the alternative? We were passionately fond of each other and legal marriage was not, at that time, possible. Then we received news of my wife's death. Naturally I was horrified to learn of her terrible end, yet I could not but see that it simplified my own position. I could now marry the girl I loved; and, after a decent interval, I did—in Rio de Janeiro."

Harler paused before going on. When he spoke again, it was hesitantly at first, then with growing assurance.

"I have mentioned Sir Victor's will. By the deaths of Lady Warringham and Rosalie before the death of Sir Victor, their interests in the will ceased completely. But what did *not* become void was my own life interest in Rosalie's share. I have taken legal opinion, so can speak with authority on the point. Were Sir Victor to die today without making a fresh will, Rosalie's share would come to me, and the share originally intended for Lady Warringham would go to the old boy's next-of-kin, whoever that may be. If Rosalie and I had had a child, the child would have got it as the next-of-kin—and would have got *my* share, too, incidentally! . . . You'll readily see, then, that it was—and is—greatly to my financial advantage for the old boy not to alter his will. There was a danger, however, that he would. With his wife and daughter both dead—and, as he thought, myself dead as well—the will had lost all its original meaning. If he died, the estate would go automatically to his next-of-kin—his cousins or his sisters or his aunts. I don't know enough about the Warringham family to tell you who it would be . . . But he might not have wanted his next-of-kin to inherit. He might have decided that, as his wife and daughter were no longer alive, he preferred to leave it to the Dogs' Home. So, in my own interests, it was up to me to ensure that he didn't change his will. If he did, I was going to lose a fortune. You can see that, can't you?"

They certainly could. They could also sense that Harler was

still telling the truth. As if in confirmation of their thoughts, his next remark was:

"You need not take my word for it. Mr. Howard, my father-in-law's solicitor, will verify everything I have said . . . To proceed. As soon as possible, I came back to England, leaving my wife in Rio de Janeiro. A great deal depended on the success of my mission. Things had been difficult for some time past. I was hard pressed for money . . . Sir Victor was very surprised to see me, but after the first shock had worn off, he gave me a friendly welcome. I was compelled to invent a story to account for my long absence and failure to contradict the report of my death. I told him that the train smash had caused me to lose my memory and that I had only recently regained it. Scarcely more than a little white lie, in the circumstances! It was Sir Victor who suggested that I should come and share this big house with him. When he heard that I had married again, he was old-fashioned enough to be shocked at first, but when I told him, quite bluntly, that he couldn't have me if he didn't have my second wife as well, he agreed to her joining us. I wired for her to come. When she arrived, my father-in-law gave us the exclusive use of a suite of rooms upstairs, where we have lived ever since."

He looked at Charlton.

"I don't know what sort of yarns you've been hearing about me, Inspector Clayton. What story did the old boy pitch you? It's more than likely that he charged me with every crime under the sun. All I'll say in reply is that, although my conduct may not have been particularly ethical, I have done nothing illegal. I will admit that it is rather sordid to expect one's first wife's family to keep one's second wife, but beggars can't be choosers. Towards the end of our stay in South America, things were getting desperate on the money side, and I clutched at that legacy as a drowning—"

"I take it that you and your wife have been living here as Sir Victor's guests?"

"You mean, we don't pay for board and lodgings? Poor

relations, in fact? Yes, that's quite true. In addition, Sir Victor has made me a small weekly allowance. In return, of course, he has had our companionship. During our stay, we've been able to do many little things to help. For instance, up to a week or two ago, my wife, who has some knowledge of shorthand and typing, was spending much of her time assisting Sir Victor with a new book he was writing. Something to do with bird-life . . . Everything, in short, was going along in the friendliest possible fashion. The old boy had accepted me back as his son-in-law and heir to half his fortune. He had accepted my wife as a pleasant and useful addition to the household. He was content . . . And so were we. Life here was dull, but we were prepared to put up with it. It was better than living from hand to mouth in a back street in Rio or Santos. But there was a snag—and the snag was Mrs. Winters."

He got out his cigarette-case, offered it round, was refused and, with a nervous shrug of his shoulders, snapped the case shut and returned it to his pocket.

"Mrs. Winters resented our presence in the house. She had a racket of her own and she didn't want any interference with it. In the time that had elapsed since the death of Lady Warringham, she had managed to get a considerable hold on my father-in-law. This was made easier for her by the fact that, slowly but surely, his mind was giving way. I think it was directly caused by the tragic loss of his wife and daughter. At first his oddness showed itself in nothing more than a slight eccentricity. As I told you yesterday, Inspector Clayton, he would have long conversations with his dead wife and daughter. He took up spiritualism. He bought himself a planchette. When a circus visited this district a couple of months back, he spent a great deal of time in the menagerie, which was attached to the circus as an additional attraction, studying the habits of the wolves. He claimed, quite seriously, to have found one with a distinct resemblance to George Washington! . . . And we even caught him practising Black Magic . . . Yes, you'll hardly credit it, but it's a fact. Late one night, I came down to the kitchen for a glass of water. I found Sir Victor, in his dressing-gown, at the gas-cooker. He was boiling up some revolting mixture in a saucepan—I'd say, from the filthy smell, that it was largely composed of stale fish—and he was muttering incantations over it. On my word of honour, he was. When I asked him what on earth he was up to, he turned round and looked at me very queerly with the remark, 'Clement, my boy, in his claims regarding the efficacy of ichthyomancy, Cagliostro was a misleading charlatan.' . . . With that, he turned out the gas under the saucepan, nodded me a friendly good night, and calmly went back to bed."

This little anecdote impressed Charlton profoundly. It had all the hallmarks of fact.

"That brings me to the events that led up to our meeting yesterday morning, Inspector Clayton. For some time past, my wife and I have been concerned over Sir Victor and extremely suspicious of Mrs. Winters. We felt certain that she was plotting against us. Sir Victor was in the care of Dr. Stamford, who had arranged for a brain specialist to come down tomorrow. We know now—Mrs. Winters told my wife so yesterday morning—that she had prevailed on the old boy to cut me out of his will and insert her name instead. Previous to that, we could only guess at the mischief she was up to but our suspicions were thoroughly aroused on Saturday last, when we learnt that Mr. Howard was to call on Monday morning. Mrs. Winters was delighted. Which could mean only one thing, for anything that pleased Mrs. Winters was bound to be unpalatable for us . . . We had one trump-card left."

He spaced out the last four words dramatically, with thumps of his clenched fist on the palm of his other hand.

"My wife and I were convinced that the old boy was—well, if he wasn't mad, he was the next thing to it. Dr. Stamford thought the same. If we could only stave off Mr. Howard until after the brain specialist had delivered his verdict—and we knew what that verdict would be—any fresh will of Sir Victor's would be virtually useless. We decided, therefore, that the solicitor must be put off until after tomorrow. I can confidently claim that there was nothing morally or legally wrong in our efforts to safeguard my legacy. As a sane man, he had wanted me to inherit. Only insanity and the disgraceful machinations of Mrs. Winters caused him to alter his mind—mind that was deranged and irresponsible."

Oratory did not suit the shabby little man. Charlton was reminded of Sergeant Martin's comparison of Harler with the chairman of a mushroom company. He had the words, but not the trick of making them sound convincing.

"So you will appreciate my dismay, gentlemen, when you arrived yesterday morning. We wanted no trouble, no awkward incidents, until such time as Sir Victor's insanity had been officially established and our own financial future assured. I did the only thing possible; I persuaded you to go away. Little did I guess the dreadful event that was to follow."

At this point, Charlton decided that Harler had been given his head long enough. The time had not been wasted. He had given them some useful information; and, for the most part—so Charlton imagined—had confined himself to the truth. But now the real interrogation must begin.

"Thank you, Mr. Harler," he said briskly. "Now I'm going to ask you to answer one or two questions."

Harler looked crestfallen. He had lost his nervousness and grown pompous towards the end of his peroration. At Charlton's interruption, his apprehension returned.

"You're not compelled to answer them now, Mr. Harler," Charlton went on in the deep, agreeable voice that had lulled many a malefactor into a sense of false security, "but you'll probably have to answer them sooner or later. . . . First of all, Mr. Howard's visit. You say that you decided he must be put off until after tomorrow. What steps did you take to ensure this?"

"I simply told him that the old boy was not in a fit condition to see him—which, of course, he wasn't."

"Why not?"

Harler looked surprised. "You know as well as I do!" he protested. "His brainstorm on Sunday night had left him in a very bad state."

"What caused this brainstorm, Mr. Harler?"

"I've not the least idea. His mental attacks came and went. There was no accounting for them. They might happen any time."

"Are you of the opinion, Mr. Harler, that the phosphorescent hands that Sir Victor claims to have seen were merely an hallucination?"

"Oh, undoubtedly; just as he thought he saw the spirits of Rosalie and Lady Warringham."

"You do not agree that the phosphorescent hands were a physical fact?"

"Good heavens, no!"

"You do not agree that some person entered Sir Victor's room with the intention of bringing on a brain-storm of sufficient seriousness to prevent Sir Victor from seeing his solicitor?"

"Look here!" cried Harler wildly. "You're not trying to suggest, are you, that I did that?"

"I don't suggest it, Mr. Harler. I ask whether you did."

"Of course I didn't! It's preposterous!"

"A pair of rubber gloves, covered with luminous paint, has been found here."

"That proves nothing. They weren't in my pocket, or hidden in my wardrobe, were they?"

"No, they were not. They were discovered this morning by John Campbell in what he describes as Falcon's Nest."

"What, that tree arrangement? Well, anybody might have put them there."

His face screwed up into an expression—perhaps he imagined—of reluctant surmise.

"I wonder whether that young monkey had anything to do

with it? Just the sort of trick a boy would get up to, you know. Have you considered that?"

"Official police tests," Charlton said grimly, "have established that the gloves have been worn on *your* hands, Mr. Harler. Do you still deny that you were Sir Victor's visitor on Sunday night?"

"I most emphatically do! On several occasions I borrowed those gloves from Mrs. Winters. Only a short—"

The Superintendent was a fraction ahead of Charlton.

"How do you know," he pounced, "that the gloves belonged to Mrs. Winters?"

Harler faltered badly, then rallied.

"Inspector Clayton has just said they were found here. I know of only one pair in the house. I naturally assumed that they were the pair in question."

The Super jumped up and stood menacingly over Harler, who winced and edged back, as if fearing a blow.

"Harler," he snapped, have you ever been in Mrs. Winters' bedroom?"

"No! No!" Harler's voice rose hysterically. "For God's sake leave me alone!"

"We're looking for the man who broke open her bureau. We're looking for the man who opened her bedroom window. We're looking for the man who twisted out her life with a paper-knife . . . *Your* fingerprints, Harler, were on the bureau drawer, *your* fingerprints were on the window, and *your* fingerprints were on the paper-knife.

How did they get there, Harler? . . . I'm asking you, how did they get there?"

The small man was almost weeping.

"I don't know! I don't know anything about it! I tell you, I didn't do it! . . . For God's sake believe me! I didn't do it!"

"Sergeant," ordered the Superintendent, "take this fellow outside."

Martin closed his notebook and obeyed. When the door

had shut behind him and his frightened charge, the Super said to Charlton:

"Better arrest both the Harlers on suspicion."

"A bit hasty, isn't it?" Charlton asked doubtfully.

"I'm not through with my inquiries yet. Tiny."

The Super brushed his objections aside with:

"We can't afford to take any risks. They're a tricky pair of customers. Or the woman is. The man's a fool. Won't do any harm for them to cool their heels for a day or two. Might make 'em talk. Anyway, we've enough evidence against Harler to justify an arrest."

"I don't think he did it, Tiny."

Superintendent Kingsley made much the same reply as Harler himself had made to his wife in the privacy of their sitting-room that morning.

"And if he didn't," he demanded, "who did?"

Charlton's reply was: "I've a very shrewd idea."

PART III

CONSTRUCTION

CHAPTER SIXTEEN

(i)

NOT without angry protests, Clement Harler and his second wife, Gladys, had been arrested on suspicion of being concerned in the death of Mrs. Enid Winters and had been forcibly removed from Elmsdale to even more unattractive surroundings. They had been searched before being taken away and now Inspector Charlton, the only police officer remaining in the house, was examining their rooms on the first floor.

There were two rooms, one on each side of the corridor; a sitting-room at the front and a bedroom at the back. The sitting-room was heated by a gas-fire. The bedroom had a small electric fire standing in the hearth. The grate behind it had been recently cleared, but not thoroughly enough for Charlton not to notice something that caused him to summon Lily Higgins.

"Lily," he asked, "did you clean this room today?"

The little housemaid was delighted with a second chance to be talked to by her hero.

"Yes, sir. Went over it with the vacuum."

"Did you clear the grate?"

"Yes, sir. It needs doin' every mornin'. Mistrer-missizarler throw cig'ret-tends there."

"Were there any burnt papers in the grate this morning, Lily?" She nodded. "They weren't there yesterday?"

"Not when I done it in the mornin', sir."

"And the paper-ash went into the vacuum, did it?"

"Yes, sir. Cig'ret-tends an' all."

"Was all the paper burnt?"

"No charred bits, d'you mean, sir? No, nothink like that, sir. It was all burnt to a cinder."

"Did Mr. or Mrs. Harler say anything about it to you?"

"No, sir; never a word."

"Have you emptied the vacuum-cleaner since this morning?"

"Yes, sir."

"What did you do with the dust?"

"Tipped it out on a newspaper, sir, then wrapped it up and put it in the dustbin."

"Can you get it for me now, Lily?"

Breathlessly eager to serve her demigod, Lily ran down to the yard and brought back the package. Regardless of the custom that precludes demigods from debasing themselves before their worshippers, Charlton went down on his knees on the carpet, spread out the paper in front of him and carefully winnowed the vacuum-cleaner's miscellaneous harvest.

Results repaid him for the fiddling task. He found these things: thirteen thin metal staples, as used for exercise-books and the like; a scrap of charred blue cardboard; and the remains of a letter that had been torn up with some thoroughness. He examined the blue fragment. It was small and irregular in shape. On one side of it was printed in quarter-inch characters of a darker blue enough to identify the three letters "VIN." On the reverse, he was able to read, in much smaller characters, "can also" on one line and "National" on the line below.

The pieces of letter had not been touched by fire. On one of them was written in ink ". . . ar Eni . . .," which he took to be a part of "Dear Enid."

He placed the scraps of letter on the dressing-table for assembly later, then felt in his pocket for one of the small envelopes that he always carried around with him. In this he placed the fragment of card and the thirteen staples. Under

Lily's awed and adoring gaze, he stepped to the fireplace and went down on his heels. A patient search of the grate produced two more staples. He put them with the others, licked the flap of the envelope and stuck it down. As he wrote on the outside, he said to Lily:

"Where did your hungry vacuum gobble up that torn up letter, Lily? Was it in here?

"No, sir. It was in the wastepaper basket in Mrs. Winters' sitting-room. I didn't think the vacuum would take it, 'cause it doesn't usually like little bits of paper, which get stuck in the nozzle, but I managed to get them all up the spout."

"When was this, Lily?"

"Yes'd'y mornin', sir."

"Did you clean out the grate at the same time?"

"Yes, sir."

"You didn't leave a cigar-end behind, I suppose?"

"Oh, no, sir. I left it all neat and tidy."

"Did you do Mrs. Winters' room this morning?"

Lily shook her head. "I couldn't today, sir, 'cause you was in there, so I 'ad to leave it."

"Thank you, Lily." He pointed to the newspaper on the floor. "Right, I've finished with that. It can go back in the dustbin."

Lily knelt down and refolded the paper round the refuse. Charlton went across to the dressing-table and began to arrange the scraps of letter on its polished ton Lily asked him:

"Did you want anythin' kelse, sir?"

"No, thank you, Lily."

With the crumpled bundle clutched to her flat chest with one hand, and the other hand ready to open the door she said timidly:

"If it's all the same to you, sir, I'd like to go 'ome, sir. I don't want to stay on in service 'ere, sir."

"Where's your home, Lily?"

"Whitchester, sir. 29, Back Eldon Street."

"Yes, of course you can go." He got out his notebook and jotted down the address. "You'll have to speak to Sir Victor, of course. He's your employer. Do you know whether Mrs. Gulliver is staying on?"

"Yes, she is, sir." Her face went long and solemn at the cook's reckless bravery as she added, "She says as what she'll stick to the master till the 'eavens fall."

"I'm very glad to hear it, Lily."

With one last adoring glance at him over the top of the newspaper, and with a shy, "Thank you ever so, sir," she left him.

He turned his attention to the torn-up letter. Some of the pieces were missing, but enough of the original missive remained for him to understand its contents.

They interested him vastly.

(ii)

He went from the bedroom into the Harlers' sitting-room, There he found the dummy revolver, which Harler had confiscated from John Campbell, and a screw-driver—a cheap thing with a yellow wooden handle and a blade still bent from some strain that had been put upon it.

He slipped the revolver in his pocket and took the screwdriver along to the dead woman's bedroom. He found that the blade fitted very neatly into the indentations in the drawer and rail of the escritoire. On the evidence so far collected, he considered it reasonable to assume that the Harlers had broken open the drawer, removed the contents, taken them along to their own apartments, where they had gone through the papers and subsequently burnt all, or some of them, in the bedroom grate.

He was walking down the stairs a few minutes later, when Sir Victor Warringham came out of the library.

"Ah, Inspector," the old gentleman greeted him affably. "I was just coming in search of you. My housemaid, inconsiderate child, has just expressed her desire to leave here and return to her parents. I had no alternative but to consent. Mrs. Gulliver, my cook, remains loyal, which is extremely fortunate. I shall not starve!"

"Wouldn't you be more comfortable at an hotel, sir, until you have decided on your plans for the future?"

The old man looked pained.

"Plans, Inspector? What plans can I make? My whole world has crashed about my ears. It crashed once before and I built it up with labour and tears. Now it has crashed again. My housekeeper is brutally murdered. My son-in-law and his wife are arrested for the crime. My housemaid is proposing to desert me. Little John Campbell, always a great consolation to me, has been spirited away to Peartree Cottage . . . I am left alone . . . But I shall not leave Elmsdale. For many years it has been my home and I shall remain here, abandoned and forgotten, until the day comes for me to join my beloved wife and daughter."

It was a quietly spoken speech. Charlton was touched by its sadness and simple dignity.

"I expect you have relatives, sir?"

"That is so; I have relatives." He smiled slightly. "Which is not to say that I want them here. My attempts to give sanctuary to indigent relatives have already proved calamitous, Inspector. I have no wish to invite further catastrophes."

Charlton gave a helpless gesture. There was so little he could do.

"I have been wondering," Sir Victor went on, "whether John could return here, to bring back a little sunshine into an old man's life. What do you think of that, Inspector? I would like you to answer not as a police officer, but rather as one to whom I feel I can turn for advice."

This was getting difficult. Charlton answered at length:

"John might be company for you, Sir Victor, but would it be quite fair on the boy?"

"I see your point. He would be lonely in this big house. Yes, it would be selfish of me. With Tom Blackmore, he is in the company of a younger man; a man who can join in his boyish pursuits. I must dismiss the thought from my mind."

He turned sadly to go back into the library, then, struck by an idea, faced round to Charlton again.

"There is a solution, Inspector—an admirable solution that has just occurred to me. Why should not Tom Blackmore come here also? I have a great regard for Tom Blackmore. He is the son of my boyhood friend, Andrew Blackmore, who died many years ago. Tom has all the virtues that his father possessed. . . . Yes, that would be an excellent scheme. I already have some extremely suitable applicants for a tenancy of Peartree Cottage, which forms part of the Elmsdale estate."

He rubbed his hands together with great satisfaction.

"Yes," he repeated, "it would be an excellent scheme. . . . Are you passing anywhere near Peartree Cottage this evening. Inspector? It would be a great convenience if you would kindly put the suggestion to Tom Blackmore on my behalf. The cottage is not on the telephone and I am so helpless here, with no one to run errands."

It might have been more diplomatic to leave the last sentence unsaid. Charlton, however, was not unduly sensitive and replied that he would be pleased to carry out the small commission.

"Would it perhaps be better, sir," he suggested, "if you gave me a note for Mr. Blackmore?"

Sir Victor agreed. He went into the library and came out again in a few minutes with the letter, which he handed to Charlton. As they walked to the front door together, Charlton said:

"Have you been able to find Mrs. Freshwater's address?"

"No, the name is Tucker," was the old gentleman's surprising response. "A widow woman with two children. Her present accommodation is extremely cramped. I understand her to be sharing a cottage with another family. She mentioned to Tom Blackmore that if, at any time, he should move out of Peartree—"

After being badly away, Charlton caught him up at the first bend.

"A moment, Sir Victor. You misunderstood my question! Mrs. Freshwater is the sister of the late Mrs. Winters. You'll remember you were going to try to find her address for me."

Sir Victor pulled open the front door.

"Ah, yes, of course," he agreed without warmth. "I fear that I have been unsuccessful."

Charlton went out on to the doorstep.

"I'm having inquiries made through official channels. If we can trace Mrs. Freshwater, perhaps some permanent arrangements can be made for John Campbell."

The old man's eyes lighted with sudden anger.

"I take little interest in this Mrs. Freshwater," he said sharply. "It is necessary, I agree, for her to be informed of her sister's death. Nevertheless, I do not welcome her intrusion, if intrusion it proves to be. Any suggestion on her part that John be handed over to her, or into the keeping of some other—and doubtless undesirable—relative of my late housekeeper, will be resisted by myself."

He took hold of the door-knob.

"Stubbornly," he appended, "and to the last."

Upon which unequivocal pronouncement, he gently closed the front door on the Inspector.

(iii)

They were having a late tea in the kitchen of Peartree Cottage: Tom Blackmore, John Campbell and Raymond Valentine.

From the moment that he had first set eyes on Valentine in the porch of Peartree Cottage, John Campbell had taken a fierce and unhidden dislike to him. When he had been recalled from the garden at the end of the conversation between the two men and told that this was Mr. Valentine, an old friend of Uncle Tom's, who would be staying a night or two at the cottage, the boy's hostility had been obvious, even to the drink-dulled perceptions of the visitor. His feelings had been somewhat assuaged when he had been assured that he would sleep in 'the blue room in the east wing,' while Valentine would have to shake down on the couch in the den; yet his antipathy to Valentine remained as great as Thomas Brown's to a certain Doctor Fell.

The afternoon had passed in an atmosphere of steadily increasing tension, like a length of elastic being slowly and unceasingly stretched. Valentine had maintained a manner of flippant good-fellowship towards Blackmore, with many an "old darling" and "dear old horse." With John he had been damply jocund, dragging him constantly into his one-man conversation by ending almost all his sentences with such phrases as, "Isn't it, John?" or "What do you think, young feller?" John had seldom answered more than "Yes" or "No," and had made up for it by talking continuously to Tom Blackmore, in the reckless, quiveringly off-hand tone that boys use under stress, of all the fun they had had in the past without Uncle Tom's old friend, Mr. Valentine, and all the fun they were going to have in the future, again (by implication) without Uncle Tom's old friend, Mr. Valentine. Blackmore had responded in his usual kindly way to John, and had been terse with Valentine.

Halfway through tea the elastic snapped.

Blackmore had heard a familiar honk-honk on a motorcar horn and had gone out to the front gate to talk to an acquaintance who had pulled up outside.

Valentine chose the moment to say to John:

"And what's going to happen to you, young man, now that your Aunt Enid can't look after you any more?"

The boy gave his longest answer of the afternoon.

"I'm going to live here with Uncle Tom," he asserted stoutly.

Valentine leant past the paraffin-lamp on the table to say in a hoarse, confidential undertone:

"How would you like to come and live in my home in London?"

Wincing from a waft of stale whisky, John answered briefly:

"Not trificly."

"It's in a great big block of flats," wheedled Valentine, who had the hide of an extrovert rhinoceros. "It's on the fifth floor and you get to it in a lift, which works by pressing a button. How would you like to go whizzing up to the fifth floor by just pressing a button, eh, young feller?"

Said John: "I've worked a lift in Harris & Green's at Southmouth."

"But wouldn't you like to live in London—vast, exciting London?"

"I'd much rather stay with Uncle Tom."

"Mrs. Valentine would look after you just as kindly as your Aunt Enid."

"Aunt Enid wasn't kind. She was trificly strict."

"Well, Mrs. Valentine wouldn't be. You'd like her, John. She'd take you round to see all the sights—the British Museum and the Tower of London. My wife is a great sport."

"She's not your wife," John said with great clarity and distinctness. "She's Uncle Tom's wife and I'm quite sure I shouldn't like her. And I don't like you either."

He helped himself nonchalantly to another cake as Valentine began to splutter like the fuse of a firework just before the big bang. Then:

"You impudent whelp. I'll tan the hide off you for—"

"You'll do what, Valentine?"

Tom Blackmore had come back into the room.

It was John who answered: "He wants me to go back and

live with him and your wife in London. I've told him three times that I don't want to go."

"Once should have been enough. Valentine, I'll trouble you not to—"

He stopped when he heard the click of the front gate. Inspector Charlton had arrived.

(iv)

Tom Blackmore greeted Charlton with a smile.

"We're just having tea," he told him. "Care to join us?"

"A very sound suggestion," Charlton agreed and followed him into the kitchen.

Blackmore introduced him to Valentine.

"Raymond Valentine, an old friend of mine. He dropped from the clouds at lunch-time, as old friends have the thoughtless habit of doing, and expected me to find him a bed. Valentine, this is Inspector Charlton of the C.I.D."

Valentine gave a whinnying laugh and held out a hand that Charlton took and then let drop because it felt like something dead and flabbily unpleasant.

"A detective, eh? Whenever I meet one of you splendid band of sleuths, I always think about the score or so of naughty little crimes I've committed since last week!"

John Campbell gave up his chair to Charlton and poured him out a cup of tea. Charlton accepted both with a smiling word of thanks, then turned back to Valentine, who had pulled a packet of 'Manikins' from his pocket.

"Yes," he said, making himself agreeable, "we unhappy policemen always spread alarm wherever we go. Quite harmless folk exaggerate their recent tiny faults into felonies as soon as we knock on the door."

Valentine held out the packet. Charlton shook his head.

"No, thanks. I'll have a cigarette, if you don't mind."

"Can't smoke the things myself," Valentine said, extracting

a 'Manikin.' "Always chew the ends of cigarettes into a soggy mass. Even with these, I have the same trouble. I'm one of those wet smokers."

He held out a match to Charlton, who lighted one of his own cigarettes.

Charlton said to Blackmore:

"I only dropped in for a few minutes. I have a note for you from Sir Victor."

"Very kind of you to bring it."

"Not at all."

He handed the envelope to Blackmore, who opened it and read the message. Halfway through it, he looked up and gave Charlton a meaningful glance. Charlton surmised that Sir Victor had mentioned the arrest of the Harlers. Blackmore finished reading and slipped the note away in his pocket.

"John," he said, "Mr. and Mrs. Harler have been called away on business. That leaves Sir Victor all alone and he wants to know whether you'll go back and keep him company."

"Well, Uncle Tom. . . " John began, looking exceedingly unhappy.

"And he asks me to go with you."

"Oo! That's trifficly different. When does he want us to go?"

"Tonight. Rather short notice."

"I think it would be as well if you went, Mr. Blackmore," Charlton suggested.

Raymond Valentine said: "Don't worry about me, old fruit. I can rub along here quite well by myself and I shan't have to sleep on the jolly old couch. Just tell me where you've hidden the Scotch."

CHAPTER SEVENTEEN

(i)

THE long day's work was not yet over. When Charlton got back to Police Headquarters from Peartree Cottage—where he had handed over the dummy revolver to Blackmore before leaving—Sergeant Martin was waiting for him with a message from Dr. Lorimer, the police surgeon.

"'E says 'e's got something important to show you, and will you make it convenient to meet 'im at the mortuary at seven-thirty."

Charlton glanced at his wristwatch.

"Just time for a snack before we go along there."

"We?" grumbled the Sergeant. "Not content with runnin' me off me feet since seven-fifteen ack-emma, you now want me to spend a pleasant social evenin' in the perishin' morgue. 'Aven't you got no 'eart? What about me wife and kids?"

"Kid, surely? There's only one, isn't there?"

"That was when I was last 'ome," Martin flashed back.

Charlton opened the door and led the way along the passage.

"What would you have said," he asked over his shoulder, "if I'd told you not to come with me?"

"I should've bin deeply offended," said Martin.

Over sandwiches and coffee in a cafeteria, he told his chief that word had been received from the Croydon police that afternoon that Mrs. Freshwater had moved from the district and had not yet been located.

"But they'll let us know, the moment they contact 'er."

Charlton felt in his waistcoat pocket for the small envelope containing his salvage from the vacuum-cleaner. He slit it open with a knife off the table and extracted the charred fragment of blue card, which he passed across to Martin.

"What do you make of that, Martin? It came out of the fireplace in the Harlers' bedroom—or, at least, it came out of the vacuum-cleaner that had been used on the fireplace in the Harlers' bedroom."

"Sounds like the 'Ouse that Jack built," commented the Sergeant, picking up the fragment.

"'V-I-N'," he read. "French for wine. Many's the bottle of Vang Blong and Vang Roodge I've sunk. I remember one night in '16, just before the first big show on the Somme. We was resting in a little place by the name of—"

"Spare me the sordid details," beseeched Charlton.

"You've no soul," complained Martin, and turned the piece of card over to examine the other side. "'National.'

National—what?. . . National Gallery? Grand National? National Debt?. . . Government?. . . Health?. . . Service? What haven't I thought of?. . . National Anthem? No, it wouldn't be that."

Charlton opened his mouth to speak, but Martin stopped him with a flat-palmed hand, as a policeman stops oncoming traffic.

"Don't tell me: I 'aven't given it up yet. That's the rule in riddles, you know." He pondered for a full minute, then announced in triumph, "I've got it! National Savings! And the V-I-N on the front is the middle letters of 'Savings.'"

He found a crumpled packet of Woodbines somewhere about him, removed a cigarette and, regardless of the fact that it was curved like a boomerang, lighted it with a flourish and sat back in his chair to blow a jet of smoke towards the *ceiling* of the cafeteria.

"Quite correct, Martin. I was hoping to have the satisfaction of enlightening you. Yes, I'd say it's a piece of the cover of a book of National Savings Certificates. With it I found fifteen metal staples, which suggest that there was more than one book—not necessarily all National Savings, of course."

"And Snaky 'Arler's fingerprints was on the writing-desk drawer. Looks as if 'e pinched Mrs. Winters' savings and then burnt 'em." He clicked his tongue. "Wasteful, ain't it?"

"We can guess why he did it. He wasn't interested in her savings; he was looking for something else. What it was, and whether he found it, we don't know yet; but he took the other stuff to create the impression that a cat-burglar had broken in. Hence the ladder and the open window. Had he just extracted the papers he needed, he could be sure that Mrs. Winters would look at him with more than a suspicious eye when she discovered her loss this morning."

The Sergeant's mouth fell open.

"You mean... You mean 'e didn't do the murder?"

"I'm quite sure he didn't."

"But look at all that evidence!" expostulated the Sergeant with a note of real grief in his voice.

"Evidence, yes. But evidence of what? Purely and simply evidence to prove that he broke open the bureau and handled the paper-knife. Evidence of larceny, I grant you, but not of murder.... No, Martin, had Harler murdered anybody at all, it would have been Sir Victor."

"Or Gladys," was Martin's unkind alternative.

Charlton got up from the table.

"That wouldn't have been murder," he said. "It would have been a crusade."

(ii)

Attaché-case in hand, Dr. Lorimer was waiting for them when they arrived at the mortuary. He apologised to Charlton for having kept him waiting so long for the report for which Charlton had asked that morning.

"But," he added, "I've one or two little things that will interest you."

The mortuary officer took them to where Mrs. Winters' body lay.

"Now, this is the first thing," said the young surgeon.

"When Sergeant Peters arrived at Elmsdale this morning, he and I removed the flex—and you can take my word for it that we did it damn carefully. Before being tightened up, it had been tied round the neck by a reef knot, with the paper-knife slipped between the two loops of the knot, if you follow me?"

"Yes, I noticed that this morning."

"Right. . . . Now, to effect strangulation"—he took off his horn-rimmed spectacles and gestured with them as he talked—"you must have sufficient pressure to close the veins. This, coupled with the post-mortem swelling—and taking into account the time-lapse between the strangling and my examination—would mean that the flex should have been half-buried this morning. I grant you that it *was* buried pretty deeply, but what I do say is that the flex wasn't twisted tightly enough when I came to look at it to have caused such a serious weal."

"Could it have loosened itself during the night?"

"It's not impossible, but I doubt it. Her jaw stopped the paper-knife from shifting. Well, that's my first point. My second point is that, before producing enough tension to cause a weal like that one, that paper-knife thing would have snapped in the murderer's fingers."

He opened his attaché case.

"That's only my theory. I thought we'd better prove it, so I popped along to the stationer's and bought this." He produced a paper-knife from the case and held it up.

"I can't guarantee it's exactly the same quality, but it looks identical with the other one—except that it's got an 'L' on the seal, instead of a 'W'. Being of an economical turn of mind, I thought that, if we didn't succeed in wrecking it, I could use it myself."

"Where did you buy it?"

"Horwill, Adams. I tried several other shops first, but couldn't match it."

"That seems to clinch it. Sir Victor bought the other one there. He gave it to Mrs. Winters for a Christmas present."

"Little did he know—but this is no time for dramatic stuff. I suggest we reconstruct the murder. I've brought along this piece of flex"—he took it from the case—"so all we want now is a neck."

He looked at Martin.

"Oh, no, you don't!" said the Sergeant firmly.

They compromised on Charlton's leg. He placed his foot on a chair and pulled up his trouser-leg. Lorimer knotted the flex round the calf, inserted the paper-knife and began to turn. After a couple of revolutions he stopped and asked:

"How does that feel? It's about as tight as we found the other one."

"It's not too bad, but I shouldn't like it round my neck."

"Naturally not. Now, I'll carry on till I think it's as tight as the one that strangled Mrs. Winters. The fellow gave it a really savage twist, you know, to cause such a weal."

Before he had made a complete turn, the blade of the paper-knife snapped at the knot in the flex.

Lorimer smiled his satisfaction; he could see that Charlton was impressed by the demonstration.

"That should settle it, Charlton. So there you have my first two points: that the flex wasn't tight enough and the paper-knife wasn't strong enough."

Charlton undid the knot. Lorimer put the flex and broken paper-knife back in his case. Then, with a beckoning finger, he drew Charlton to the side of the body.

"Here is my third point—and a very important one." He felt in his waistcoat pocket and produced a small magnifying glass, which he handed to Charlton.

"Do everything for you, don't I?" he grinned. "Take a look just *there*, where the knot in the flex was." He indicated a point below the jaw. "You'll see a little cluster. It's a collection of short, tiny strands of fibre. . . . Can you see them?"

With his eye to the glass, Charlton grunted assent.

"It can't be a coincidence," Lorimer went on, "that they're in that one spot and nowhere else on the neck. When tension was put on the flex, the silk covering parted at the knot and the fragments got transferred to where you see them now. Isn't that feasible?"

"Very." Charlton stood upright and passed the glass back to the doctor. "Lorimer, I congratulate you. That's the most important clue I've met in this case."

Hovering in the background, Sergeant Martin scratched his head.

"Well," he observed, "I s'pose you know what you're up to, but if it *was* flex what was used, what did you expect to find if it wasn't bits of the covering?"

"The flex on Mrs. Winters' bedside lamp," Charlton explained with a note of excitement in his usually composed voice, "was coloured gold. Those strands on the neck are maroon."

(iii)

"Which brings us," said Lorimer, "to my fourth and last point. You told me this morning, Charlton, that you wanted me to make sure that the strangling was actually done with the flex we found round the neck. With that in mind, I was careful how I took it off. I needn't tell you that flex makes a very distinctive mark on flesh. So as I removed the flex from the weal, I matched it against the marks. It was a tricky job, believe me, especially when I had to turn her over. But it was a trickier job still for the murderer—and he failed. The fit at the back was not quite exact."

He waved his spectacles towards the body.

"We won't turn it over now. You can take my word for it that, at the back of the neck, there are two sets of marks—the firm weal of Flex Number One and the fainter marks of Flex Number Two."

"Splendid," said Charlton. "Just what I wanted to know. Martin, here's another little job for you. Either go yourself, or send someone else, tomorrow, to all the shops in Lulverton where they sell light-flex. The fellow we're after would have bought two or three yards of maroon-coloured flex during the last few days."

"Bit of a shot in the dark, ain't it?" queried the dubious Sergeant.

"I've a very good reason for it," Charlton answered calmly.

"But a chap doesn't 'ave to go out and buy a piece of—"

"Do as I ask, Martin, and don't argue. If you've got your notebook handy, I'll give you a detailed description of the man."

CHAPTER EIGHTEEN

(i)

THE following day, Wednesday, was to see the end of the Winters case, as far as Inspector Charlton's investigations were concerned. It was a day of mist and drizzle.

The white frost had disappeared overnight and given place to a depressing and all-pervading dampness. When Charlton arrived at Police Headquarters in the morning, there was a note from the night duty sergeant lying on his desk. It was to the effect that the Croydon police had rung up late the previous evening to say that Mrs. Constance Freshwater had been located in Leatherhead. She had been informed of her sister's death and was coming down to Lulverton by an early train on Wednesday. Charlton was pleased; certain ideas had taken definite shape in his mind, and he was hopeful that Mrs. Freshwater would prove him to be on the right track.

Also awaiting him was a report from the analysts on the brown stain on the neck of Mrs. Winters' nightdress. Tests had shown, said the report, that the stain had been caused not by beef-extract, but by tobacco-tar, commonly called nicotine. He was pondering on this when he received a third message—this time by word of mouth.

Clement Harler wished to see him.

When they brought Harler in, he showed signs of having passed a sleepless night. His normally unimpressive appearance was not improved by the fact that he had not shaved that morning.

"I have asked for this interview, Inspector Clayton," he explained with a hang-dog air, "in order to clear up some serious misunderstandings. Yesterday I was not frank with you; today, if you will be good enough to listen, I will tell you the whole truth. It will be a confession of guilt, but not of murder."

Without replying, Charlton lifted the telephone receiver and asked for a police stenographer to be sent along to his room. When the constable arrived with his notebook, Charlton said to Harler:

"The stenographer will take down your statement. When it has been typed out, I shall ask you to sign it. I remind you once again, Mr. Harler, that your statement will be entirely voluntary and may be read out in court. Take a seat."

Harler shrugged his shoulders and sat down.

"I don't relish it, but I have no alternative. Needs must when the devil drives." He turned to the stenographer, who sat with pencil poised. "If you are ready, I will start."

The constable nodded. Charlton told Harler to proceed.

"My actions throughout this disastrous affair," Harler began his statement with characteristic perfidy, "have been prompted entirely by the ambitions of my wife. It was she who, on hearing in South America of my interest in Sir Victor's estate, insisted on my re-establishing myself in the Warringham *ménage.* It was she who forced me, against all my better instincts, into doing what I have done during the last few days. I remember that the first stage performance of my wife's that I ever witnessed was in a small part in Shakespeare's *Macbeth*. By nature she is better fitted for the leading female role."

Charlton recalled that Sir Victor Warringham had made a similar comparison.

"She has driven me," Harler went on, "not to murder, but to other serious transgressions or the law. I propose now to admit them all, without keeping a single thing back. Perhaps the confession will send me to prison, but it will keep me from the gallows."

"Mr. Harler," Charlton said sharply, "you're wasting my time! Get on with your statement, please."

"Very well, then. My part in this ghastly business can be divided into two sections: the first concerning my father-in-law on Sunday night; the second concerning Mrs. Winters on Monday night. I will take them in chronological order. Yesterday, you suggested to me that I tried to prevent the meeting between Sir Victor and his solicitor by giving the old boy a fright in the middle of the night. I denied it then; now I admit it. It was my wife's damnfool idea and I was crazy when I agreed to it, but you know what wives are! On Saturday morning, my wife took a telephone-call from Dickson, Parrish, Willmott & Lister, the solicitors, to the effect that Mr. Howard, the senior partner, would call on Sir Victor at ten o'clock on the Monday morning. My father-in-law was not in the house at the time; he had come into Lulverton to do some personal shopping. When my wife passed the message on to him on his return, his manner instantly became so strange and secretive that her suspicions were aroused. She passed those suspicions on to me. We decided there and then that Mr. Howard must be kept away from Sir Victor until such time as the old boy was certified insane. I told you of this yesterday. What I did not tell you was that on Saturday afternoon, reluctantly and under great protest, I went into Southmouth and bought a pot of luminous paint. On Sunday night, after the household had retired to rest, I went down to Mrs. Winters' room and took the rubber gloves from her table drawer. I treated the gloves with the luminous paint and, at two o'clock on Monday morning, went into Sir Victor's room. I took the precaution of removing the electric lamp from the table, so that he would not be able to switch it on and catch me in the act. Then, having slipped on the gloves, I awakened him by giving a series of ghostly groans. When these aroused him, I went through threatening motions with the luminous gloves. . . I must admit that Sir Victor's reactions took me by surprise. I had imagined that a man so gullible when it came to psychic phenomena would treat such a serious visitation with respect."

Harler, as Sir Victor himself had suggested to Charlton, should have read *England's Haunted Houses*. On his own testimony, Sir Victor was not a believer; he was a sceptic.

"My wife and I had anticipated that spectral hands in the night would make the old boy's already rocky state of mind still more rocky. We expected him to go into a flat spin, arouse the whole household and, by wild talk of phantoms in the presence of Mrs. Winters and the other members of the staff, give us a very strong excuse for turning Mr. Howard away on the following morning. Unluckily for us, my ghost act had a contrary effect on the old boy. He greeted it in silence and, by suddenly lunging out with his fist, nearly managed to punch me in the stomach. I saw it was time to leave. I slipped out of the room, locking the door behind me. In a second or two, he was thumping on the panels and demanding to be let out. I just had time to get back to my room and hide the gloves away before everyone else was awake.

"To the consternation of my wife and myself, his behaviour in front of the staff was completely rational. He refused to accept the ghost theory, insisting that his room had been entered by a human being. That he was not raving, but spoke cold truth, was evidenced by the door having been locked from the outside. He pointed that out to us himself. I could not claim that he was mistaken, because Mrs. Winters arrived on the scene too soon for me to unlock the door and remove the key before it was noticed. In spite of this awkward fact, my wife and I did our best to play up the ghost idea. We failed miserably. The old boy would not part from his assertion that some person bad made an attack on him. Apparently he did not suspect me, for he demanded that a thorough search of the house should be made. On the other hand, Mrs. Winters, though she did not say as much then, was clearly of the opinion that I was the guilty party... Well, I don't think it is necessary for me to tell you any more. You know the rest. I will turn, therefore, to—"

"Just a moment, Mr. Harler. What did you do with the gloves: and pot of luminous paint?"

"At first I merely locked them away in our bedroom. Later, with the sinister trend of events, I disposed of them elsewhere. I placed the gloves in John Campbell's 'Eagle Nook'—or whatever he calls it. The pot of luminous paint I put at the back of a drawer in his bedroom dressing-table. I did this so that, should there be further police inquiries into the matter, it would be thought that the whole thing had been a boyish prank on John's part. When the rule is, 'Every man for himself,' nobody will deny that such a precaution was justified."

Angry words sprang to Charlton's lips at the little slug's revolting smugness. He swallowed them back and said instead:

"Why did you break open Mrs. Winters' bureau?"

"That is an incident in the second section of my statement. I will continue to be completely frank with you and deal first with my motive for that action. I should have said *our* motive, for my wife is as concerned in this as I am. You will recall the provisions of my father-in-law's will? I have received his frequent reassurances that the original document remains unchanged, except for the codicil added at the time of my first marriage... It seems, on the of it, a simple straightforward state of affairs. But is it? That was the question my wife and I asked ourselves; and we decided that the real position was more intricate. We also decided that Mrs. Winters could supply the solution the mystery."

"Why?" It was Charlton's favourite question.

"Well, consider her position, Inspector Clayton. Look at it as you will, she was a hired servant of the Warringham family—a housekeeper and no more. Perhaps we should concede that she was a friend and companion of the late Lady Warringham and, as such, deserved to receive some sort of annuity on the death of her employer. Perhaps we might even concede that, if Sir Victor were not anxious for his next-of-kin to inherit the share in the estate that was to have been Lady Warringham's, he might have decided that Mrs. Winters should have it instead. My wife and I would have put forward not the slightest objection to such a plan. We are neither of us of a grasping nature and would have been well content with my own legal share of the estate. I remember once saying as much to Sir Victor in Mrs. Winters' presence. . . Why, then, the mystery? Why the plot? You can take it from me, Inspector Clayton, that there *was* a plot—a plot to which my father-in-law was not party, but which was directed against him. We could believe that Mrs. Winters had so worked upon Sir Victor that he had agreed to her having Lady Warringham's legacy. In fact, we had been prepared for such a move . . . But we could *not* believe that Sir Victor would ever consent—except under extreme pressure—to leave her his whole fortune. It must run into hundreds of thousands of pounds. I spoke jokingly yesterday of the Dogs' Home, but it was not entirely in jest. Sir Victor is interested in several organisations. I am convinced that he would place their interests before those of Mrs. Winters. . . And that was our motive for breaking open the bureau—to find out whether she possessed any papers that would throw light on the mystery. Briefly, we suspected blackmail—and it could be said of us that, in doing what we did, we were acting in the best interests of Sir Victor as well as ourselves."

"Give me the whole story, please, Mr. Harler. I want to know exactly what you did, right from the moment when you doctored Mrs. Winters' beef-extract with Sir Victor's phenobarbitone."

"So my wife told you that, did she?"

"No, she didn't. She denied it."

"Then my wife is a liar, because she did. We wanted to ensure that Mrs. Winters would not be disturbed while her room was being searched. . . When she was in a deep sleep, after having taken the drug, we went along to her room and—"

"What time was that?"

"Some while after midnight. We found that all the drawers in the room were unlocked, with the exception of the lower drawer of the bureau. I had come provided with a screwdriver and we forced the drawer open. We found some papers in it—"

"What were they?"

"Nothing of interest to us. Mrs. Winter' marriage certificate, a cheque book, some books of National Saving certificate—"

"How many?"

"Five, if I remember rightly."

That accounted for the fifteen staples. Three for each book, two for fixing the pages in the blue cardboard cover, and the third for preventing the holder's card from slipping through the bottom of the pocket in the back cover.

"Was there anything else?"

"Yes; six ten-pound notes, a small packet of love-letters from her husband during their courting days and some papers concerning his death on active service. . . That was all, I think."

"What did you do with them?"

"We replaced everything except the Savings certificates and the Banknotes. These we took away, to give the impression that a burglar had broken into the house. They were too dangerous to keep, so, when we got them back to our rooms, we burnt them. If you had told me last week that I should be consigning ten-pound notes to the flames—"

"Were any of the documents in sealed envelopes?"

"Yes, the marriage certificate. To open it, I used the paper-knife from the desk—and it was then that my fingerprints must have got transferred to it."

"What did you do with it afterwards?"

"I laid it back where I had found it—on top of the desk. . . In order to heighten the impression that the house had been burgled, I threw up the window, then went out into the garden and placed the ladder against the wall. Then my wife and I retired to bed, bitterly disappointed that our search had been so fruitless."

"Did you look in the other drawers?"

"We made a thorough search of the whole room. We even lifted her pillow as far as we dared. We looked behind the pictures on the wall and turned back the carpet. We found nothing—absolutely nothing."

"You say that you replaced the papers in the desk. Did you put them back in the same drawer—the lower one?"

"Yes, I think so. . . " He rubbed his stubbly chin. "No, I wouldn't like to be too positive on that point. You'll appreciate that I was somewhat agitated. I certainly replaced them in one of the drawers of the desk."

"And when you last saw Mrs. Winters. . . ?"

"She was sleeping soundly in her bed. We had not disturbed her. I give you my solemn assurance, Inspector Clayton, that we left her alive and well. . . I do ask you to believe that. . . We did wrong, but we were playing for high stakes. Yet the stakes were not so high that we committed a foul murder. At least *I*"—he drew a sharp breath and screwed up his eyes, as if struck by a blinding light. "I can only suggest," he went on hurriedly, "that, after we quitted her room, some person took advantage of the ladder and strangled Mrs. Winters in her sleep."

"You heard nothing after you got back to your own room?"

"Not a sound."

"Mrs. Harler told me yesterday that she returned to Mrs. Winters' room some time after her first visit and found it empty."

"Yes, she slipped back to see whether the drug had taken effect. She was most surprised to find Mrs. Winters not there."

"Do you know where she was?"

"No, I have no idea—unless she had gone along to the end of the corridor, if you follow me. . . Be that as it may, she was safely in bed when we looked in again later."

CHAPTER NINETEEN

(i)

AT ten o'clock Mrs. Constance Freshwater arrived in Lulverton. She was taken along to the mortuary to identify the body and, later in the morning, was interviewed by Inspector Charlton in his room in Police Headquarters.

She was very like her sister, except that she was some years younger, less gaunt and was dressed in a fashion not so uncompromisingly Edwardian. Her brown hair was expensively waved and set; and Charlton's first impression, when she was shown into his office, was that her husband had either a good income or a number of unpaid draper's bills. She was still visibly affected by her sister's death and, from time to time during the interview, dabbed at her eyes with an inadequate little handkerchief.

Charlton was tactful and sympathetic. After expressing his condolences and regret for the necessity of questioning her so soon after the shock she had sustained, he said:

"In my investigations so far, Mrs. Freshwater, I have been able to discover very little concerning your sister's private life, and I'm hoping for some help from you. No one at Elmsdale seemed to know much about her. In fact, it was only from the cook that I got your name; and even then, she didn't know your address. So will you please give me—well, let me call it a background."

Mrs. Freshwater looked woeful.

"Is this really necessary? Wasn't my sister killed by some man who broke in to steal? Wouldn't it be better to look for *him* than poke about in other directions?"

"I'm afraid my questions are essential, madam. We have reached the conclusion that the crime was not committed by a professional thief, but that it was done for a more personal reason. So will you please give me whatever details you can of Mrs. Winters' history."

"Very well, then." Her tone was reluctant. "She would have been fifty-three next February, ten years older than myself."

He would have put the difference at very much less than that, but was too courteous to contest the point.

"Our father was a man of considerable means, but lost all his money through the dishonesty of his partner. It broke my poor father's heart. . . When he died, a few years after the crash, and was followed by my mother, my sister and I were left to fend for ourselves—or rather, my sister was left to fend for both of us. In 1914, when she was in her early twenties, she fell deeply in love with an officer in the Royal Navy and married him in the following year. After a married life of tragic shortness, her husband was killed in the Battle of Jutland. . . She never really recovered from the blow. I think she died the day she got the telegram. . . But she had to go on living—and to do that she had to work. So she obtained employment. For some years she was a school-teacher. Then, in 1926, she answered an advertisement for a companion and was accepted. Her new employer was Lady Warringham—a perfect dear—who was then just plain Mrs. Warringham. Sir Victor wasn't knighted until some years; afterwards—1933, I think it was. . . My sister has remained with the Warringhams ever since. She became almost one of the family. Poor Lady Warringham was killed by one of those dreadful buzz-bombs—why they ever came up to London when they were perfectly safe from the things down here, I've never been able to understand—and my sister took over the responsibility of running Elmsdale for Sir Victor . . . And that's her very ordinary history, Inspector. It *is* Inspector, isn't it? . . . I hope that's what you wanted to know?"

"Extremely helpful, Mrs. Freshwater. You yourself were married when?"

"In 1926, a month or two after my sister came to Elmsdale."

"You have no children?"

"No."

"Is your husband still alive?"

"Oh, yes! He's on the Stock Exchange, you know. We've just bought a house in Leatherhead."

Two simple statements, yet they told Charlton quite a lot about Constance Freshwater. He waited for her to tell him how many bathrooms the house contained, but she forbore.

"Thank you, Mrs. Freshwater. . . Now, about young John Campbell—"

"Oh, you need have no anxiety over him. My husband and I will be delighted to have him with us at Leatherhead. The house is quite big enough for us to take in one small boy!"

There it was. No mention of bathrooms or the landscape-garden, but the same impression of opulence more subtly imparted.

"I should like some facts about him, please. I understand that he is a nephew of your sister. Is that so?"

"Yes."

He waited for her to go on, but she confined her reply to the monosyllable.

"Will you tell me the precise relationship, Mrs. Freshwater? I take it that the boy was on her husband's side of the family?"

She dabbed her eyes with a corner of her tiny handkerchief and was silent. He gave her plenty of time before gently reminding her of his last question.

She answered tearfully: "All this is very distressing to me, with my poor sister not yet in her grave."

"But it's not a very painful enquiry," he remonstrated mildly. "It's essential that we trace the boy's parents."

"Oh, you don't understand!"

"I quite agree, Mrs. Freshwater. I should like you to help me to understand."

"Then if you really *insist* on knowing, I'll tell you. John is the child of our other sister."

"I gathered that there were only two of you."

"That's what I wanted you to think. She was the youngest

of the three and she went—she was a great disappointment to us. For years my sister Enid and I have refrained from even mentioning her name. In disgracing herself, she disgraced us—and we put her out of our lives."

"Is she still living?"

"I should imagine so, though I have had no news of her for a long time."

"How did Mrs. Winters come to adopt John Campbell?"

"My younger sister—her name is Vera—eventually married a man called George Campbell. He was a—publican."

The word came out like a stubborn tooth.

"Nearly ten years ago, my sister Enid visited my husband and myself in Croydon, where we were then living. She told me that Vera had had a baby and was already beginning to neglect it. Enid and I decided that, whatever our feelings towards our sister, the child could not be allowed to grow up with such parents and in the surroundings of a public house. So we made up our minds to take the little boy into our care. Enid called on Vera and put the suggestion to her. Vera was only too pleased to be rid of what was to her a burden, and the child was taken away from her. For some months, I looked after him, then, when he was old enough to toddle, he went to live at Elmsdale, where he has been perfectly happy ever since. . . He is going to a good school—Paulsfield College—and there is no reason why he should ever know the miserable truth about his parents. . . My husband and I will be happy to pay for his schooling. If necessary, we will take him into our home and will bring him up in the way my poor, dear sister would have wished. . . You can understand now, Inspector, why I didn't want to tell you all this."

"I quite appreciate your feelings, Mrs. Freshwater, but it is my duty to see that the boy's parents are informed. Will you please give me their address?"

"Must you *really* have it?"

She was getting weepy again, but he was firm with her in

his reply. She had to capitulate.

"Then it's the 'Lord Nelson,' in Southmouth. I can't tell you exactly where it is, because I've never been there."

"I'm obliged to you, Mrs. Freshwater. What are your immediate plans?"

"I'll put up at a hotel until after the funeral. In the meantime, I'll send my husband a wire."

"When you've arranged your accommodation, will you please let me know where I can find you?"

He walked across to open the door for her. She collected her fur coat around her. As she was about to pass him through the doorway, he asked:

"By the way, Mrs. Freshwater, what was the maiden name of you and your sisters?"

She answered, "Valentine."

(ii)

Southmouth, three miles to the south of Lulverton, was one of the smaller ports on England's southern coast. During the last twenty-five years, there had been progressively grafted on to the old town a new and much larger district that extended for some distance along the coast and had been developed into a prosperous seaside resort, with a handsome pier and one of the most impressive promenades in the country. In order that its name might be in keeping with its civic splendour, it was renamed Southmouth-by-the-Sea, while its shabby parent, the ancient borough, came to be known as Old Town.

The Lord Nelson was in Old Town, right down on the waterfront, on the corner of a narrow street that led up to the main road and the trams. The little window of its Public Bar gave a view of the harbour and shipping. Its only other section, the tiny Private Bar, was round the corner and looked out on the fried fish shop opposite.

A few minutes after midday opening time, Charlton parked

his car on the quay, walked across to the Lord Nelson, hesitated between the two entrances, then went through the side-street door into the Private Bar.

The only occupants were two shrivelled grandams perched alongside each other on a mahogany seat covered with worn, stained velvet that had once been crimson. In front of them was a round wooden-topped table with ornamental cast-iron legs; on it stood two glasses of stout. The counter and partitions had that yellow grained-and-varnished finish that was so much in favour with a preceding generation; and above the narrow counter were the movable, frosted-glass-panelled screens that saved our forefathers—or that was the intention—from being recognised by the licensee when they covertly ordered a whisky, and prevent those of this generation from getting, without shouting, any attention at all.

There was no one behind the bar when Charlton entered. Between sips at her stout, one of the grandams was giving the other a detailed account of a recent altercation between herself and a Mr. Young who, Charlton gathered, while he stood waiting at the counter, was her butcher. Her companion was not sufficiently engrossed to be neglectful of another customer's thirst and cut into the recital by calling out on Charlton's behalf:

"Mr. Campbell! There's someone wanting serving!"

Oblivious of the interruption, the toothless narratress was going blissfully on:

"I never was one to mince me words, dear, and I certainly wasn't going to with Mr. Young, an ounce over the ration or not. Yes, dear, them was 'is very words. 'Mrs. Bristow,' 'e says, 'you're a two-faced, lyin' old 'arridan,' 'e says—right in front of the 'ole queue, mind you! But I wasn't going to be put upon by the likes of 'im, with 'is motor-car on Sundays and Mrs. Young with another one on the way sooner than is decent. Two-faced, lyin' old 'arridan, 'e called me. But I 'ad me answer ready, dear. 'Oh, no, I'm not!' I comes back at 'im."

The curtains across the entrance from the back parlour were pulled aside and a man came through into the bar. He was nearer fifty than forty-five. His stocky body had a curious rigidity, as if whisky had hardened his arteries till they had set like concrete. He gave the impression that, were he to have been given a slight tap on the chest, he would have fallen flat on his back, as might a tightly stuffed teddybear, with no change of expression on his drink-coarsened features, which had the set, red appearance of rusted iron. Despite the time of year, he was in his shirt-sleeves. In his mouth were the tattered remains of a cigar.

He walked up to the counter, took a cloth and wiped it, and, expecting Charlton to do all the peering under the screens, announced from his full height in a hoarse voice:

"No draught. Only bottled stout or Cointreau."

"Are you Mr. George Campbell?"

The licensee nodded and said with the affability that characterises the retailer of the New Age:

"What of it?"

The Inspector flicked out his warrant card.

"I'd like a word with you in private, please."

Mr. Campbell's countenance did not change.

"Like that, is it?" he grunted, and jerked his head to the right. "Go round to the side door up the street and I'll let you in."

Charlton complied. With a polite smile, he stepped past Mrs. Bristow and her friend, who had now gone in to bat and was getting busy on the deplorable private life of the grocer, and went out into the drab street. Rain was beginning to fall in a fine, penetrating drizzle.

By the time he got to the side door, Mr. Campbell had it open, and led him through into the back parlour, where he produced a box of cigars, a bottle of Scotch and two glasses. It is to a licensed victualler's lasting benefit to keep well in with the police.

Charlton saw that the cigars were as good as the whisky and accepted both. There was a bright fire in the hearth. Mr. Campbell pushed easy chairs forward and invited his guest to be seated.

"Now," he said, when the cigars were alight and the drinks poured out with a generous hand, "'oo are you after this time—Inspector, is it?"

"Yes, Inspector Charlton."

"Charlton, eh? I've 'eard talk of you. The hoodlums don't take very kindly to you in these parts. Always pleased myself, of course, to 'ave you drop in any time you're passing. Can usually manage to bring out a bottle of the real stuff, you know!"

He held up his glass, clicked his tongue appreciatively, then took the small sip of the practised tippler, who, it has been said, is so habitually drunk that only the abnormal is normal.

"Thanks, Mr. Campbell. I don't think I need keep you many minutes."

The host waved his cigar.

"Long as you like. I've put one of the girls on to serving. The missis is away for a few days, which makes things a bit difficult, but we'll manage. Let's have it."

"I believe you're a relative of a Mrs. Enid Winters?"

Somehow he sensed that, at this question, Campbell went over to the defensive.

"Yes, that's true. She's my wife's sister. Anything wrong?"

"I'm afraid so. She died suddenly on Monday night."

"That's bad news, Inspector. P'raps I can't feel as bereaved as I ought, because I only saw 'er but once—and that was years ago. For all that, I'm sorry and I know the missis will be cut up when she 'ears. What did she die of?"

"She was murdered."

This abrupt reply startled Mr. Campbell so much that the muscles of his face nearly creaked into action. He mentioned his Maker in husky astonishment and demanded further details. Charlton told him as much as he considered necessary.

"Well, if that doesn't beat the band!" said Mr. Campbell at the end of it. "Fancy poor old Enid bein' done in like that!" He took another sip and relighted his cigar. "Right in the prime of life. Just shows, don't it?"

He put his hands on the arms of his chair, as if about to rise, and had got as far as, "Well, it's very decent of you to come along—" when the Inspector's next remark made him sink back into his chair.

"In the care of your sister-in-law, there has been living a boy whose name is John Campbell. I've been told that he is your son."

It was unaccustomed exercise, but Mr. George Campbell made up his mind with great speed.

"'E's no son of ours," he retorted.

CHAPTER TWENTY

(i)

"OH, no!" said Mr. Campbell. "I'm not wearing that!"

"Mrs. Freshwater, your other sister-in-law, told me that he is your son and was adopted by Mrs. Winters at an early age."

Mr. Campbell shook his head. "Connie Freshwater may think so, but 'tisn't true. Look 'ere, Inspector, I've always made it a standing rule to keep on the right side of the law. I'm going to do the same this time. Anyway, it was a part of the original bargain that if the balloon ever did go up, I'd 'ave the right to spill the beans."

"Will you give me the facts?"

"A good few years back—must be getting on fer ten years now, I got a letter from my sister-in-law, Enid Winters. She said she wanted to see me—me and the wife, that is. It came as something of a surprise to us, because the wife 'adn't bin on speaking terms with 'er sisters since the Lord knew when. Difference in temperament was the cause. The missis liked to see a bit of life, while they was a couple of sour-pusses. Never really forgive 'er, they didn't, fer choosing me fer an 'usband. Said she was marrying beneath 'er and wouldn't come to the wedding. Slap up do it was, too. Twenty-five-fifteen-six for the liquor alone. The cake was—"

"You were saying that Mrs. Winters wanted to see you?"

"That's right. Soon as I got the letter, I said to meself, ''Ullo! What's come over Enid? 'Ard up fer a quid, is she?' Not that it was much good coming round to me for a sub just then; I 'adn't two pennies to rub together. It was before I took on this 'ouse, you understand. . . Well, the missis dropped a line to Enid, saying we'd be glad to see 'er; and a couple of days later up 'er ladyship turned, looking as if she'd just tasted an olive for the first time and didn't much care for the flavour.

She wasted no time in coming down to brass tacks. A friend of 'ers, she told us, 'ad just 'ad a baby. It was all on the right side of the blanket, as the saying goes, but the parents wasn't able to look after it, and Enid wanted to take it over from them and bring it up prop'ly. The kid'd bin correctly registered with its right name—"

"And that was. . . "?

"Enid wouldn't say, though the question was put. It was registered with its right name, but just to save any tittle-tattle, Enid wanted to call it John Campbell, so's she'd be able to say, if ever she was asked, that it was 'er sister Vera's kid—Vera being my missis. . . Well, Inspector, it all sounded very fishy to me, as it would 'ave done to you. But as I say, I was up against it at the time, and when Sister Enid went on to say that we wasn't expected to do it fer nixes, I pricked up me ears. ''Ow much?' I enquired. There's no need to go into all the 'aggling that took place. The long and the short of it was that on the one side, the missis and I agreed to say the kid was ours if anyone took it into their 'eads to ask us; and on the other side, they put up the money for me to buy the Lord Nelson, an 'ouse I'd 'ad me eye on for some time, always 'avin' fancied the idea of running—"

"Did Mrs. Winters supply the money herself?"

"Lord, no! She never 'ad that many 'ape'nies."

"Then who did?"

"I couldn't say. It was all done through solicitors."

"Who were the solicitors?"

"Dickson and somebody of Lulverton. . . As I mentioned earlier on, I've never gone against the law yet; and I made it clear at the time to Sister Enid that, though I'd no objection to them calling the kid John Campbell and saying it was Enid's nephew, if it suited them, and that, though I'd be prepared to give the same answer to any casual enquiry that might come me way, I wasn't going to get meself mixed up in anything illegal. I told Sister Enid that, as soon as I saw the red light, or if ever there was any official investigation, or anything in writing, I'd—"

"Have you ever seen the boy?"

"Never. Matter of fact, after the legal business relating to the Lord Nelson 'ad bin completed, I never 'eard another word from 'em. Sister Enid never called or wrote again and, as time went by, I fergot it'd ever 'appened. It all came back to me with a nasty shock when you brought up the subject just now, Inspector!"

"Have you any idea who the boy really is?"

"Not the foggiest. It didn't suit my book to ask too many questions."

"Do you know where he was born?"

"That's different. I can 'elp you there. When Sister Enid was doin' 'er best to persuade us there was no shenanigan in progress, she said that the kid was brought into the world in one of the poshest nursing-'omes in Whitchester."

Charlton finished his whisky, brushed some cigar-ash off his overcoat and rose to his feet.

"Many thanks, Mr. Campbell. You've helped me a lot."

"Only too pleased," replied that gentleman with something approaching a smile. "Another couple of fingers to keep the cold out?"

Charlton agreed. It seemed an occasion for moderate celebration. He was getting somewhere.

(ii)

The C.I.D. men attached to the Lulverton Division of the Downshire County Constabulary included, besides Charlton and Sergeant Martin, three plain-clothed constables: Hartley, Emerson and Bradfield. Hartley did not figure in the Winters murder case, but Emerson was to play his small part before the affair was over. Peter Bradfield, the third of them, was in the early thirties. The son of a London solicitor, he had taken up police work because the life had appealed to him more than the sober calling of his father. He was tall and athletic, good-looking except for a wide, flat nose (and there were those of the other sex who averred that it was only the nose that made him handsome), with a sunny disposition, a gay manner and a swashbuckling air that would have taken him a long way when Elizabeth was queen. He had served in the Second World War, had been released from the Army with Release Group 33 and was now back in his old occupation at Lulverton. Martin had not long to go before retirement. Peter Bradfield's name was down to take his place as detective-sergeant and Charlton's first assistant.

When Charlton got back to Lulverton from the Lord Nelson at Southmouth, he summoned Bradfield.

"Peter," he asked, "what are you doing at the moment?"

Bradfield answered with engaging frankness:

"Nothing."

"Then you're just the man I need."

"But I have been busy. I've been walking round Lulverton, chatting to shopkeepers about light-flex."

Charlton was immediately interested.

"Any results?"

"Yes. A man answering to the description Sergeant Martin gave me bought two yards of maroon-coloured flex from a little shop called Macfarland's in a side street called King Edward Street. It was the seventeenth shop I went into. Macfarland, the proprietor, is quite definite about it, though he'd never seen the customer before."

"When was this?"

"Just as he was closing up, a few minutes before seven o'clock on Monday evening. The customer bought a screwdriver and two yards of flex. Macfarland says that, when he'd cut off the flex from the roll, the fellow picked it up from the counter, wound it round his fists and tested the strength of it. Macfarland said to me that he thought it was a funny thing to do."

"Yes, wasn't it," Charlton said grimly. "Thanks, Peter. That's another little piece of our jigsaw puzzle dropped into place. Now, I've another job for you—an assignment that calls for your unique talents."

"I know what that means," growled Bradfield. "I've got to hold hands in the dark with some confounded serving-wench."

"No, not this time. I'll admit that, in the past, you've sometimes had to play Pan in the pantry, in the interests of justice, but this is something different. Listen to me. . . "

(iii)

Ten minutes later, Bradfield left for Whitchester. It was mid-afternoon before he returned, wet but successful. Charlton was waiting for him in the office—waiting with impatience, for a lot depended on the results of Bradfield's mission.

"Any luck, Peter?" he asked before Bradfield had got all of himself into the room.

"Everything you wanted to know," replied his assistant, shaking the rain off his hat. "Let me get out of my swimsuit and I'll tell you all."

He took off his dripping mackintosh and hung it up. Then he came across and sat down. Charlton gave him a cigarette.

"There are three really classy nursing-homes in Whitchester," Bradfield began. "I didn't have to go any further than the second one, which is called the Stanborough Park Maternity Home. I had a chat with the Sister—a terrifyingly efficient female, fairly exuding personality and antiseptic. I passed on all the facts you gave me and she caused one of her satellites to consult the records. The satellite shot back in fifteen seconds, grovelled abjectly for having been away so long, and produced the gen. Thanking my stars I hadn't come into the place as a customer, I edged out of the presence of F. Nightingale, spinster, and hurried round to the registrar of births and deaths. He was a very pleasant and obliging man, and he gave me this."

He felt in his pocket, produced a document, unfolded it and handed it across the desk to his chief. It was a copy of a birth certificate. Charlton picked it up and scanned it eagerly.

"Well, well," he said at length. "Most interesting and just what I expected."

The name of the child was recorded as John Campbell Harler; the name of the mother, Rosalie Elizabeth Harler, formerly Warringham; the name of the father, Clement Harler, car-manufacturers' traveller; and the name of the informant, Victor Warringham, knight.

(iv)

In sending Bradfield to Whitchester, Charlton had worked on a very few facts and a good deal of supposition. This was how he had put it to Bradfield:

"One day last week Sir Victor Warringham gave a small boy a wristwatch on the occasion of his tenth birthday. So it would be at the end of October or beginning of November, 1936, that the boy was born. The scene was a Whitchester nursing-home."

"What was the name of the place?" Bradfield had asked.

"I must leave you to find that out. It was described to me as 'one of the poshest nursing-homes in Whitchester.'"

"Shouldn't be difficult to locate. Can you give me the name of the kid?"

"I know what he's called now: John Campbell. But I don't imagine you'll find that name in the nursing-home files. This is roughly the story, Peter. I'm looking into the murder of a woman called Enid Winters. Perhaps the news has reached you already in the corner of this building in which you skulk when you should be working? Mrs. Winters was housekeeper to Sir Victor Warringham. Some eight-and-a-half years back, an eighteen-months-old boy came to live at Elmsdale, the

Warringham home. It was given out that his name was John Campbell and that he was a nephew of Mrs. Winters. I've already established that neither statement was true. Sir Victor had a daughter Rosalie, who has since died. She was married to a man called Clement Harler. It's my firm conviction that this boy, John Campbell, was the child of Rosalie Harler, and that the birth was hushed up. But it isn't likely that the boy was known by the surname Campbell at the nursing-home. That would have been too risky. It's much more probable that the thing was done quite openly; that Rosalie went into the nursing-home as Mrs. Harler and that the child was duly entered in the birth registry as—well, maybe John Harler. Who were in the plot, I can't be sure yet. Certainly Mrs. Winters. Perhaps Sir Victor and Lady Warringham."

"I take it that this little excursion into motherhood was a *faux pas* of Rosalie's?"

"Everything points to it. Harler, the husband, had been out of the country too long to have been the father. That is, I've been told so. I haven't confirmed it officially. . . . So there's your briefing, Peter. Get the facts—and bring back a copy of the birth certificate."

Bradfield had jumped to his feet.

"Oh, and one other thing," Charlton had added. "Find out the name of the doctor."

(v)

Now Bradfield was back. Charlton folded the copy of the birth certificate and put it away in his pocket-book.

"Any other points of interest, Peter?"

"Yes. The Sister remembered the case, principally because those well-known figures, Sir Victor and Lady Warringham, were involved. They were both on the spot, waiting in the vestibule for the glad news to be announced. Your Mrs. Winters was there too. Created a somewhat bad impression by trying to teach the Sister her job. In the absence abroad of the proud father, Sir Victor undertook the registration. Mrs. Harler was in the nursing-home for three weeks, then left with her mother and child for a holiday in Scotland. No address available."

"Who attended Mrs. Harler?"

"A certain Dr. Stamford of Lulverton. In other words, Old Mortality."

"What do we know about him, Peter—apart from the fact that he's the worst medico in the district?"

"We know that it's better to have scarlet fever in the house than Old Mortality. We know that his practice is falling away like thawing snow off a roof. We suspect that, if it hadn't been for a wrong diagnosis on his part, old Mrs. Burtenshaw might have realised her ambition and lived to be a hundred. We've reason to think that the old gentleman's a trifle too fond of his noggin of fire-water. We also have it on good authority that last week his butcher threatened him with a summons for not paying his meat bill."

An expression of amazement had spread over Charlton's face.

"How did you come by all this information?" he wanted to know. "A lot of it's news to me."

"I'll let you into a secret, sir. When I heard that the delivery had been in the bungling hands of Old Mortality, I said to myself: 'If the Warringhams wanted to keep this dark in Lulverton, why have a Lulverton doctor? Why not have a Whitchester man? Whitchester's a nice big town. Mrs. Harler had been living there for some months before she went into the Stanborough Park, so she could easily have called in—'"

"You say she was living at Whitchester?"

"Yes. I got it from the Sister. Mrs. Harler had a flat in Riverside Mansions, a big block that had just been put up in Arundel Road. I didn't think it was necessary to go along there. Where was I?... Oh, yes, I said to myself, 'Bradfield, maybe that doctor was squared. You'd better find out something about him in Lulverton before you report back.' So there it is, sir."

"You showed initiative, Peter. You'll get on, my boy."

"Once," replied Bradfield, "I was a bombardier in the Royal Artillery. Can I climb higher?"

CHAPTER TWENTY-ONE

(i)

CLEMENT HARLER had to be seen again. He had shaved since their meeting that morning and looked more presentable. His manner, too, was more assured, as if, having made a clean breast of it, he had nothing more to fear.

"I want to consult with you, Mr. Harler," Charlton told him, "because a very serious fact has come to light—a fact that concerns you deeply."

Harler gained still more confidence from this opening remark; Charlton's choice of the word 'consult' seemed to put his association with the police on a new and more agreeable footing.

"Please tell me what it is," he invited. "I only hope it is something which will get me out of this terrible predicament."

"When did you leave this country for South America, Mr. Harler? I want the exact date."

"I sailed on the 25th of August, 1935."

"And you were in South America continuously from the day you disembarked until your return to this country?"

"Quite so. I arrived back in England just before Christmas, 1945."

"During the whole of that period you did not see your wife? I mean your first wife?"

"No. . . . I must confess that I don't see where this is leading, Inspector Clayton. I have already given you all this information."

"I wanted the dates. It may be necessary to produce proof that your statements are correct."

"There would be no trouble about that, I imagine. I could produce ample evidence."

"Good. . . . Now, this is what I have to tell you. On the 1st of November, 1936—that is, a few days over fourteen months after you sailed for South America—your wife gave birth to a child."

There was no play-acting about Harler's reaction. He was dumbfounded. Charlton gave him time to digest the news before he added:

"The child is the boy we know as John Campbell."

Stupefaction gave place to an eruption.

"Well, I'll be damned! Do you mean to tell me we've been living in the same house all this time without knowing?"

"You didn't know, did you, Mr. Harler?"

"Good Lord, no! The biggest surprise I've ever had. She didn't waste much time, did she? I suppose the father was—"

"According to the birth certificate, Mr. Harler, *you* were the father."

He passed the document over the desk. Harler took it.

"'Name and surname of father, Clement Harler. 'What a lie! 'Rank or profession of father, car manufacturers' traveller.' That's another lie; I was out of the firm before I left England. 'Informant, Victor Warringham, knight.' So the old boy was in it, was he?. . . Well, that beats everything! I can picture his feelings when I returned from the grave!"

He laughed harshly, threw the certificate on the desk, then sprawled back in his chair, chewing the nail of his little finger.

"I can see it all now," he said after a period of cogitation. "That was the mystery I told you about this morning. Can you see the implications, Inspector?"

"I can. John Campbell Harler will inherit the whole of Sir Victor's fortune, half as the child of Sir Victor's daughter and the other half as his next-of-kin."

Harler sat up.

"Oh, no, he won't! I'll see to that! Why, this birth certificate's nothing less than perjury! John Campbell's not the issue of Rosalie's marriage. He's illegitimate! And I can prove it, just as I can prove that Victor Warringham, knight, made a false declaration! Believe me, Inspector Clayton, I shan't take this lying down! God, if I'd only known this before!"

His excitement abated. He brooded for a while, savagely biting his nails. Then he said:

"It's obvious now what Winters was up to. So long as she kept control of the boy, she'd have her fingers on the purse-strings. . . . But she wasn't a relative. As soon as old Warringham died, I should be appointed sole trustee, under the terms of the codicil to the will."

"Why?"

Harler jerked forward to slam his hand down on the certificate on the desk.

"Doesn't it say there that I'm the father of the brat? She was in a cleft stick. If the boy was to inherit, she'd have to prove that he wasn't her nephew, but Rosalie's son; and if she did prove it, she'd cut her own throat at the same time, because the boy's legal father—myself—was still alive. . . . Why, it would have been of advantage to me to get rid of Mrs. Winters and accept the parentage."

"Yes," was Charlton's dry comment, "that has already occurred to me."

"Meaning exactly what? . . . Oh, getting rid of Mrs. Winters? I didn't need to murder her, if that's what you're hinting at. All I had to say to her was, 'Right, Mrs. Enid Winters. You've looked after the boy and you've been well paid for it. Now I can dispense with your services, thank you, and leave you to find new employment elsewhere.'"

"And suppose, Mr. Harler, that she had answered, 'I can prove that you are not John's father. If you dismiss me, I'll take the matter to court.' . . . What then?"

"Yes, I see your argument," Harler admitted grudgingly. "But she was far worse placed than I was—and so was the old boy, come to that. I wonder how they were proposing to get round the difficulty. . . . Probably leave the money to her under a new will, and pass it on to John Campbell at her death. How did you find all this out, Inspector Clayton?"

"In the course of my investigations," was the vague reply.

"So you're still sleuthing, are you? That's a good sign for me. It suggests that you don't still think I'm your quarry. May I be allowed to give you a pointer?"

Charlton nodded.

"I was not the only one standing to lose by a change in the will in Winters' favour. There's one other man who would not have liked to see all that money, and complete control of the kid, going into her hands."

His lip curled maliciously.

"I mean," he said, "John's father."

(ii)

After some reflection following Harler's return to his cell, Charlton decided to go and see Sir Victor. Accordingly, he summoned Peter Bradfield and drove with him out to Elmsdale. By that time, darkness had fallen and it was still raining hard.

The front door was opened to them by Tom Blackmore.

"Why, hullo, Inspector!" he smiled a welcome.

"What brings you out on this black and dirty night?"

"I want to have a word with Sir Victor, if he's free."

"Yes, I think he is. Come in out of the wet."

When they stepped into the hall, Charlton introduced Bradfield to Blackmore, who then took them into the library. Charlton enquired:

"How are you settling down here, Mr. Blackmore? "

"Very well, thanks. Mrs. Gulliver's worked like a Trojan and got me fixed up in one of the spare rooms. Young John's gone back to his old room."

"What about your friend, Mr. Valentine?"

"He's still at the cottage. Seems quite happy. If you'd like to wait for a minute or two, I'll go and fetch Sir Victor.

He's in the dining-room, trying to teach John how to play chess!"

As soon as they were alone, Charlton said to Bradfield in a low tone:

"Peter, I didn't bring you along for the fun of the thing. Things are liable to get lively and I want you around. This evening we're going to meet Mrs. Winters' murderer face to face, with the buttons off the foils. . . . Dear old Bert Martin's not as young as he was, so I've left him behind. . . . But before the big moment, I've another job for you. For the time being, just wait out in the hall. I'd better see Sir Victor alone. Wait till I've introduced you to him, then scram."

Bradfield nodded. In a few minutes, Sir Victor joined them. He greeted Charlton with a smiling inclination of the head.

"Good evening, Sir Victor," Charlton smiled back. "This is my assistant, Detective-constable Bradfield, who may have to take this case over from me. I'm expecting to be called up north."

This was news to Peter Bradfield, which was understandable, inasmuch as Charlton had invented it on the spur of the moment.

"I am pleased to make your acquaintance, Mr. Bradfield," said the old man with magnificent courtesy. "Would that I could welcome you to my home in happier circumstances."

Bradfield said something appropriate and faded out into the hall, where he was soon discovered by Mrs. Gulliver, who bore him off and fêted him with tea and cakes. Peter Bradfield had a way with him.

In the library, Sir Victor invited Charlton to be seated and politely enquired his business.

"I feel," he added, "that it must be something of importance. Nothing trivial would surely have brought you out here on such a terrible night."

"Yes, sir," Charlton agreed gravely, "it is important. I have a most serious matter to raise with you."

"Is it concerned with the death of my housekeeper?"

"It is."

"Then I will endeavour to assist you to the best of my ability. Pray proceed."

"Sir Victor, during my inquiries today—"

"But are not your inquiries at an end? I should have imagined that the arrest of my rascally son-in-law and his—ah—concubine would have brought your investigations to a successful conclusion."

"The case goes on, sir, until I have positive proof. As I was about to say, during my inquiries today, I uncovered what has been, up to now, a closely guarded secret."

Sir Victor's thin frame grew rigid.

"Do not speak in riddles," he snapped. "Come to the point, man!"

"I have found out," answered Charlton, who was not to be stampeded, "that the boy, John Campbell, is not the nephew of the late Mrs. Winters, but the son of your daughter."

At this calmly delivered statement, the old man flared up.

"You impudent, prying fellow! What are my private affairs to do with you? Have you no consideration, no thought for the feelings of others, that you must stir up more unhappiness, more misery, than there is for some of us already? You are a policeman. It is your task to apprehend the murderer of Mrs. Winters. You are exceeding your duties—I repeat that you are grossly exceeding your duties—by intruding yourself into matters that are not your concern!"

Charlton listened to this tirade completely unmoved, except to think what a majestic presence the English stage had lost in Sir Victor Warringham. When the old man finished, he was white and breathless. He had a hand on his heart. Charlton said sharply:

"I can't agree with you, Sir Victor. Mrs. Winters was murdered because John Campbell Harler is your grandson. It was left to me to find out the relationship for myself. I'm not doing all this because I like it. I have a job to do—and it is your business, Sir Victor, to help, not to hinder!"

This timely piece of dignified remonstrance, delivered by Charlton with his tongue in his cheek, had the desired effect.

"I beg your pardon, Inspector. My remarks were quite uncalled for. You have a right to know the facts. My only excuse is that you have touched on a subject that I would far rather you had not had cause to mention. Now that you have hit upon the secret, I have no alternative but to give you such facts as you require. I will begin by admitting that little John is my grandson, my daughter Rosalie's child."

"May I hear the whole story, sir?"

"It is a sad story, Inspector—a story of heartbreak and bitter anguish. It opened for me when my beloved wife told me that our daughter had come to her with a terrible confession; that she was going to have an illegitimate child. Some months previously, we had had news from South America that Clement Harler had been killed in a train disaster. With that in mind, I suggested that a speedy marriage with the father of the child-to-be was the only solution. My wife informed me that there were factors that made this impossible. I was never entrusted with the identity of the father. My wife admitted that my daughter had confided his name to her, but I myself was kept in ignorance. I think they feared that I might attempt some form of vengeance, as I well might have done ten years ago, when I was more vigorous than I am today.

"At the time when she discovered her condition, my daughter was living in this house. I immediately took the necessary steps. I got a tenancy for her of a flat in Whitchester, where she would be far enough away to avoid the critical scrutiny of those who knew how long she had been a widow, and near enough to be under the care of my dear wife. As she drew near her time, I was faced with a terrible problem. . . . For better or worse, I made my decision. In the absence of the child's father, it fell to me to lodge details with the registrar of births and deaths.

I gave the name of the father as Clement Harler. . . . Only a loving parent, placed in a similar position, can be a real judge of my action. . . . Clement Harler, as far as I knew then, was dead, but only a few people shared the knowledge that he had left this country too early to have been the father of the child. In these circumstances, I gambled that I would not be found out. . . . However, there did remain the danger that, were the boy publicly acknowledged as my daughter's child, some ill-disposed person might see fit to cause an unpleasant scandal. To guard against that eventuality, John was adopted as her nephew by Mrs. Winters, who was also in the secret."

Charlton asked: "Did Mrs. Winters know who the father was?"

"I am convinced that she did. She would never admit as much, but I have always had the impression that she knew. As confidante of my wife, she could hardly fail to know. . . . But to return to my story. . . . When she left the nursing-home at Whitchester, my daughter took the child to Scotland. When he was old enough to leave his mother, the little boy was passed into the keeping of Mrs. Freshwater, who, as you know, is a sister of Mrs. Winters. . . . I fear I was grievously at fault, Inspector in diverting your attention from Mrs. Freshwater during our previous interviews. I feigned little knowledge of her, because I wished to keep you from questioning her."

"Did she know the truth?"

"I cannot tell you whether she ultimately discovered it, but it was never our intention that she should. It was arranged that Mrs. Winters should tell her that John was the son of their second sister, a Mrs. Campbell. I should add that Mrs. Campbell and her husband were—ah—suitably recompensed for their connivance. . . . So, as I have told you, little John was handed into the care of Mrs. Freshwater, while my daughter returned to take up her normal residence at Elmsdale. After a suitable period had elapsed, the boy was also brought here and grew from infancy to boyhood in the belief that he was Mrs. Winters' nephew.

"With no more than a brief mention of the loss of my wife and daughter in the heart-rending sequence of events, I will bring the story up to the calamitous day when my son-in-law reappeared without warning. . . . I need not describe my emotions. . . . When he suggested that he should take up residence here, there was no alternative but to accede to his request. I could not send him away."

"Why not, sir?"

"It would have aroused his suspicions that something was amiss."

"I don't quite see that. Hadn't you sent him away once before?"

"Not exactly, Inspector. It is more accurate to say that I had prevailed upon him to go. I have always been one to avoid scandal at almost any cost. My daughter's married life had not been of the happiest. On an occasion when my son-in-law chanced to mention the openings in Brazil for a man of enterprise, I took the opportunity to suggest that he should go out there and try his luck. The conversation developed into a man-to-man talk. He agreed that all was not well between him and my daughter, and consented to go abroad for a time, in the hope that things might straighten themselves out. I supplied him with the necessary funds and, in due course, he departed for South America."

"Was it understood, sir, that if he made a success in South America, your daughter would join him there?

"No. He may have imagined so himself, but such an idea was never in my own mind—nor, I am sure, in my daughter's. All we wanted to do was to get rid of him with as little fuss as possible. . . . But for all practical purposes, he went off to Brazil with my blessing. How, then, could I turn him away when he ultimately returned?"

This account of Harler's South American expedition did not seem to square up with other versions Charlton had heard, but he did no more than nod agreement with Sir Victor's closing remark.

"It was not long," the old gentleman went on, "before Mrs. Winters began to get difficult. I could see her point of view. She was aware of the provisions of my will. She saw that, as far as she herself was concerned, the future was financially uncertain. . . . A long series of wearisome conversations between us culminated last week in an explicit demand on her part for me to alter my will in such a way that she would be the principal beneficiary. In exchange for this, she undertook to look after little John until he gained his majority and to bequeath to him, on her death, the whole of the money obtained from my estate. She added, I am sorry to say, that if I did not do as she desired, she would not continue to hold her tongue about John's parentage.

"I equivocated. I promised to consider the matter. I told her that if I decided to fall in with her request, I would instruct my solicitors to prepare the necessary document."

"Was that why you asked Mr. Howard to call?"

"No, Inspector, it was not. To be frank with you, I was not at all desirous that my fortune—which is not inconsiderable—should pass into the hands of Mrs. Winters. Admitted that she was a close friend of my wife's during her lifetime, that she rallied to our aid at the time my daughter's child was born, that she has been a dependable, hard-working employee of the family for many years. Yet I neither liked nor completely trusted her. What guarantee had I that she would act towards my grandson in the manner she had promised, when I was dead and gone? No, Inspector, I had another reason for summoning Howard. I had a different plan."

"You told me yesterday, Sir Victor, that you had decided to accept Mrs. Winters' suggestion."

"Pardon me, Inspector, but I did no such thing. What I did tell you was that I had so informed Mrs. Winters. I employed this subterfuge to put her off the track until such time as I could confront her with a *fait accompli*."

"You also succeeded," said Charlton with some bitterness, "in putting *me* off the track as well."

Sir Victor beamed happily at him.

"For that I cannot be blamed. It was only that you placed a wrong construction on my words. . . . Now, let me come back to my story. . . . Deep and anxious thought had brought me to one conclusion: the Harlers must be told the truth about John Campbell. There no other way of safeguarding the lad's future. He must be brought out into the open as John Campbell Harler, my grandson. This could not be done unless Clement Harler acknowledged him, at the same time, as his son. The difficulty was that, in so doing, my son-in-law would automatically forego his own legacy under my will. I will not go into the details now. In fact"—this was added with more than a trace of acidity—"I fancy your inquiries have been exhaustive enough to make you fully acquainted with all the clauses of that document!"

Charlton disregarded the taunt.

"I felt, however," Sir Victor went on, "that something could be done to compensate my son-in-law."

"Were you prepared to have Mr. Harler take over the care of John?"

"Oh, no! Quite definitely no! Never would I have consented to that. I should have made it a condition that his would be only nominal parentage. I proposed to entrust the little chap to Mr. Tom Blackmore, whom I hold in great esteem. Mr. Blackmore would have been appointed trustee. My son-in-law would have been prevailed upon to take his wife and—ah—bribe back to South America. He would have had the custody of neither my grandson, nor of his finances. You can accept my assurance on that, Inspector!"

"Did Mr. Blackmore know your intention?"

"Yes. He is a man in whom I can confide. I had a long talk with him on the subject on Friday evening last. He agreed to accept the trust and we decided that Mr. Howard should be consulted as to the best way of achieving our purpose."

"I wish I'd known all this before, Sir Victor."

The old man shrugged his shoulders in deprecation.

"Reticence was unavoidable. I could not shout the truth about my grandson from the housetops."

He rose from his feet and began to pace restlessly up and down the long room, with his hands clasped behind his back. Charlton, who remained seated, switched to another topic.

"Whose suggestion was it in the first instance, Sir Victor, that Mrs. Winters should adopt John as her nephew?"

"It emanated from Mrs. Winters herself. My wife and I were apprehensive, but were finally persuaded."

He turned at the window and retraced his steps as Charlton put his next question—or began to.

"Do you know a man—"

He broke off. Sir Victor had paused in his walk to turn his head and glance down over his shoulder. Charlton watched him curiously. Sir Victor resumed his pacing.

"You were about to say . . .?"

"Do you know a man called Raymond Valentine?"

"I certainly do. He is a brother of Mrs. Winters—a drunken ne'er-do-well of the worst type and a great anxiety to her, I believe. I was once prevailed upon to give him employment. I was later compelled to order his dismissal."

"May I know the reason, Sir Victor?"

"He thrust his attentions on my daughter."

"Was that after Mr. Harler had left for——"

Once again Sir Victor had stopped dead and turned his head as before. Then he looked across at Charlton with a delighted smile on his face.

"It *is* getting long and bushy, isn't it?" he said brightly.

Charlton was puzzled. "What is?"

"My tail."

CHAPTER TWENTY-TWO

(i)

TEN minutes later, Charlton left Elmsdale with Peter Bradfield. As they emerged from the drive, instead of turning to the right for Lulverton, he swung the car to the left. Half a mile along the lonely rainswept road, he slowed down, but did not stop, outside the first dwelling since Elmsdale. A light was on in one of the ground-floor rooms.

"That's Peartree Cottage, where the man Blackmore usually lives," he told Bradfield. "At the moment, the only inhabitant is a fellow called Raymond Valentine, the brother of Mrs. Winters."

He accelerated the engine and drove on into Mickleham, where he could turn the car round without difficulty. On the way back to Lulverton, he told Bradfield what he wanted him to do.

Immediately they arrived at Police Headquarters, Charlton's place at the wheel was taken by a uniformed constable, who drove Bradfield back the way he had come, dropped him twenty yards short of Peartree Cottage, and then went on alone to the cottage. He bore a message for Raymond Valentine to the effect that Inspector Charlton would be obliged if Mr. Valentine would come at once in the car to Police Headquarters.

Bradfield waited until Valentine had been collected and the rear light of the Vauxhall had disappeared into the wet darkness before he proceeded to carry out his chief's instructions.

(ii)

It was still early evening, but Raymond Valentine was already mellow. He had worked his way steadily through Blackmore's whisky and was well into a bottle that he had had the foresight to bring with him from London. He had reached the stage when every man was his friend and, by the time the police car reached its destination, had warmly invited the driver and his wife, if any, for a weekend in his Sloane Street flat. As they pulled up outside Police H.Q., he was saying:

"The wife's a great shport. She'd take you round to see all the shights—Weshminstrabbey, Buckinerpals, the Shavoy Grill. And there's a li'l place jussoff Gronersquare. Fourn-six for a double Scotch, but we'd have a rattling goo' time, wouldn't we, ole darling?"

Though not quite easy in his mind about being called 'old darling' by a gentleman with such a superb moustache, the driver decided to humour his passenger.

"No doubt about that, sir," he said, and led him in fatherly fashion, almost by the hand, out of the car, into the building, up the stairs, along the passage and into the office where Charlton stood waiting, with his back to the dying fire.

Greetings were exchanged, on the one side reserved, on the other, fulsomely friendly.

"I'm sorry to bring you out on such a night, Mr. Valentine, but it's unavoidable."

"Thash all right, dear old detective. Everything points to happiness. My time's your time—and all that drip. Lesh get the business shide finished, then repair to a neighbouring ale-housh."

"Sit down," Charlton suggested with a wave of his hand, adding silently to himself, "before you fall down."

"Thanksh. Your driver chappie just caught me in time. I was about to be off to the village for a shnorter. Now, what'sh trouble?"

"I'm investigating the murder of Mrs. Enid Winters. I believe you're her brother?"

"Squite correct. Loving brother. Great shock to hear that poor old Enid'sh been rubbed out. Very great shock indeed. Firs' murder in the family. Famoush family, the Valentines. Why, at the Battle of Nayshby——"

"I met you yesterday afternoon, Mr. Valentine. Why didn't you tell me you were her brother?"

"Because I din't think you'd be in the teeniest bit interested. Thash why. After you'd joined us in the odd beaker of tea and had gone your way, I passed the remark to my dear ole pal, Blackmore. 'Tom, ole frien',' I dishtinctly recall shaying to him, 'Tom, old frien', 'sgreat honour to have Crim'al 'Ves'gation 'Partment dropping in for a snack, but it's not an everyday occurrench. Wassat distinguished looking dick shnooping round for? Picture my feelingsh, dear old sleuth, when Tom 'sponded, 'Somebody's murdered your shishter.' Din't break it very gently, did he? But Tom Blackmore was alwaysh li' that. No finnesh."

"Mr. Valentine"—there was a rasping note in the usually smooth tone—"do you expect me to believe that?"

"Nashrally. Life couldn't go on if people din't speak the truth, splendid old Sher——"

"Mrs. Winters was murdered on Monday night, Mr. Valentine. Mr. Blackmore told me yesterday afternoon in your presence that you had arrived at Peartree Cottage at lunch-time. Are you suggesting that between those hours Mr. Blackmore was negligent enough not to inform you of your sister's death?"

"Thash what I jus' said 'bout Tom. Too damn full of his own affairsh. No finer feelingsh at all."

Charlton sickened of the man. There was something repellent about Valentine. His flippancies lacked life and sunshine. He was like a character created by a humorist who had written himself out. Drunk or sober, he was a caricature of a caricature, until an evil temper made him drop the mask—and then he was more repellent than ever.

"There's a fellow's shishter," Valentine was going on, "brutally done to death like Cock Robin and——"

"Mr. Valentine! Pull yourself together! This is a serious matter! . . . Now, on Monday evening you called at Elmsdale and saw your sister, didn't you?"

"No. I've not seen Enid for months. If you want the truth, dear old inquisitor, I never could hit it off with Enid. Not my type at all. Too shtrait-laced. Thish child hankers after the fleshpotsh of—"

Without a word, Charlton had leant across the desk to place something in front of him. It was a sheet of card on which had been pasted such fragments as Charlton had managed to collect of the tom np letter from Mrs. Winters' wastepaper basket. Valentine picked it up, glanced at it and threw it back on the desk.

"You will see," said Charlton, "that it is signed, 'Ray,' and is to the effect that the writer will call at Elmsdale at eleven o'clock—a time when, the writer suggests, 'the rest of the household will be safely tucked up in their little cots.' Do you deny that you wrote this letter, Mr. Valentine?"

"Can't very well, can I?" was the naïve reply.

"And do you deny that you kept the appointment; that you sat with your sister in her private room on the ground floor of Elmsdale and smoked one of your 'Manikin' cigars? I shouldn't try to deny it, if I were you, Mr. Valentine."

Raymond Valentine sat in fuddled thought, automatically pushing his moustache up from his lip with the balls of his fingers. Charlton watched his efforts to get a grip on himself. Valentine was just drunk enough to know that he was not sober. At length he said, feeling for his words, building up his sentences as if erecting, storey by storey, a house of playing-cards, and only occasionally lapsing into slurring:

"I told you a naughty little fib, old chappie. In point of fact, I did see Enid on Monday."

"At eleven o'clock?"

"In round figures. Wouldn't be sure to the exact minute."

"How long were you with her?"

"Quarter of an hour or so. Then she got too sleepy to go on chatting. She shaw—saw me off the premises and I came back to my hotel in Lulverton."

"Mrs. Winters mentioned that she felt sleepy?"

"Funnily enough, she did. Said she didn't know what had come over her. Couldn't keep her eyes open. I wasn't feeling too wide awake myself. Been on my tootsies since first thing. So when Enid suggested calling it a day, I was damn glad to say goo'night."

"What was the subject of your conversation?"

"Have a heart! That's more than somewhat shteep, isn't it? Confidential chat between brother and sister. Scarcely expect me to retell it to you, could you, old darling?"

"I can't compel you to answer my question, Mr. Valentine. Nevertheless, I'd like to know why you called on your sister at that hour of the night."

"There's a quick answer to that. Our aged friend, the Archbishop of Elmsdale, is no warm admirer of Mr. R. Valentine. As far as he's concerned, I'm a dead loss. So to carry out the old brotherly obligations, I had to move stealthily and by night. I knew that one shingle hint that I was in the house and the Venerable Bede would set the jolly old bow-wows on me. I admit that on this particular occasion, he—"

Under his heavy moustache he bit his lip.

Charlton prompted, "You were going to say. . . ?"

"Nothing, old horse. Completely as you were."

"So you saw Sir Victor on Monday night?"

"Tremendous wheedler, aren't you? Yes, I did have a few words with the ancient."

"What about?"

"Oh, general gossip, you know. Surprised to find him so genial."

"Did you talk with him in your sister's sitting-room?"

"No. Enid and I happened to bump into him in the hall, while she was showing me out."

"How was Sir Victor dressed?"

"Grey lounge suit—single-breasted, if I remember rightly. Starched white collar. Tie, some quiet—"

"And your talk with him was limited to—"

"Small talk, old boy. Utterly idle nothings. Ships that pass in the night. Can't remember a word of it."

"Had your sister asked you to come down to Lulverton?"

"Yes. I had a line from her by the evening post on Saturday. She said she wanted to see me, so I came down from the metropolis hot-foot."

"Why the haste, Mr. Valentine? Was it an urgent summons?"

"Yes, I suppose you'd call it urgentish."

"Did it concern Sir Victor?"

"His name was certainly mentioned during our chinwag, but only in a vague, passing sort of way."

"You're not prepared to give me fuller details?"

"There's really none to give you. I think you're making a mountain out of a molehill, old darling."

Charlton changed the subject.

"Mr. Blackmore is a friend of yours?"

"Known him since boyhood almost. Boon companions at one time. Fidus Achates and so forth. Drifted apart these last few years, though."

"Were you acquainted with Sir Victor's daughter, Mr. Valentine?"

For an instant, he thought the man was going to refute it. Then Valentine replied in a casual tone:

"Curious you should ask that. Rosalie was an old flame of mine in the dear, dead days beyond recall. A boy and girl affair, you know. The moon in June and all that caper. It was soon over."

"I am wondering, Mr. Valentine," Charlton said suavely, "whether the subject of your conversation with your sister on Monday night was—John Campbell." Valentine stiffened. With swift anger, he snapped:

"I'm standing no more of this! I'm—if I'll put up with your questions and—innuendoes! you want to know anything else, you can. . ."

As the diatribe proceeded, there was a knock on the door and Bradfield looked in. Before Valentine could stem his flow of invective and look round, Bradfield had given Charlton a silent signal. He had extended his clenched hands—and both thumbs pointed towards the ceiling.

(iii)

Peter Bradfield did not have to break into Peartree Cottage. He entered by the front door, which Valentine, in his temporary geniality towards mankind, had left unlocked. Nor did his quest take long.

On the transfer of Tom Blackmore and John Campbell from the cottage to Elmsdale the previous evening, Valentine had installed himself in the second bedroom, which was to have been John's. During his general, but expertly detailed, search of the little building, Bradfield found under the bed in the second bedroom the much labelled suitcase that Valentine had brought with him from London. It was locked, but suitcase locks are child's play to a man of experience.

When Bradfield slipped out of the cottage ten minutes after his entry and walked back to meet the car, which was returning to fetch him, he left no trace behind. Everything in the cottage was as he had found it. But he could take back news to his chief of three interesting discoveries. The first was a copy of John's birth certificate. The second was a length of electric-light flex, which, though now untied, showed clear signs of a reef knot on which had been put sufficient tension to part the strands of the maroon-coloured covering. And the third was a briar pipe, with the vulcanite mouthpiece snapped off at the point where it plugged into the wooden stem.

(iv)

He met the police car a hundred yards along the road and arrived back in Charlton's office just in time to hear Valentine's outburst.

When Valentine paused for breath, Charlton said:

"I'm sorry you're adopting this attitude, Mr. Valentine. In the circumstances, I won't trouble you any further." He rose to his feet before adding significantly, "At the moment. The car is ready to take you back to Peartree Cottage. Please don't leave the neighbourhood without referring to me first."

Valentine left them with no more than an angry grunt of farewell. The moment he was out of the room, Charlton lifted the receiver of his telephone, asked to speak to Detective-constable Emerson and gave that stalwart young man a few terse instructions.

Then Bradfield delivered his report. Charlton smiled with satisfaction.

"More than I'd hoped, Peter," he admitted. "Did you leave everything tidy?"

"Not a trace that I'd been there," was the confident reply.

"Good. We don't want to arouse his suspicions until we're ready to act. Where did you find the birth certificate?"

"In the suitcase, slipped into one of the side pockets. There was also a nice little collection of bills and dunning letters, some addressed to R. Valentine, Esq., but most of them to the female of the species. They were fixed together by an elastic band—and the birth certificate was amongst 'em."

"That's rather interesting, Peter. It looks as if—"

He broke off to answer the telephone.

"Inspector Charlton here. . . . Yes, Mrs. Gulliver. What's the trouble? . . . Right. I'll come immediately." He slammed down the receiver, jumped to his feet and took a swift stride across the room for his coat and hat.

"Get another car, Peter—and for God's sake look sharp about it! We're wanted at Elmsdale. Old Warringham's gone stark, murdering mad!"

PART IV

PROOF

CHAPTER TWENTY-THREE

(i)

A SHORT while before Mrs. Gulliver's urgent telephone-call for help, there was a scene of quiet domestic happiness in the dining-room at Elmsdale. Mrs. Gulliver had cleared away the dinner things from the table at one end of the big room and was now washing them up in the kitchen. At the other end of the dining-room, a big log burnt cheerfully in the fireplace, on one side of which sat Tom Blackmore and on the other, Sir Victor Warringham and John Campbell. Blackmore, with Bugle curled on the hearthrug at his feet, was in an easy chair, busy with his pencil on the *Daily Telegraph* crossword puzzle. Sir Victor and John faced each other across a chessboard, which was on a small occasional table.

"Now ought I to move my castle, sir?" John was saying.

"Rook, my boy!" smiled the old gentleman genially. "The piece may resemble a castle, but it is most improper to call it one. Yes, I think you can safely move your rook, but remember that a rook can be moved only in a straight line, never diagonally."

John, his face screwed up with the complexities of the game, tentatively moved his rook to another square. Sir Victor crowed in triumph.

"You have played right into my hands, my boy!" he chuckled, and advanced his queen. "Now get out of that, if you can!"

"But you said it would be all right, sir," the boy ventured.

"And so it would, had you moved it in the right direction! Similarly, you might enquire whether it would be safe to catch an omnibus into Lulverton. I should naturally answer in the affirmative, but it would be *your* responsibility to ensure, before boarding the vehicle, that it was bound for Lulverton and not Timbuctoo!"

"Chess is trifficly difficult," John complained.

"Couldn't we play draughts, sir? I'm good at draughts. I once beat Uncle Tom twice running."

"No, let us confine ourselves to chess, the finest game invented by man."

All boys are opportunists. John saw his chance to defer his next move under the quizzical eyes of the old gentleman. He asked:

"Which country invented it, sir?"

The bait was swallowed whole. Tom Blackmore grinned behind his paper.

"Its origin," said Sir Victor, "is uncertain. Persia seems to have been the first country in which it gained real popularity, but there is every reason to believe that, in the first instance, it was introduced into Persia from India. It is your move, my boy."

The diversion had proved too short-lived. John mastered a sigh and ruffled up his already untidy hair. The game continued with many frowns of concentration on John's part and much delighted critical comment on Sir Victor's, until there was a knock on the dining-room door.

Sir Victor called out, "Come in! . . . Ah, Ada."

Mrs. Gulliver was carrying a tray of cutlery.

"Excuse me, sir," she said. "I just want to put the knives and forks back in the sideboard."

With arms outstretched to keep the tray clear of her waistline, she stumped across to the sideboard. As she pulled open the drawer used for cutlery. Sir Victor said to her:

"My teeth proved that the joint tonight was tender, yet I found difficulty in carving it. The fault must lie with the carving-knife. Please leave it on top of the sideboard, Ada, and I will see that it is sharpened."

Mrs. Gulliver looked surprised.

"I can attend to that, sir. I'm sorry it wasn't as sharp as it might be. Leave it to me, sir. There's a man comes every—"

"Ada!" Sir Victor's tone was testy. "Please do as I tell you! Put the other cutlery away, place the carving-knife on the sideboard, and go back to your kitchen. We shall probably require some coffee later in the evening, after Master John has gone to bed."

"Very good, Sir Victor," answered the chastened cook, and proceeded to carry out his instructions, not without the melancholy thought that the master hadn't been himself lately.

The players went back to their game. At length, having check-mated with a victorious jab with his queen that shook the flimsy table and set all the other pieces rocking, and having explained in detail to John how the disaster might have been avoided. Sir Victor drew Blackmore's attention from his crossword puzzle.

"Tom, my dear fellow, I feel we are guilty of culpable neglect in leaving your guest alone in Peartree Cottage. Would it not be an act of tardy hospitality to invite him to take some coffee with us? There is also some excellent brandy on the sideboard. It should have occurred to me to ask him to dinner, but my memory is beginning to play tricks with me. Would you care to walk along to the cottage and bring him back with you?"

This suggestion perplexed Tom Blackmore. He knew how Raymond Valentine stood in the old man's esteem. It had embarrassed him earlier in the evening, when John had blurted out a reference to Valentine's sojourn at the cottage.

"I see you hesitate, Tom. Please hesitate no longer. In the light of his sister's tragic end, the ugly past must be forgotten."

"As you please, sir. I'll fetch him now."

As he got up from his chair, Bugle grew animated. It looked to him as if a stroll with the boss was in prospect. He was to be disappointed. Tom Blackmore decided to leave him behind; the weather was too foul. He went out into the hall, closing the dining-room door behind him. Bugle scratched at the panels and whined for some time after Tom Blackmore had left Elmsdale.

Sir Victor showed no inclination to begin a new game. He sat gazing meditatively into the fire, a splendid study for a painter of dignified old age, with his fine-drawn, ecclesiastical features and noble head of pure-white hair. John sat opposite him for a while, then got up and wandered across the room to pick up a book and glance idly through its pages.

A gust of wind blew the rain against the window and rattled the sashes. The log hissed from a spattering of rain down the chimney . . . The big house was very quiet. In the kitchen, Mrs. Gulliver, the only other occupant, was reading a novelette beside the domestic boiler, which had its front open to show the comforting glow of the coke.

Turning his head, Sir Victor said across the room to John:

"Come over here and sit by me, my boy. I have something I wish to say to you."

John obediently closed the book and came back to his chair. When he was seated, the old man went on:

"John, the time has come for you to be told certain facts about yourself. You are at present under the impression that your parents are dead and that Mrs. Winters was your aunt. I can no longer defer telling you, dear lad, that this is not strictly correct. Your poor mother, alas! is no more, but your father still lives . . . Your mother was my own beloved daughter."

John drew a sharp, frightened breath; and his hands clenched on the chair-rail beside his bare knees.

"Then—then Mr. Harler is my—"

"No, John, Mr. Harler is not your father."

He raised himself from his chair and began to pace the room, just as he had loped—a long, lean figure—up and down the library while he had talked to Charlton in the afternoon.

"Your father, John, was your Aunt Enid's brother. Although there was no legal relationship between you and your Aunt Enid, there was a tie as strong as any that the law can recognise

. . . I did not know until last Monday night the identity of your father. But I know him now. Oh, yes, I know him now."

He turned at the end of the room and came back towards John, his body bent forward, his hands behind his back.

"The death of your aunt has precipitated a crisis, crisis, John—a crisis that has been impending for a long time past . . . Your father has come to claim you."

John, on his chair at the chessboard, cried out desperately:

"I don't want to go, sir!"

"Have no fear, dear lad," the old man paused in his stride to soothe him. "He'll never take you away from me."

He moved on. John followed him with his eyes.

"No grandchild of mine shall be left to the tender mercies of such a base villain as Raymond Valentine." John whimpered: "*Valentine,* sir? Is *that* man my father?"

"Alas! he is. But be easy in your mind! He shall never have you!"

The resonant voice shook with emotion. He came to a stop by the sideboard and looked across at John.

"No one shall ever have you, my dearly beloved grandson—not while there is still one way to stop them . . ." He dropped his voice to a cooing murmur. "Did you ever guess, dear lad, that your grandfather was a *wolf?*"

He spat out the last word, then spun round to the sideboard. Thin fingers clutched like talons at the carving-knife. By the fireside, the chessmen went flying as John sprang to his feet. Bugle began to bark.

In the kitchen, Mrs. Gulliver looked up from her book with a start at the distant sound of barking, and John Campbell's high-pitched scream of terror.

(ii)

Not without serious misgivings, Tom Blackmore put on his heavy trench-coat and, with his cigarette fighting a battle with the wind and rain, set off from Elmsdale to Peartree Cottage. After ten minutes walking, he reached his home, to find it empty and in darkness. The front door was still unlocked, as Valentine—and Peter Bradfield after him—had left it. At that particular time, the slowly sobering Valentine was reaching the end of his interview with Inspector Charlton.

On finding the cottage empty, Blackmore walked on into the village, expecting to find Valentine in the Mickleham Arms. Enquiries there elicited only negative information: the gentleman Mr. Blackmore described had certainly not called there that evening, and what was Mr. Blackmore taking now he was there? Blackmore ordered some beer and sat in the bar for a quarter of an hour. When Valentine still did not put in an appearance, he left a message for him with the landlord and started back for Elmsdale. By the time he reached Peartree Cottage, Valentine had returned from Police Headquarters.

(iii)

With Bradfield now at the wheel, it did not take the police car long to cover the distance from Lulverton to Elmsdale. Under his expert hands, the car turned off the road, spraying the water from the puddles, and swept through the entrance gates into the drive. As they drove on towards the house, there came from the thick, dripping undergrowth of the spinney the long, mournful howl of a wolf.

At a sharp word from Charlton, Bradfield brought his foot down on the brake with a suddenness that churned up the gravel of the drive. Charlton had the door open and was out of the car before it stopped. With Bradfield at his heels, he left the drive and broke through the bushes, pulling a powerful flashlamp from his pocket as he went.

Again the loud, protracted howl. It led them to Falcon's Nest. Ten yards from the foot of the big chestnut tree, Charlton stopped dead. The beam from the flashlamp shot upwards.

With his feet feeling wildly for the wooden rungs of the swinging rope-ladder, and his body half out of the tree-shelter, was Sir Victor Warringham. And gripped in his thin right hand was a carving-knife.

When the brilliant beam fell upon him, he screwed round to face the light. His long white hair hung dankly over his brows and his teeth were bared in an animal snarl.

Charlton called out:

"This is Charlton, Sir Victor. I think you'd better come down."

His voice had an instant effect. A howl died on Sir Victor's lips and his expression changed from savagery to bewilderment.

"Why, bless my soul!" he exclaimed. "Where am I?"

Charlton gave a warning shout.

"Be careful! Get your foot on the ladder, Sir Victor, or you'll fall!"

He shifted the beam. With the lower part of his body on the threshold of Falcon's Nest, Sir Victor felt round with his feet for a rung, found it and shifted his hands to get a grip on the ropes. But with his full weight on the ladder, the fastenings parted with a jerk.

Below, both men jumped forward. But with a frightened cry, the old man threw up his hands, letting go of the carving-knife, and fell the twelve feet to the ground, to lie without movement among the tangled ropes and rungs of the ladder.

Charlton went down on one knee beside him. Then he grunted and said over his shoulder to Bradfield:

"Looks as if his neck's broken."

He reached out and picked up the knife, which had fallen near. On the wet blade of it were smears of blood.

He scrambled to his feet and called up:

"John! . . . John! Are you all right?"

But from Falcon's Nest there came no sound.

"Stay here," he said to Bradfield; and ran off to fetch the ladder that hung from the wall of the wash-house.

CHAPTER TWENTY-FOUR

(i)

WHEN Tom Blackmore opened the front door and walked into Peartree Cottage, Raymond Valentine was upstairs in the second bedroom, pushing his pyjamas and shaving-kit untidily into his suitcase, by the light of the candle on the mantelpiece. Blackmore heard him and called up:

"Is that you, Valentine?"

The other man came out to the top of the stairs.

"Yes; I'm clearing out."

"This is very good news," Blackmore said up to him. "Why the sudden panic?"

"That's my business," grunted Valentine and stepped back into the bedroom.

Blackmore went up the stairs and followed him into the room. Valentine was relocking the case. Without turning round, he said:

"You can consider yesterday's arrangement as cancelled."

His voice had its normal hoarseness, but his words were to the point, without the usual tiresome persiflage.

"Too hot for you to hold, Valentine?" the big man jibed.

"Yes, if you want to know. I've just had a bad ten minutes with that Inspector fellow and I'm getting out quick."

"That won't do you much good, you know. He'll find you fast enough if he wants you. You wouldn't get—"

He broke off suddenly, struck by a thought.

"And why should he want you, Valentine? What's he been questioning you about?"

"He asked what I was doing at Elmsdale on Monday night."

"Oh, he's found out that you were there, has he? And what did you tell him?"

"Nothing—only that I had a chat with Enid. Then he mentioned Rosalie and demanded to know whether I'd come down to talk to Enid about John Campbell."

"Did you admit that you had?"

"Of course I didn't. What do you take me for?"

"He'll be after you again about that, you know. He's a tenacious fellow, is Charlton. Yes, I think you're doing the right thing by skipping out. But I shouldn't go back to Sloane Street for a time, if I were you ... I suppose you wouldn't like to take coffee with Sir Victor before you go?"

His tone was ironic.

"Good God, no! The last man I want to see."

"He's just sent me here with the invitation."

Valentine picked up the suitcase.

"Tell him I've gone to the Solomon Islands."

He pushed past Blackmore and bumped downstairs with the suitcase. Blackmore stopped to blow out the candle. Valentine went into the den for his overcoat, which was on the back of a chair. As he was putting on the coat, he noticed something lying on Blackmore's desk... By the time Blackmore descended, the thing was in Valentine's pocket.

Blackmore asked: "Any address in the Solomons for forwarding mail?"

The other man did not reply. He buttoned his overcoat, turned up the collar and slammed his hat on his head. Blackmore put another question:

"What shall I tell Charlton, if he asks?"

This got an answer: "Look, Blackmore, I'm in a jam. Don't tell him I've made a run for it, there's a good chap. Tell him I've—well, that I've finished my stay here and gone off for a holiday, you don't know where. Will you do that for me?"

Blackmore smiled grimly. "I told you yesterday, Valentine, that you'd got gall. I'm more convinced of it than ever now! Why are you so damned anxious to get away from Charlton? Come on, let's have the truth!"

Without a word, Valentine pulled open the front door, heaved up his suitcase and went stumbling off down the path. Blackmore called after him with a mocking laugh:

"Goodbye, old darling!"

But after he had closed the door on the parting guest, the smile faded on his lips and he stood in deep thought for some minutes. A dark suspicion was forming in his mind. . . . Then, with a decision made, he lighted a cigarette and prepared to leave the cottage. He would talk to Charlton.

(ii)

The extending ladder was on its hooks on the wall of the wash-house. Charlton carried it back to Falcon's Nest. He was breathing heavily by the time he arrived, for the ladder was no light weight for one man. He left it to Bradfield to place it against the chestnut tree and climb up to Falcon's Nest, while he waited below in a fever of apprehension.

Bradfield shone his flashlamp into the interior. The tree-house was empty.

"He's not here."

"Thank God for that! I was afraid you'd find him with his throat cut. Right, Peter. You'd better come down. I've got to find out what's happened."

He left Bradfield to stay by Sir Victor's body and went up to the house. The front door was open and swinging in the wind. He walked into the hall and shouted:

"Mrs. Gulliver!. . . Mrs. Gulliver!"

He had to repeat the call again before she emerged, timidly and with difficulty, from the cupboard under the stairs. She was white and terrified.

"Oh, sir, it's *you!* Thank the dear Lord for that! I couldn't be sure 'oo it was, because I 'ad me fingers in me ears, to stop from 'earin' that poor little boy's death shrieks. Oh, but I *am* glad you've come, sir! The master's gone mad—stark, raving mad. Mr. and Mrs. 'Arler was right after all, for all their wickedness. What 'appened outside, sir? 'Ave you got little John safe? Poor little chap, 'e must 'ave bin frightened out of 'is life!"

"No, we haven't found him yet, Mrs. Gulliver, but I expect he's all right."

"And the master, sir?"

Gently he led her into the dining-room and put her into a chair. He found the brandy on the sideboard and poured some into a glass. It brought some colour back into Mrs. Gulliver's cheeks,

"The master, sir?"

"I'm afraid he's dead, Mrs. Gulliver."

"Oh, *sir!*" The tears ran down her homely features; she wiped them away with a corner of her apron. "Still, p'raps it's all for the best, sir. The dear old gentleman would've 'ad to be put away in a padded cell for the rest of 'is days—and 'e was always so kind and natural. Wouldn't 'ave 'urt a fly, 'e wouldn't, sir. . . And little John. . . The master worshipped 'im, sir, just like as if 'e was one of 'is own flesh and blood."

Again she was overcome by a fit of weeping. While she recovered herself, he went out into the hall to telephone for Dr. Lorimer and the ambulance. By the time he came back, she was more composed.

"Will you tell me what happened, Mrs. Gulliver?"

"I was reading by the kitchen fire, sir, when I heard, first a dog barking and then a scream of fright. I went all limp for a moment, then thought I'd better go and see what was up. Just as I come out into the 'all, the dining-room door was pulled open and John ran out, with the master be'ind 'im waving the carving-knife. I thought it was some silly game, till I saw the looks on their faces. The master was 'owling out at the top of 'is voice like one of them dervishes they tell of; and what with 'im and John and Mr. Blackmore's little dog jumping round barkin' 'is 'ead off and snappin' at the master, the din was terrible. My legs went all trembly and I couldn't get any further 'n the end of the 'all, but I saw little John get the front door open in time and dart out into the darkness. The master went to go after 'im, but the dog got in 'is way with 'is jumpin' and snarlin'. The master shouts out after John, 'oo must've bin off down the drive by that time, 'I'll catch you up, my boy! I know where you're bound for! Raymond Valentine shall never have his son!' What d'you think the master meant by that, sir?"

"Please go on with your story, Mrs. Gulliver."

"There's not much more to it, sir. The master kicks the dog out of the way and runs out into the rain after John, waving the carving-knife in the air. The poor little dog yelped from the nasty kick in the ribs and slithered across the 'all. Then 'e picks 'imself up and chases after the master... That was the last I seen of any of 'em, sir. I managed to pull meself together and hurried to the telephone. Then, when I'd talked to you, I went and 'id."

"Where's Mr. Blackmore?"

"I don't rightly know, sir. I think 'e must've gone out; I 'eard the front door go earlier on. But where Mr. Blackmore went, I couldn't say."

"Thank you, Mrs. Gulliver. Now, you'd better wait till we can arrange something for you. You'll be quite safe now. Have you any relatives in the district?"

She told him of a sister in Lulverton. He went out again to the telephone and made the necessary arrangements. Then, after a few more reassuring words to Mrs. Gulliver and a suggestion that she should go upstairs and pack, he turned up the collar of his overcoat and left the house, pulling the front door closed behind him.

He reached the foot of the front steps and took a few paces forward before his foot hit something soft and yielding. He stepped back and flashed his torch. On the gravel lay a body with a bloody gash across the throat. It was Tom Blackmore's spaniel, Bugle.

(iii)

He went back to Bradfield, took over from him and sent him to the gates to wait for the ambulance. A few minutes after his assistant's departure, a twig snapped and there was the sound of bushes being thrust aside.

"Is that you, Peter?" he called out.

A voice answered, "No, it's Blackmore. Where exactly are you?"

Charlton switched on his torch, and Blackmore found his way to him.

"Glad to find you here, Inspector. This is a dreadful business. Have you got Sir Victor under control? He's dangerous."

"He'll never be dangerous again, Mr. Blackmore."

He turned the torch-beam on to the body.

Blackmore drew a sharp breath. "How did this happen?"

"He fell out of John's tree-house and broke his neck. I'm very anxious about the boy."

"He's all right," Blackmore instantly assured him.

"He had the sense to run for me. I met him on my way back here from the cottage. He's now in good hands. I took him along to Mrs. Tucker... John has told me what happened. A ghastly affair."

They waited till Dr. Lorimer arrived with the ambulance. The young police surgeon confirmed that Sir Victor Warringham was dead. The body was transferred to the ambulance and, with Lorimer in attendance, was taken off to Lulverton. Charlton, Blackmore and Peter Bradfield walked back to the house together.

As they neared the house, Charlton said:

"I've some bad news for you, Mr. Blackmore. Your little spaniel is dead."

He switched on his flashlamp. Blackmore stood in silence, looking down at the body of his pet. At length he said quietly:

"I suppose Sir Victor did that?"

"Presumably. Mrs. Gulliver told me that the dog was snapping round him and holding him back from John. Sir Victor must have slashed at him with the knife, to get rid of him."

"Poor little devil... But it was a good death. If he hadn't been there, John's throat would have been slit instead."

He turned and walked up the steps. The two detectives followed. Charlton told him:

"You'll have to bang hard on the knocker. Mrs. Gulliver's at the top of the house."

Blackmore answered: "No need to disturb her. I've a key. I'm *persona grata* in the household." He turned the key in the lock and added with a short, ironic laugh: "Or was, while there was any household left."

They went into the dining-room. Blackmore lighted a cigarette, then fetched the brandy and glasses from the sideboard.

"We all need a small one, I think."

He poured the drinks and they sat with them round the fire. When the first small one was being followed by a second, Blackmore said:

"Well, Inspector, I suppose this latest tragedy doesn't make things any easier for you?"

Charlton answered:

"My investigations are now finished, Mr. Blackmore, and my case is complete."

"You mean—Sir Victor murdered Mrs. Winters?"

"He had very good cause." He lighted a cigarette and went on with an expansiveness that Bradfield attributed to the brandy: "I've found out a good deal since Monday morning. My inquiries went back to over ten years ago, to the time when Sir Victor's daughter, Mrs. Rosalie Harler, became infatuated with a man who was not her husband, and bore him a child. In the absence abroad of Mr. Harler, the birth of the child was registered by Sir Victor, who, knowing he was making a false declaration, gave the father's name as Clement Harler. For fear of awkward questions by those who knew that the child could not be Harler's, the child—a little boy—was adopted by Mrs. Winters as her nephew and came to be known as John Campbell."

He drew at his cigarette.

"By Sir Victor's will, his fortune was to have passed on his death to his wife, Lady Warringham, and his daughter, Rosalie, in equal shares. When Rosalie married Harler, a codicil was added to the will. This altered the will to the extent that, if Rosalie died before her father, her share of the fortune would pass to Harler, provided there was no issue of the marriage. As things turned out, Rosalie did die before Sir Victor. Lady Warringham lost her life at the same time. This meant that the boy registered as John Campbell Harler would inherit the whole of the fortune on Sir Victor's death. . . Mrs. Winters was well content with this. John would grow up under her guardianship and, if he had normal human feelings, would see that she wanted for nothing in her old age. There might be some awkward moments during the metamorphosis of John Campbell into John Campbell Harler, but a way could doubtless have been found; and once the boy was firmly established as the heir, the danger of the real facts coming out was negligible.

"There was, however, one unknown quantity: Clement Harler. At the time of the boy's birth, Harler was believed to be dead. In fact, he was very much alive, and caused Sir Victor and Mrs. Winters quite a lot of worry by suddenly turning up out of the blue. With Harler on the scene, John Campbell could not be introduced to the world as Sir Victor's grandson and heir to the Warringham fortune. If that were done, Harler would have two very good reasons for kicking up a fuss. Firstly, why should he tamely play father to another man's child? And secondly, why should he give up his share of the inheritance?. . . With these thoughts in mind, Mrs. Winters got busy. Her own future must be assured. It was no use depending now on the subsequent generosity of John, because, with Harler in the offing, John would never see a penny of the money. So she had to persuade Sir Victor to alter his will in such a fashion that she herself became the principal legatee. Sir Victor was more than reluctant to do this; and finally Mrs. Winters had to threaten him with exposure unless he fell in with her wishes. As a result, Sir Victor fixed an appointment with his solicitor."

"But not to change the will in her favour," Blackmore threw in, not as a question, but as a statement.

"No, Mr. Blackmore. Sir Victor, who, I should imagine, had a fairly quick brain during his periods of sanity, had no such intention. He had entirely different plans."

"I see what you mean. Instead of letting Mrs. Winters virtually blackmail him, he—got rid of her?"

"Again, no. Sir Victor didn't strangle Mrs. Winters. That little job was done by John's father."

(iv)

Raymond Valentine hesitated at the gate of Peartree Cottage, then turned to the left towards the village. He could have a quick double Scotch and then catch the bus to Lulverton. In the Mickleham Arms, he was given the message that Blackmore had left for him. He grunted an acknowledgment, ordered his double and gulped it down. When politely refused a second, on the score of shortage of supplies, he retorted with a coarse remark and went out to wait in the rain for the bus.

A young giant in a raincoat and a brown felt hat, who had entered the Mickleham Arms at the same time as Valentine, but had gone into the other bar, had listened with interest to the conversation and Valentine's abrupt departure. But being one who had to do quite enough standing about in the wet, the young man avoided it when it was not necessary, and therefore tarried with his pint in front of the bar-parlour fire until he heard the bus arrive. Then he drained his tankard and went out to the car that he had left just up the road.

When the bus had taken him into Lulverton, Valentine got off at the Public Library stop and, suitcase in hand, walked along to the station, after calling in at the Marquis of Granby, where, for the lack of whisky, he had a double rum. At the station barrier, he produced the second half of a monthly return; and his shadow was near enough to hear him ask for the time of the next train to Waterloo.

There was half an hour to wait. Valentine was not one to waste a single minute of licensed hours if he could avoid it, so he passed the time in the Railway Tavern, just outside the station. His follower, who had not such an insatiable thirst, lurked in a dry corner outside, while Valentine consumed a couple of South African brandies, a Guinness topped up with a gin, and, because by that time there were no spirits left—at any rate, for such casual customers as Valentine—two pints of mild-and-bitter.

With the large young man not far behind him, he arrived on the platform less than a minute before the train was due. It came in on time. As it drew to a stop, Valentine hurried up and down, looking for an empty compartment. He found one. His hand was on the door-handle when a voice asked:

"Excuse me, sir, but are you Mr. Raymond Valentine?"

By this time, Valentine was drunk again, but now, from the incautious variety of his potations, was not convivial, but in fighting mood.

"You mind your own—business!" he retorted, using the same word as he had used to the landlord of the Mickleham Arms.

He turned the handle, pulled open the door and, with a heave and a shove, got his case into the compartment.

"Inspector Charlton would like a word with you before you leave, sir," said the young man politely.

"—Charlton! If he wants me, he can come and find me!"

With abnormal agility, he jumped into the compartment and tried to slam the door shut behind him. Up and down the platform, doors were closing. The train was about to start.

The young man had hold of the door-handle. Valentine's other hand flashed to his overcoat pocket and came out again.

"Stand away or I'll fire!" he shouted.

But the other man was not disposed to stand away. With a savage wrench he pulled the door out of Valentine's grasp. Then his other hand shot out and got Valentine's wrist in a grip that made that gentleman yelp and drop the weapon. His captor pulled him out of the compartment like a small boy caught in the larder.

"Naughty, naughty," he murmured reprovingly.

By now, the station staff had noticed that something unusual was afoot. The guard hurried along the platform and demanded to know what they thought they were playing at. The young man produced his warrant card and was allowed to retain possession of his captive, despite vehement and extremely alcoholic protests.

The train drew out, leaving behind it the two men, the suitcase and Tom Blackmore's toy revolver, which Valentine had snatched up from the desk, against an emergency, while Blackmore had walked down the stairs of Peartree Cottage.

"I'll trouble you to come along with me, sir," said the young man. "I have a car outside the station."

And, as Detective-constable Emerson could crush a tobacco-tin with his bare hand as if it were made of tissue paper, Raymond Valentine had no alternative but to comply.

(v)

Inspector Charlton threw his cigarette into the fire.

"You see, Mr. Blackmore," he observed, "John's father had every reason for wishing Mrs. Winters out of the way. In the first place she knew too much. While she lived, she was a thorn in his side. At any time, or for any reason, she could publish the facts; and her case would be very hard to disprove. What were these facts? Number One, John was not the issue of the marriage between Rosalie Warringham and Clement Harler. This could be demonstrated by the absence of Harler from this country during the—er—critical period—an absence that could be established without question by the Passport Office, the shipping companies' sailing-lists, the Brazilian authorities—and probably others . . . Fact Number

Two, Sir Victor Warringham made a false declaration when he registered the birth. Fact Number Three, in so far as he was not the issue of the Harler-Warringham marriage, John had no legal claim whatever to the legacy . . . So, in disposing of Mrs. Winters, John's father achieved four important objects. Number One—to enumerate once again!—Number One, he ensured that Mrs. Winters would never lay hands on the money as a direct beneficiary under any new will that Sir Victor might make. Number Two, he got John out of the clutches of Mrs. Winters. This was a vital consideration, because, even though Mrs. Winters did keep her mouth shut, she would undoubtedly do so only on the understanding that she continued as the boy's guardian. Number Three, he made certain that Mrs. Winters would never publish the truth about his relationship to John. And lastly, Number Four, he secured John's future. Unless anything very unforeseen happened, Mrs. Winters' death put an end to any possibility that John's rights under the will would ever be called in question."

Blackmore asked: "What about Harler?"

"That brings me to Sir Victor's real purpose in summoning his solicitor. His design was to tell Harler the truth and buy his silence—and Harler's silence wouldn't have been a very difficult purchase! Then the will would have been allowed to stand, except that you yourself would have been appointed as John's trustee. I believe you were aware of this?"

"Yes. I'm afraid I wasn't frank with you yesterday on that point, but Sir Victor had asked me not to mention it."

"Mrs. Winters was the lioness in the path, of course. It was probably Sir Victor's intention to ask Mr. Howard whether there was any way of baulking an attempt on her part to upset the plan."

"Yes, that's quite correct."

"But John's father was apparently of the opinion that the only way to stop her was to strangle her—an effective, if somewhat drastic, proceeding."

Blackmore got up to pour out more brandy as Charlton continued:

"This evening Sir Victor announced that he knew John's father to be Raymond Valentine."

The big man pursed his lips in a whistle of comprehension. "So *that's* it, is it?"

"Valentine came down to Lulverton from London on Monday. He left his bag in an hotel and arrived at Elmsdale late in the evening—at eleven o'clock to be precise. Mrs. Winters was waiting for him and let him into the house without the knowledge of the rest of the household. They talked together for a short while, then Mrs. Winters complained of feeling sleepy. Valentine left her and she went to bed."

He raised his glass and sipped the brandy with evident pleasure.

"The murder itself," he went on, "was beautifully simple and well executed. Mrs. Winters was in a deep sleep. A length of light-flex was slipped under her head as it lay on the pillow and twisted until she died. A pair of gloves prevented any tell-tale fingerprints from being left behind; and our homicidal friend left by the way he had come."

"Down the ladder?"

"No, by much more conventional means—through the front door."

"I don't like to dispute what you say, Inspector, but it doesn't seem likely that Valentine would use the front door. I shouldn't imagine he had a key."

"He didn't need a key."

"Then how the devil did he get in?"

"He didn't."

"But aren't you suggesting that he murdered Mrs. Winters?"

"No, Mr. Blackmore, I'm not. What I am suggesting is that *you* did."

CHAPTER TWENTY-FIVE

"AND," Inspector Charlton went swiftly on, "it is my duty to tell you that anything you say will be written down by my assistant and may be used later in evidence."

Tom Blackmore took this with apparent tranquillity. He answered without a tremor or trace of excitement in his pleasant voice:

"Naturally I deny this startling accusation, Inspector. I'll be interested to hear how you arrived at such a fantastic conclusion."

"I'm going to ask you some questions, Mr. Blackmore. You're at liberty to refuse an answer. First of all, are you the father of the boy known as John Campbell?"

"Yes . . . I flatly refute the charge of murder, but I'm ready to admit that John is my son. Now that Sir Victor is dead, secrecy is not so important. You see, my father was Sir Victor's closest friend, and I myself was very high up in Sir Victor's regard. John's mother was Rosalie Warringham—or Rosalie Harler, as she was then. If Sir Victor had ever known the whole truth, I shudder to think what would have happened." He frowned slightly as he added, "Not that it could have been much worse than what *has* happened."

"Who besides you and Mrs. Harler were in the secret?"

"Lady Warringham knew and so did Enid Winters. There were one or two others—but I'll come to that in a minute. When poor Rosalie and I first met each other, we discovered that, after the bad choices we'd both made in the past, this was the real things at last. We were both married, but separated—she from her husband, Clement Harler, and I from my wife, who now describes herself, quite inaccurately, as Clare Valentine . . . Harler was in Brazil. Three months after he'd gone, I got my decree nisi; and a couple of months later we had word that Harler had been killed in a railway smash. My decree hadn't been made absolute, but Rosalie and I were very deeply in love and—well, we anticipated.

"My wife had left me for Raymond Valentine, the creature I introduced you to yesterday. I imagined that she would be only too pleased to be divorced from me and be able to marry Valentine, but she wasn't. She put a private detective on my tail. He earned his fee by supplying her with certain authentic details. She passed these on to the King's Proctor—and bang went my decree absolute. It meant that I couldn't marry Rosalie. Legally, I couldn't have married her in any case, but we didn't know then that Harler was still alive . . . It was a ghastly predicament. Rosalie had to tell her parents. They took a realistic view of it and hushed it up as best they could. By this time, you know how it was done. After a decent interval, I rented Peartree Cottage from Sir Victor, so that I could be near the ones I loved. Then . . . Then Rosalie was killed by a bomb . . . All I had left was John . . . And he called me 'Uncle Tom.'"

His mouth set in hard lines, he sat in silence until Charlton put his next question. Bradfield was scribbling busily in his notebook.

"Is Mr. Valentine still living with your wife?"

"Yes—and good luck to both of them! They make a splendid pair!"

"Are you and he on good terms?"

"I'd rather be friends with a jackal."

"Yet he was your guest at Peartree Cottage."

"I couldn't help myself; the crafty, drunken swine had me by the short hairs . . . It wasn't until yesterday, Inspector, that I found out why my sweet-natured wife had stopped the decree absolute from going through. The prime mover was Enid Winters. She was a schemer—a long-term strategist. All the Valentines had a bad streak in them. The father was a wrong 'un, and the four children weren't much better. Raymond, the son, turned into a lounge lizard of the worst type. Vera, the youngest daughter, found her own level, then made herself an honest woman by marrying a bookmaker's tout, who subsequently blossomed out as an innkeeper. Vera's now behind the bar of his dockside beer-house. The other two, Enid and Connie, outwardly led a more ladylike existence. Connie did very well for herself by netting a stockbroker called Freshwater; and Enid, after a short married life, became the eminently respectable companion of Lady Warringham, wife of the famous car-magnate. But all four Valentines were tarred with the same brush . . . And Enid had all the brains.

"It was Enid who engineered the affair between Rosalie and Raymond Valentine. That was before Rosalie married Harler. Enid might have succeeded, for Raymond Valentine was a presentable enough young fellow in those days. She first got him a job in Victor Motors, then brought him into the Warringham home. Rosalie reacted very favourably and there might have been wedding-bells if Valentine hadn't just casually abandoned her for a worthless little piece in the chorus of a London show. Sir Victor gave him the sack. Rosalie was very cut up at first, then—which is the sort of thing that often happens—married Harler on the rebound.

"In those days, I was no more than a distant observer. Valentine was just a name to me then. He was later to be forcibly brought to my notice! In his unending quest for feminine variety, he found my wife. They appealed to each other so much that she ran off with him, leaving me with a lot of bills to pay, but no regrets. I'd already discovered her true character.

"Well, as I mentioned just now, Enid's first plan failed. We come to the second plan. Plot is a better word. In some way or other, she found out that Rosalie and I had formed an attachment. She did nothing until news of Harler's death came through. Then, knowing that, as soon as my decree became absolute, I should ask Sir Victor for his permission to marry Rosalie—which wouldn't have suited her book at all—"

"Why not?"

"She didn't want me in the family. To all intents and purposes, she was running the show. I might have cramped her style. In fact, I definitely would have done—I should have made a point of it. The woman had altogether too much rope."

"I see . . . Please go on."

"To stop my decree from becoming absolute, Enid Winters went to my wife and told her what was going on between Rosalie and me. My wife replied that she couldn't care less. But when the Winters woman hinted broadly that it would be to their subsequent financial advantage if I was prevented from marrying into the Warringham family, my wife and Valentine changed their minds—with a result that I have already described. We played right into their hands—and the plot was an even greater success than Enid Winters had dared to hope, in that Rosalie gave birth to John and thereby supplied Enid with a beautifully sharp weapon to carve slices off the Warringham fortune at her leisure."

"Clement Harler seems to be under the impression that his wife's *affaire* was with Raymond Valentine, not with you. Can you explain that, Mr. Blackmore?"

"No, I can't. I didn't know that he even knew she had an *affaire*. Who told him?"

"I don't know."

"She was certainly friendly with Valentine at one time, but that was before her marriage. I can only suggest that either Harler was given the wrong story by somebody, or he told you a lie to save his own face for deserting his wife. . . . To get back to my own story, Valentine didn't call at Peartree Cottage yesterday merely to explain why I was still a married man. He had a far more practical purpose—nothing less than blackmail . . . Enid Winters hated me like poison. I had too much pull with Sir Victor; and always the thought must have been in her mind that one day I might get John out of her clutches. So she decided that I must go. She wasn't particular where I went, so long as it was a thousand miles or so from Elmsdale. That was the message Valentine brought: if I didn't leave the district and make no future attempts to communicate either with Sir Victor or my son, she would climb up on the tallest soap-box she could find and publish the truth in the market-place.

"When Valentine had said his piece, I took the opportunity of telling him that his sister was in no position to carry out her threat, because she was dead ... Whether this news was fresh to him, I don't pretend to know, but he expressed great surprise and horror. However, he got over the shock very quickly, and, being a born opportunist with no scruples, altered his tactics to suit the new set of conditions. He ceased to be Enid's emissary and introduced himself as a blackmailer on his own account ... His suggestion was that he and my precious wife would continue to keep their mouths shut provided that, in due course, I diverted a generous proportion of John's legacy into their pockets.

"If I had had only myself to think about, Inspector, I would have told him to open his mouth as wide and as often as he liked—and be damned to him. But there were other considerations. There was John; and there was Sir Victor. By kicking Valentine out of the cottage and daring him to do his worst, I was throwing everything on to the scrap-heap. John would be a social outcast for the rest of his days; Sir Victor would receive a blow that might snap the thin thread of his sanity, and would probably involve him in legal proceedings for faking the details on the birth certificate. So I agreed to be blackmailed ... Just to turn the knife in the wound, Valentine forced himself on me and insisted on putting up at the cottage for a couple of days ... It may interest you to know, Inspector, that I saw Valentine just before I came along here. He packed his bag and left. He told me before he went that I could regard his blackmailing venture as definitely off. He was a very much frightened man."

Charlton made no comment on this, but asked his next question:

"Mr. Blackmore, where were you between eleven o'clock on Monday night and two o'clock yesterday morning?"

"In bed—most of that period, at any rate. I spent the evening listening to the radio and went to bed somewhere between quarter and half-past eleven."

"Have you any witnesses to that?"

"Unfortunately, no. I was by myself all the time, except for poor little Bugle."

"You didn't come to Elmsdale?"

"Definitely not. I didn't go out of the cottage."

"During my first conversation with you on Monday evening, Mr. Blackmore, you were smoking a pipe. On my meetings with you since, you have smoked cigarettes. Why is that?"

The answering smile was plainly an effort.

"A very odd question, Inspector! There's a very simple answer. That pipe was the only one I had. I was careless enough to snap the stem. I always buy my pipes from a firm in Piccadilly, so rather than spend money locally on an inferior pipe, I'm making do with cigarettes for the time being. I shall be popping up to Town for some other things in a day or two and I'm proposing to buy a new pipe then. Is that what you wanted to know?"

"How did you come to break the pipe?"

"Tapping it too fiercely on the fireplace—an old failing of mine."

"Was anyone else there when you broke it?"

"No. Had I known that you would be so interested, I could have arranged to have someone there to watch the accident."

Sarcasm has great power to annoy. Charlton's voice took on a sharper note as he pursued his interrogation.

"After you left Police Headquarters last Monday evening, what did you do?"

"Caught the bus back home."

"Before you went home, did you go to Macfarland's shop in King Edward Street?"

"Yes, I did—well, I went to *a* shop in King Edward Street. I didn't notice the name of it."

"What did you buy there?"

"A screwdriver."

"Did you also buy two yards of light-flex?"

Blackmore hesitated before he answered:

"I suppose you've checked up with the shopkeeper, so it's a waste of time to say I didn't."

"And before you bought it, did you test its strength by pulling on it?"

"I don't recall doing that. If I did, it was done subconsciously."

"Why did you buy this flex?"

The big man shrugged his shoulders. "The same reason as most people; to do a little electrical job."

"Where?"

"At home."

"Peartree Cottage has no electric light, Mr. Blackmore. How did you use the flex?"

"Well, I haven't done anything with it yet. There hasn't been much time for odd jobs since I bought it. I was going to fix a light in the outside lavatory—worked with a flashlamp battery. It's a bit awkward without a light in there, these dark evenings."

"Can you produce the flex?"

A flicker of uncertainty before, "Yes."

"I shall be asking you later to do so, Mr. Blackmore."

"You know, Inspector, you're attaching a great deal of importance to a very trivial thing. You've really no right to go running round accusing me of this murder, just because I bought a piece of flex. The strangling was done with the flex of the bedside lamp."

"Oh, no, it wasn't!" Charlton retorted. "I can bring unshakable evidence to show that it wasn't done with that, but with maroon-coloured flex. On the neck of the dead woman were found strands of the silk covering, and you can take it from me, Mr. Blackmore, that the forensic laboratories won't have much difficulty in identifying those strands with the flex you bought at Macfarland's."

Blackmore considered this.

"Why can you be so sure," he asked at length, "that the other flex wasn't used?"

"Firstly, when you removed the first flex and replaced it by the second flex, the marks made on the neck by the second flex didn't coincide with the marks already made by the first. Secondly, the deep marks made by the first flex could never have been caused by that paper-knife. Tests have shown that it would have snapped. Even as it was, Mr. Blackmore, you broke your pipe, twisting the first flex. And when it broke a drip of nicotine fell on Mrs. Winters' nightdress. . . . Do you still find my accusation startling and my conclusion fantastic, Mr. Blackmore?"

Tom Blackmore got to his feet and, under the watchful eyes of the two detectives, took a turn up and down the room. He saw the chessmen scattered over the floor, where John had shot them when he had jumped up to escape Sir Victor. He collected them and put them away in their box. Then, having inserted the lid in its grooves and slid it shut, he looked across at Charlton and said quietly:

"All right. You win. I suppose you realise what this is going to mean to John? You're smashing up his whole life."

Charlton stood up to face him.

"You should have thought of that," he said sternly, "before you strangled a woman in her sleep."

CHAPTER TWENTY-SIX

(i)

RAYMOND VALENTINE was far too drunk to be questioned that night? He was put to bed in one of the cells and brought into Charlton's office the following morning, crestfallen and with a severe hang-over.

With no polite preliminaries, Charlton began:

"You have in your possession, Mr. Valentine, a copy of the birth certificate of John Campbell Harler. How did you come by it?"

"My sister gave it to me."

"When?"

"Monday evening."

"Why?"

"Dear old horse!" Valentine protested plaintively. "Don't keep firing off questions! It's like red hot needles. I'm not in my usual rude health this morning. Enid gave me the certificate to take along and show Blackmore."

"Where had she been keeping it?"

"She said she'd had it locked away in the bureau in her bedroom."

"Why did she want Mr. Blackmore to see it?"

"Because she thought he'd be interested."

"Don't waste my time," Charlton said tartly.

"That's all very well, but I'm feeling my way step by step. How much do you know, old Sherlock?"

"Quite enough to put *you* in the dock, Mr. Raymond Valentine!"

"But don't be ridiculous! I've done nothing criminal."

"Valentine, I was too lenient with you yesterday. This time I don't feel so generous and I want no more evasions. I can't force you to talk, but later on there may be someone who can. Why did your sister bring you down from London?"

Valentine gave a weary gesture.

"If I've told you once, I've told you a thousand times, she wanted to have a chat with me. Much water has gone under the old bridge since—"

"I'm suggesting to you that she had you down here to help her with a little blackmail. I'm suggesting that she offered you a share in the loot if you managed to get Blackmore to quit the district and leave his natural son to her tender mercies. I'm suggesting that, on the death of your sister, you threatened Blackmore with exposure unless he closed your mouth with a fat bribe. I'm suggesting that your so-called 'few words' with Sir Victor were, in fact, an attempt to extort money by threats; that, by arrangement with your sister a few minutes earlier, you endeavoured to pass yourself off as the father of John Campbell and so intimidate Sir Victor into leaving the whole of his fortune to Mrs. Winters. . . . Do you or do you not admit all those things?"

From the expression on Valentine's face, it seemed that his brain must be fighting for life under a ton of swan's-down. Charlton pursued him unmercifully.

"Speak up, man!"

Ultimately Valentine said faintly:

"Anything you say, old horse. D'you think there's somewhere quiet and dark where I could go and lie down?"

(ii)

Charlton later had a brief chat with Mr. Howard. He told him of the death of Sir Victor and of the arrest of Tom Blackmore for the Winters murder. Then he asked the solicitor:

"What happened at your interview with Sir Victor yesterday morning? To relieve your mind, Howard, I know all about John Campbell Harler."

"I thought you wouldn't be long finding that out. Altogether a very curious affair. I was not fully in Sir Victor's confidence until yesterday. I knew that the boy was his daughter's child by a man who was not her husband. What I did not know was that Sir Victor had registered the father as Clement Harler. Neither was I aware until yesterday that the real father was a man called Raymond Valentine."

"Oh, no, he wasn't. The father was Tom Blackmore."

Mr. Howard whistled.

"Was he, by Jove! That explains a good deal . . . Anyway, Sir Victor thought it was this man Valentine, a brother of Mrs. Winters. What he wanted me to do was work out a method whereby John would inherit the whole fortune—with Blackmore as trustee—without having trouble either with Valentine or with Harler. I advised him to tell Valentine to go and jump in the lake, and make a new will, leaving half the fortune to John and the other half to Harler. Much more than the Harler fellow deserved, but an effective way to keep his mouth shut."

"Was this new will executed?"

"No. I was going to get Sir Victor's signature to it today, after the two of us had had a conference with Harler."

"So what's the position?"

"If Harler creates a stink—to put it crudely—he'll get his half and the other half will go to Sir Victor's next-of-kin, who, as far as I know, is a younger brother. John will get nothing . . . On the other hand, if Harler takes it lying down, John—once we've established him as John Harler—will inherit the whole fortune."

(iii)

There was one last interview—with Clement Harler.

Charlton said: "Mr. Harler, I'm glad to tell you that you and your wife are to be released from custody."

"So I should think!" retorted that seedy individual. "You haven't heard the last of this, Clayton! I shall speak to Sir Victor at the first oppor—"

"That won't be possible, Mr. Harler. Sir Victor died last night."

"Died? But that's not . . . Are you trying to tell me . . . How did he die?"

"He fell out of a tree and broke his neck."

"Fell out of a tree? What the hell was he doing up *there?*"

"He climbed the tree with the intention of murdering John Campbell with a carving-knife. Luckily, he didn't succeed."

Harler laughed unpleasantly.

"I think that's rich! Here have my wife and I been saying for weeks that he was a crazy maniac, and nobody would believe us! Perhaps they'll believe us now!" His little mind seized on a point that meant much to him. "Did he change his will?"

"No, Mr. Harler, he didn't. That was what you wanted, wasn't it? Your trouble is now, of course, that young John inherits the lot."

"Oh, no, he doesn't!" Harler said nastily. "I'll fight the case while there's, still breath in my body."

"You're not considering accepting the parentage?"

"Why should I? I'm not taking the responsibility for another man's pup. I'm getting my share of the money and going back to Brazil. If anyone tries any funny stuff, I'll fight them in the courts every inch of the way. The brat shan't have a brass farthing."

"It is for you to decide," Charlton said, then went on as if changing the subject: "I told you just now that you and your wife were to be released from custody. That, of course, related only to your arrest on a charge of being concerned in the murder of Mrs. Winters . . . You will recall that there are two other little matters in which you were both involved: the drugging and robbing of Mrs. Winters, and the attempt to drive Sir Victor insane. There is enough evidence, Mr. Harler, to have you convicted on both counts. Sir Victor died a madman. You can take my word for that, because I was there when he died. Were you to be charged with deliberately contributing to his derangement of mind, found guilty and sentenced to a term of imprisonment, what chance do you think you would have afterwards of claiming under his will? . . . " He allowed time for this to sink in before he continued: "It is possible—I can only say that it is possible—that the police will take no action over your two serious offences . . . " Again he paused for some moments. "Did I understand you to say, Mr. Harler, that you were taking your wife back to Brazil, leaving your son in the care of a responsible guardian until he gains his majority?"

Harler chewed his fingernails. After some deep thinking, he said:

"I think perhaps you're right, Inspector Clayton."

The big detective smiled at him across the desk.

"The name," he told him sweetly, "is Charlton."

THE END